D. L. CR

HIDING
IN THE
CLOUD

Hiding in the Cloud

Trilogy Christian Publishers
A Wholly Owned Subsidiary of Trinity Broadcasting Network
2442 Michelle Drive
Tustin, CA 92780

Copyright © 2024 by D. L. Crager

All rights reserved, including the right to reproduce this book or portions thereof in any form whatsoever.
For information, address Trilogy Christian Publishing
Rights Department, 2442 Michelle Drive, Tustin, Ca 92780.
Trilogy Christian Publishing/ TBN and colophon are trademarks of Trinity Broadcasting Network.
For information about special discounts for bulk purchases, please contact Trilogy Christian Publishing.

Trilogy Disclaimer: The views and content expressed in this book are those of the author and may not necessarily reflect the views and doctrine of Trilogy Christian Publishing or the Trinity Broadcasting Network.

10 9 8 7 6 5 4 3 2 1
Library of Congress Cataloging-in-Publication Data is available.
ISBN 979-8-89333-215-5
ISBN 979-8-89333-216-2 (ebook)

CHAPTER 1

Asher flipped through his itinerary after he sat down in his aisle seat. He was heading to Anchorage from Seattle. This was to be the second of many flights that began in Denver before reaching his destination in far northern Alaska.

After putting his papers away, he watched the large plane fill with people as they clumsily lifted their oversized luggage and crammed them into the overhead bins. He exhaled heavily, disgusted with the fact that he was being sandwiched in with a bunch of strangers. Looking at the clock on his phone, Asher thought through the long hours he would be stifled in his small seat and sighed out loud, rolling his eyes.

A man walked past Asher and said to another passenger that they were in the wrong seat. This broke out into what Asher thought was a stupid conversation about reading the seating sign wrongly. The other passengers eventually had a good laugh about it.

A confident, smooth female voice came over the intercom. "Everyone, please, take your seats as quickly as you can. We will be closing the doors soon and preparing for takeoff."

"Hold your horses, lady! We just got on!" a man bellowed as he walked through the door of the plane. He then looked backward to someone following close behind, who appeared to be a business partner, and gave him a corky smile.

The other passengers quieted down slightly as the obnoxious man captured their attention. After a moment, everyone went back to what they were doing. Asher watched the two men in business suits fumble their way to their seats, sensing they had a few too many drinks before the flight. He thought to himself, *That might not have been a bad idea to have had a drink or two.* Reflecting again, he questioned, *Maybe I should start drinking? What does it matter anymore?* With this thought in mind, he slowly turned his head to look outside at the rain pouring down on all the luggage being loaded.

"Great," he mumbled miserably out loud.

"Pardon me?" a grandma asked kindly as she looked up to him from her center seat beside him.

"Oh, nothing," he answered as his eyes went back out the window trying to ignore her.

She followed his gaze, saying, "It never seems to stop, does it?" She determined he was looking at the raindrops continually falling from the gray skies of Seattle.

"I guess not," he answered her, not making eye contact.

Looking at his facial expression and hearing the tone of his voice, she understood he was not in a talkative mood, so she turned back to her magazine and let him be.

The plane soon left the gate and was up in the air, quickly hidden in the clouds that were causing the dreary, rainy scene. Asher watched the whitish-gray whiffs of thick, billowing clouds slither down the body of the plane, moving faster and faster. The plane pierced its way through the sky, trying to break itself free from the bondage of the storm. Then, in the blink of an eye, the plane emerged into the vast blue sky, looking down onto the top layers of large, soft, cotton ball-like clouds. He could feel and almost hear everyone on the plane sigh with relief as if they had been drowning and suddenly were able to come up for air. It was a feeling that everything would be all right now that they could see the blue sky again.

As the plane leveled out, the pilot came across the intercom, greeting everyone and giving the normal details of the trip. He then finished his speech with the time of their arrival. Asher looked back at his phone and exhaled again, irritated.

"It will be over before you know it," the same gentle, wise voice next to him said softly.

Asher nodded, trying not to be rude, then turned and gave her a fake smile.

"It's so beautiful and peaceful when we get through the clouds into the openness of the heavens," she stated as she purposely pointed across his chest to the windows on the other side of the plane.

His eyes followed her hand, looked out the windows, and replied, "It's nice."

"But to be honest, I love being in the thick clouds, not knowing what's coming in front of me or knowing where I am." She smiled giddily. Her small-framed body was dressed in petite clothes. She looked up to the tall, strong, young man sitting next to her and added with a grin, "It's mysterious and exciting, almost dangerous."

Asher looked down at her while attempting to figure out if she was crazy or if she truly meant what she was saying. He gave her a half smile and said, "Different strokes for different folks, I guess, ma'am?"

"Oh no, it's more than that, young man. It's a way of life!"

Not quite knowing how to reply, he hesitated, expressionless.

Seeing his face, she explained, "In the clear blue skies of life, we can plainly predict humanity as it repeats itself over and over. We get disappointed, scared, stressed, confused, or even angry when unexpected things happen or when they don't go the way we planned. But…" Drawing out the word, she excitedly clapped her hands together. "We can live free with faith, anticipating that extraordinary unknowns are truly coming. When and where we do not know. It's all a wonderful mystery because joy is there for the taking. Worry and fear are only for things that haven't happened and more than likely will never happen."

Her smile spread across her face with a look of someone who was sharing a deep secret. "This way of living is more exciting, instead of always being anchored to our limitations of what we see and hear. Everything will always work out for the good because we can put our faith in something far greater than our own human limitations. There is someone who can see through the clouds of our lives and knows what we need, when we need it, and how much of it we need. He can completely fill the desires of our heart, which we never even knew were there in the first place." She nodded with a wise grin as though she stated a fact from her vast years of experience.

Annoyed, Asher tilted his head slightly, trying to grasp what this gabby old lady was saying. Then a different voice in the aisle spoke up, "Can I get you something to drink?" Looking up, he saw a beverage cart parked next to him and the smiling face of the same beautiful flight attendant who had greeted everyone coming onto the plane. She was taller than the average woman, slender with naturally tan skin and long black hair.

Changing his train of thought and grateful that the conversation was interrupted, Asher cleared his throat. He sat up taller in his seat, attempting to be impressive, and answered, "I'll have…" Just then, the grandma sitting next to him answered the flight attendant simultaneously, jumbling their words together. Asher instantly got embarrassed that he had spoken out of turn and hadn't been a gentleman by not letting the old, fragile lady go first.

"Oh, I'm sorry. Go ahead," Asher said, trying to recover. The flight attendant gave a courteous smile, looking at the other passenger next to him. She was doing her best not to embarrass the man any more than he had himself. Taking care of the passenger next to the window, the flight attendant now looked at Asher. "So what was it you wanted?"

"I'll just take a bottle of water, please," he said, trying not to make eye contact.

"I can't give you the bottle, but I can put the water on ice if you would like."

"That would be fine," he answered, not too pleased with his request being rejected. She poured water into a plastic cup with ice and then handed it to him, saying, "Here you go," before quickly moving on to the next row of passengers.

He pulled down the tray from the seat in front of him, taking a sip as the imposing, petite passenger beside him spoke up again, "So...which one is it for you, young man? Live in a predictable, boring, trapped life full of worry and fear? Or have fun living joyfully and free with great anticipation of wondrous things to come?"

Asher, not wanting to think about anything or talk to anyone, leaned his head back on the headrest. He wanted to be left alone but gazed down at her and answered, "Ma'am, I don't mean to be rude, but I don't know what you're talking about. It sounds like some type of religious mumbo jumbo to me, and right now that's the furthest thing from my mind." He turned his head back forward, put the cup of water on the tray, and pressed the button on the side of his armrest. He leaned the chair back, closing his eyes, and exhaled heavily as he crossed his arms.

He attempted to fall asleep, but all he could do was keep his eyes closed to fool everyone, especially the grandma next to him. Suddenly, he heard the same loud voice from the man who boarded the plane late. The man, a few rows ahead of him on the opposite side, blurted out, "What do you mean you don't have that kind of beer? What do you have?" It sounded like there was a pause, though the flight attendant was answering the man softly. He replied, "Fine. If that's all you got, I'll take it! I'll even take two or three." He laughed loudly as he looked at the guy next to him, who was chuckling with him and ordering the same.

"Thanks, pretty thing. Don't be a stranger. You've got my seat number!" the man added. Both men laughed, thinking this was humorous. A soft murmur from many passengers could be heard, talking about what was said.

Asher slowly opened his eyes to see what was going on. The flight attendant unlocked the cart and moved to the next row, completely ignoring the obnoxious men. The guys quieted down as they drank their beers, adding to the alcohol that was already in their systems.

Closing his eyes again, Asher was able to drift off this time. His eyes began to move back and forth under his lids as a dream came alive. Going back almost a year ago, he saw himself alone, standing in the middle of an open cemetery on a dreary day. He was peering down at a headstone placed on a fresh grave. No words were coming out of his mouth because he did not know what to say. He was looking at what was left after his father's unexpected and sudden death.

Expressions of sorrow, relief, and anger were all attempting to come out of him. However, not even a whisper could make its way past his confused mind, let alone his tightened lips.

In Asher's dream, he was physically reliving the heavy emotions of losing his father—emotions that came out in soft but tortured moans. His shoulders slowly drooped down as he slept.

The scene shifted around in his mind until he saw himself last spring. He was in a huge ballroom with dozens of tables and hundreds of people dressed in fancy clothes. It was draft day for the NFL, and the excitement was unbelievable. He sat at a table with other college athletes and their parents, waiting for names to be called from the well-lit podium. A giant, multicolored screen glowed on the wall behind the podium, featuring the different professional teams. Names of athletes who had already been drafted were posted next to the team names.

As each team representative walked up to the microphone to announce their picks, names continued to be called but not Asher's. The draft was just about over as Asher rocked his body back and forth in his seat; he felt very nervous. Then, before he knew it, it was over. His name was never called to come up and receive a jersey.

Dejected, humiliated, and bewildered, Asher sat alone with just his mother. Guys walked past him, patting him on the shoulder and telling him, "Sorry." Then, one of the recruiters who had been talking with him months prior, walked by. Asher stood up, grabbed him by the arm, and asked, "What happened? You said I was a great prospect."

"I'm sorry, Mr. Collins, but the team's doctors said your type of knee injury is a major factor and they couldn't recommend you."

"Are you kidding me? Is that what they're saying?" he answered loudly as people around him turned to look at what was going on.

"Asher, you're a great player, and if it were up to me, you would be on our team but not right now. Show up for walk-on tryouts next month and prove yourself to them there. Maybe they'll change their minds."

As the dream continued, Asher's body tensed up; his jaw muscles flexed, and he gritted his teeth. His shoulders lifted, tightening his upper body, all while his eyes remained closed.

"But my knee has been healed for a year! I'm fine!" Asher hopelessly pleaded his case, all the while drawing more attention from the recruits and others around him. Then his mother stood up next to him and said, "Son, calm down; it's going to be okay. You'll try again, and maybe next time—"

"Next time? Next time! I'm just as good and healthy as anyone here right now. If Dad was still alive, he would be so ticked off, jumping down my throat because I didn't get drafted!" Asher slammed his hand on the table.

The smack was like a light switch being flipped off. For a moment everything went black, and then it switched back on. Now Asher was looking into his fiancée's face a month later, after the draft, handing him back her engagement ring, saying, "Asher, I'm sorry, but I can't marry you, at least not right now. We've changed. Things are different between the two of us since we graduated. My new job is taking up a lot of time, and you…?" She paused for words, then finished, "I don't know where you're going in life since you didn't get drafted. Sometimes, I don't even know who you are anymore. You're not the same person I said I would marry two years ago."

"What are you saying?" Asher's body was beginning to deflate in his dream. "I'm the same person you've known for years, Lynette. I've been a little off balance since my dad died, but I'm the same guy. And what's not being drafted have to do with you and me?"

"I'm not getting into another argument. That's all we do anymore."

"No, we don't!" Asher exclaimed.

"Whatever, Asher, take the ring back. Maybe if we see other people for a while, we'll get our bearings straight. You get on a team after the walk-on tryouts, and then we'll know if we're to be together."

"See other people? Lynette, I don't want to see other people! That's why I asked you to marry me. I love you. We love each other, right? Or…have you only been with me because I was going to be a pro football player?"

"Well, like I said, things have changed, and maybe time will give us an answer. Goodbye, Asher."

In his dream, he saw her walk away, her body slowly evaporating to nothing. He looked down at his hand, watching the ring fall to the ground and make a loud pinging sound as it hit the floor.

Suddenly, his body flinched, and he awoke from what had been a recurring nightmare. His heart and mind raced with emotions from the events that had actually occurred in his recent life.

It took a moment to come back to where he was, thirty-three thousand feet up in an airplane, flying to Alaska. The plane bumped up and down, flying through turbulence. The seat belt sign dinged overhead with a familiar sound.

Asher had graduated from college some months earlier where he had received a full-ride football scholarship. He had great aspirations of making it to the pros. In his junior year, his knee was injured during a game. It took two surgeries to get him back on the field. He played at about ninety percent of his ability during his senior year. He still did very well for his college team, helping them go to a bowl game. He had been approached by many professional team recruiters, only to be denied any invitation on draft day.

He adjusted his large-framed body in the small seat while looking out of the corner of his eye. He was staring down at the older lady next to him. He could see that she was sound asleep. *Good*, he thought to himself, still fuming about his dream. It reminded him of why he pretty much hated his life right now.

Asher's father always had high expectations for him, never letting him settle for second best at anything. The goals his father set were always out of Asher's reach, but his father did this to purposely push him to be the best he could be. Becoming a professional football player was the goal set for Asher whether he wanted it or not. Subconsciously, his father was reliving his youth through Asher, and his own dreams were eclipsing his son's life.

Their father-and-son relationship was very shallow; it was more like an employer/employee relationship. Asher struggled to understand why "the employer" disciplined so harshly, oftentimes evolving into abuse. His outlook of what a true father should be eluded him. He believed, through experience, that his father's position in the family was one of a dictator. "The employer" continually punished with harsh words or an angry hand, devoid of loving encouragement and empty of leading with a positive example.

When his father suddenly passed away, there was a cavern of emptiness that echoed in all directions. Even though Asher was a man, his father had been in charge, always telling him what to do. Now, he was lost without his life organizer. Since his father's death, Asher had, deep down, lost interest in football. This confused Asher because, for most of his life, it was his destiny. After not being drafted, he seethed with frustration and anger. He was forced to wrestle with something his father did not allow: failure.

Making things worse, the one he loved and wanted to marry walked away without remorse or regret. Ultimately, it was not him she wanted but what he was going to be. Asher's heart was ripped from him. He thought he knew this person he had spent the last three years of his life dating. They had talked about the future and how much they loved each other.

His cavern of emptiness filled with anger, sadness, pride, confusion, and self-pity, anchoring him down to the point where he had not been able to function with family, friends, or even himself. He had shut down mentally, emotionally, and physically, unable to move forward. He spent his time looking back at all the tragedies that had come his way.

A churchgoer before he went to college (because his parents made him), Asher had considered himself a religious person. Going through the motions of being a Christian, which he believed supported and strengthened his efforts in life, was failing him miserably. He struggled to see how God fit into all of this. His world had been shaken to the point that he didn't care about things, people, and especially God. How could all this happen to him when he had prayed to the One that supposedly sees and knows all? Every relationship he had and had worked hard for had vanished, and all he wanted to do now was disappear and be totally alone.

His parents told him when he first started college that when he graduated, they would send him anywhere around the world he wanted to go. Growing up in the mountains of Colorado, he loved being in the isolated backwoods, hiking, hunting, and fishing. He always wanted to experience the extreme wilderness of Alaska, so he took his mother up on the graduation present. He wanted to get as far away from everyone as he could.

Looking on the Internet, the Brooks Range in far northern Alaska above the Arctic Circle caught his attention. Seeing that it was a rolling, mountainous landscape over seven hundred miles by two hundred miles, Asher envisioned it to be the perfect place to get away, hide, and forget everything going on in his life.

The flight attendant caught his attention as he heard her footsteps behind him going down the aisle to the front of the plane. As she went by, the beer-guzzling businessman piped up loud enough for most of the passengers around his seat to hear him say, "Hey, pretty woman, how about another beer?"

Turning to him directly, she stated, "My name is Mia, and I'll check with the lead flight attendant. I think you have had enough to drink on this flight."

Everyone around them mumbled and shook their heads yes. The two men had continued their distasteful behavior the entire flight, and everyone was getting tired of them. Asher was no exception. Especially with the mood he had been in for quite some time, his fuse was always short.

"Oh, come on, Mia...," the man grumbled loudly. "We're not doing anything wrong, just celebrating on our way home. So what about those beers?"

"Like I said, I'll check with the lead flight attendant." She turned to walk away, and the man leaned out into the aisle, saying, "That a girl," and swatted her on the rear end. Her torso popped forward from the slap, and she turned, giving the guy a stern look.

Everyone in the vicinity caught their breath, stunned at what they had just seen. Asher, on the other hand, lost it. His fuse instantly burned up, and he exploded out of his seat. He swiftly placed his cup of water on the old lady's tray while flipping his own tray up and quickly approached the flight attendant. With a firm expression, he said, "I'll take care of this. You go do what you need to do."

She looked up at the well-built, handsome passenger with his short brown hair that almost touched the ceiling and shoulders that stretched out the width of the aisle. He caught her off guard more than the drunk businessman had when he swatted her on the backside. Asher could have had an intimidating appearance, but she was more smitten by him coming to her rescue than frightful of him.

She answered hesitantly, "Oh. Okay, but it's all right. Everything is fine."

"You walk away and go talk to whoever you need to talk to," he said with an encouraging smile.

"And what do you think you're doing, boy?" the obnoxious man blurted out.

Asher's smile disappeared. Then, with a nod of his head and a narrowing of his eyes to the flight attendant to go away, he quickly turned and grasped the man at the base of his neck. He pressed him hard against the back of the seat.

"What are you doing, man? You're choking him!" the guy's partner in crime yelled next to him.

As the man clawed at Asher's powerful forearm to free himself, Asher, having complete physical control of the offender, calmly said, "I'm going to let go, and you are going to be quiet until the flight attendant you assaulted comes back. Then, you will apologize to her, and you will not look at her, talk to her, or touch her again for the rest of the flight. Do you understand?"

The man's face was getting red, and, noticing that he could not breathe, Asher let go of his neck. Gasping for air and coughing, he spurted out, "What the heck do you think you're doing?"

"Do we have an understanding of what you're going to do and not do?" Asher asked, looking down at the man.

Smarting off, the man responded, "I'm not doing—" Faster than lighting, Asher grabbed the man's neck again before he could finish what he was saying.

The man's friend unbuckled his seat belt and attempted to stand up. He reached for Asher's arm and yelled out, "Back off or I'll—" He couldn't finish his threat. Asher grasped him by the neck with his other hand and slammed him back down in his seat, all while asking, "You'll do what?" Surprised at the speed and strength of the man coming to the defense of the flight attendant, the friend sat there frozen, no longer wanting to be involved.

Asher sensed the second man was no longer going to be trouble and let go as he stared him down, keeping a firm lock on the first man. The friend quietly spoke, "At least let up on Brad's neck; he can't breathe."

Asher looked at Brad with his face reddened again and eased off some with his powerful hand and said, "Once again Brad…" He drew the name out as he narrowed his eyebrows together, giving him an evil look. "Are you going to be well-behaved and apologize to the nice flight attendant?"

As Brad started to nod his head yes and verbalize, Asher let go of him. He stood up straight, giving the guy the full view of his naturally intimidating stature as their eyes locked on each other.

"What's going on here?" someone with the voice of authority questioned.

Glad that someone appeared to come to his rescue, Brad blurted out, "This guy is—"

Asher gave a slight forward jerk with his body, flexing all his muscles as though he were going to reach out and choke him again. Brad quickly stopped talking, flinching back into his seat in anticipation of what was coming.

Then Asher slowly bent over and whispered in the man's ear, "You'll do as I told you, and if you continue with your stupid, drunken self, being loud and irritating on this flight, just remember we'll soon land. And when we do, I guarantee that you'll have to use the bathroom at the airport because you have had too much to drink. And when you do, I'll be right behind you, and I will make sure you don't leave the stall. I'll break every bone in your pathetic body, and there won't be a security camera in sight." Asher slowly backed away, giving Brad a friendly smile as if he had said something kind.

He then turned to the lead flight attendant, spotted the assaulted flight attendant standing behind, and said, "Everything is fine. I thought this man was choking, but he's okay." Asher looked back to Brad with the same smile, nodding his head for Brad to agree with him. Asher then started walking back to his seat through the tense, thick air of people staring at him. They were grateful for his heroism but, at the same time, uncomfortable with the physical force that had taken place.

"I'm going to sue you!" Brad spouted, feeling safe when the big man was no longer in his face.

Asher sat in his seat, looked toward the man, and said calmly but loud enough for everyone around to hear, "No, you won't. You and your friend there are wearing wedding rings. And as soon as your wives find out what you did to this pretty flight attendant"—Asher's eyes flashed to her then back to Brad—"they will probably divorce their sorry, drunken, pitiful husbands and take them for everything they've got." The plane filled with whispers, snickering, and giggling at Asher's truthful and powerful answer. He had once again put the man back in his place.

Asher proceeded to ignore the incident and pulled his tray down, retrieving his cup from his neighbor's tray. He took a sip and leaned back in his chair again, closing his eyes with confidence.

The drunk man suddenly seemed to be fully aware of the disastrous probabilities that could happen. Darting his eyes back and forth, not looking directly at anyone until he turned forward again, he looked up to the lead flight attendant and said, "Everything is all right. He was just helping me out." Then he looked at Mia standing behind him and said with an embarrassed smile, "Sorry."

Understanding there were no more words to be said, the lead flight attendant turned to walk away, as did Mia, but not before she looked at the man down the aisle, now with his eyes closed, sitting in 23C.

***

It was midday when Asher walked off the plane from the long flight. He had decided to play mind games with the two businessmen and followed a short distance behind them as they all walked down the concourse. Periodically they looked back, only to see him watching their every move. When he got to the departure screens, Asher stopped to see what gate his next flight, to Fairbanks, was departing from. Then, only turning his head, he looked in the businessmen's direction just as Brad looked back to see if they were still being followed. Asher gave him a slow wink and produced a half smile, lowering his head as if to say, *I'm watching you.*

"I never thanked you for helping me out with those two guys." Asher heard a woman's voice come from the opposite direction. He turned to see the flight attendant standing next to him, watching the two drunks walk away. She turned to look up to him, held out her hand, and said, "I'm Mia."

Taken slightly off guard, he fumbled to get his hand up while letting go of his carry-on bag. He then gently squeezed and shook her hand. The touch of her soft skin and delicate features sent a fiery sensation throughout his body. This was followed by the chilling memories of his ex-fiancée flashing through his mind. He had not thought of another woman or even been close to anyone else until this moment. Caught in confusion, he stammered, "Oh, hi. I'm Asher."

"Asher. That's a different name." She smiled, holding on to his hand a little longer than normal. "I never had anyone come to my rescue like that before."

He shrugged his broad shoulders shyly, smiling back at her. "You must get tired of guys treating you that way."

"Most of the time it's just a flirty word here and there. Once in a great while with the fake apology of, 'Oops, sorry, I didn't mean to bump you.' But to have someone's hand actually touching me"—she looked down at their hands, then looked back up—"is very rare."

He had seen her gaze go to their hands when she said that and realized he was the one holding on. He quickly let go with an apologetic expression. "I'm sorry. I didn't mean..." He stopped mid-sentence, realizing he repeated what she was just talking about and began turning red in the face.

Each smiled at the other, sharing an awkward laugh when someone came down the concourse and called out, "Mia! Mia!" One of the other flight attendants from the flight was quickly walking in their direction.

"What is it, Jenny?"

As the woman caught up with them, she said, "We've been rescheduled to work the return flight back to Seattle, which leaves in an hour. The crew that's supposed to work it had a two-hour delay in LA."

Disappointed, Mia replied, "Are you kidding me? I was just about to get on my last flight to Fairbanks to visit my parents for a few days."

Asher interjected, "You were going to work the flight to Fairbanks?"

"Yes. Why?" Crossing her arms and putting on a big friendly grin, Mia asked, "Are you on the flight to Fairbanks?"

"As a matter of fact, I am," Asher stated, mimicking her by crossing his arms.

Jenny looked up at this large muscular athlete Mia was talking with and asked with a smile, "Is this 23C?" Mia started to blush and answered only by nodding her head yes.

"You are a big, good-looking guy!" Jenny stated enthusiastically with googly eyes.

"Jenny...," Mia said, tilting her head and giving Jenny a death look.

"You can come to my rescue anytime, 23C." Jenny flirted playfully, touching his arm with her fingertips.

"You don't want me to do to you what he did to the guy who touched me, do you?" Mia responded as she lifted Jenny's hand off Asher's arm. She could not keep her death look any longer. Smirking, she let out a laugh under her breath as Jenny mirrored her expression, and they laughed together.

Asher was uneasy and completely out of place. Even though he was deeply involved with team sports, he considered himself an introvert, especially when it came to strangers. That was one of the things his ex-fiancée and he would always argue about. She wanted them to do things with other people, but he was content with just the two of them doing things together.

However, at this exact moment, his life's frustrations and anger, which had flared up on the plane and had lately been his driving force when it came to people, disappeared. He had no defense in this brief encounter with these two women, making him feel helpless.

"Well, I've got to get to my gate," Asher said, trying to run away as guilt was building up at being this close to another woman. To him, psychologically and in his heart, he was still engaged to someone else. "It was nice meeting you, Mia." Their eyes locked despite his efforts to divert them throughout this interaction.

"It was nice to meet you too. Again, thank you for helping me out."

"No problem. I was in the right place at the right time. Lucky, I guess."

Mia started to turn to walk away before she replied, "You definitely were in the right place at the right time! But I don't believe in luck." She smiled, giving him an extra stare, and then continued on as they parted ways.

CHAPTER 2

On the horizon and as far as Asher could see, the landscape was an ocean of yellow grass. Thick green brush was standing in clumps, and pine trees dotted the countryside. At fifteen thousand feet, Asher stared at the wonder from the plane's window. Pockets of water shimmered like diamonds from marshy areas, small lakes, and streams, giving glamour to the grassy, wooded landscape. The plane was flying northward to Bettles, Alaska.

On his fourth flight of this long day, Asher left Fairbanks behind almost two and a half hours ago and was heading toward the Arctic Circle. The small settlement of Bettles was nestled there alongside the Koyukuk River. The captain of the eight-passenger, twin-engine plane had been generous in sharing different facts about Alaska with Asher and the five other passengers: two oil workers heading to Prudhoe Bay, an Alaskan state trooper, and two other tourists.

Off and on throughout the flight, the pilot banked the plane, slightly altering their course. This gave the passengers the opportunity to see one of the greatest accomplishments of modern time: the Trans-Alaska Pipeline. The pipeline started in Prudhoe Bay (the farthest northern point in Alaska) and cut straight down through the belly of this giant state. It traversed approximately fifteen hundred miles south to Valdez, Alaska.

The captain explained that most aircrafts flying north and south preferred to follow parallel to the oil pipeline, using it as a road map. This was beneficial for two reasons. First, the pipeline serves as a visual compass of where they are. Alaska has thousands of square miles of generally the exact same scenery. Secondly, and more importantly, it would be easier for search and rescue to find an aircraft if it went down if they all flew a similar course.

The scenery became monotonous after a while and hypnotized Asher. He wondered how anything living down there, whether animals, birds, or even man, knew if they were coming or going. You could not see a beginning or an end in this giant landscape unless you could see the pipeline.

The plane banked suddenly away from the pipeline, and soon Asher could make out a spot in the distance. It looked like an island next to a big river. The island interrupted the landscape's flow of grass, brush, and trees. The captain looked back at the passengers with his headgear on and said, "We're just a few minutes out from landing. Hope you enjoyed the flight to Bettles. Please make sure your seat belts are securely fastened."

Before landing, they made a pass over the dirt runway, which, when examined, closely looked like a long brown scab in the middle of the expanse of plant life. Asher found out later that in the bush, you must always do a flyover first to make sure no moose or caribou are on the runway.

After landing, Asher descended the stairs of the small plane and noticed they were parked next to one of the larger, aging buildings. It was marked with a red and white wooden sign on the front that read "Bettles Lodge."

Besides being the only motel and restaurant around, it also had a small store. Entering the lodge, you stepped into a great room that had faded and well-worn long wooden benches stretched along one of the walls. The ticketing counter for all inbound and outbound passengers also served as the register for the motel. There was an open office behind the counter that contained the radio equipment for air traffic communications.

As Asher and the other passengers entered the building, they noticed several people sitting on the benches, waiting for their plane—the same plane that he and the others had just flown in on. The center of the great room was used for foot traffic and a collection spot for luggage. Fishing pole cases, rifle cases, backpacks, and large duffle bags, all with destination tags, were piled up, waiting for departure.

As they were standing in the waiting area for no more than a minute, the door they had entered swung open abruptly. An older, short, jolly man with a bushy graying mustache and smartly trimmed beard stepped in anxiously. He asked somewhat loudly for the size of the room, "Did Mr. Collins just arrive?"

Asher took a step toward him, and before he could get a word out, the man walked right up to him with a giant smile and offered his hand, saying with confidence, "You must be Asher!"

"Yes, sir. That's me."

The man shook Asher's hand firmly, pointed toward the door, and said enthusiastically, "We need to get your stuff gathered up and to the float plane that's docked on the river so the pilot can finish loading. We leave in about forty-five minutes."

"You guys don't mess around!" Asher responded.

"You're right," he stated as his expression changed. He looked at Asher sternly in the eyes to give him a warning. "There's no messing around way up here in the bush, or you're dead!"

Their eyes locked for a moment. Asher was taken off guard, searching for words to say when a voice behind him came to his rescue, "You leave the young man alone, Rudy." Asher felt a strong hand firmly grasp his shoulder, and a man stepped up beside him as if he were being protective.

"Clay! What in the heck are you doing way up here?" Joy burst from Rudy as he opened his arms and gave the man a pint-sized bear hug. It was the Alaskan state trooper who was on the flight. Rudy and Clay patted each other on the back while they hugged. Then they stood at arm's length, holding on to the other's shoulders and both asked at the same time, "How long has it been?"

"Gee, it's got to have been two, three years at least," Rudy stated.

"If I recall, I was coming to someone else's rescue back then," Clay said loudly, rolling his eyes toward the small audience of people in the lodge. "There was someone…I don't know…about this tall." Clay put his hand out to the short stature of Rudy and continued, "Let's see," putting his hand to his chin, looking as if to be recalling the history of their encounter, "it started with a call I got just out of Tok, which is exactly halfway between Anchorage and Fairbanks. It's 400 miles each way. Someone was being chased by a grizzly about fifteen miles north, out of town, along the highway. The call came from a bush pilot who saw the horror as he flew overhead, heading to Anchorage." The trooper's tone and expression changed, reflecting the urgency of the situation. "I took off as fast as I could, hoping to get there in time to find the person alive, which would have been a huge blessing and miracle." He sorrowfully shook his head.

There were a few people catching their breath as complete silence fell in the room. You could feel the growing curiosity as they wanted to know what happened next. Asher looked at Rudy for a split second and saw that he was hanging on to every word the trooper was saying. Staring at Rudy, he thought to himself, *Rudy's still alive, so what happened to him?* Then, he looked back as Clay continued, "As I was racing down the highway, it felt like it took forever to get to the scene. But it was only about ten to twelve minutes.

"I finally saw an old white Chevy truck pulled off to the side of the road. Stopping behind the truck, I noticed that it was jacked up on one side as if someone were changing a tire. I got out of my vehicle and quickly looked around the truck… nobody." Clay paused and shrugged while gazing around at everybody. "The passenger door was wide open, and I looked in… There was no one, and the person's rifle was still on the gun rack behind the headrest. I started shouting out around the area, 'Hello! Is anyone here? Does anyone need help? It's the state police.' Not receiving a reply, I started looking toward the woods for any signs. Finally, I made out some footprints in the grass and decided to follow them.

"I called out again and again…nothing. I walked in the direction of the footprints and came upon a tire iron lying on the ground. As I kneeled to examine it closer, my heart sank as I stood up again. 'Blood…' I said out loud."

One of the people sitting on the bench exhaled the words, "Oh no!"

Clay looked over to the individual. "That's exactly what I thought as I knelt there, looking at the tire iron, trying to figure out what to do next. Then I suddenly heard a voice a short distance away. I couldn't make out any words, but I could tell by the tone that someone was under duress."

Clay glanced at Rudy with a most serious expression. Everybody in the room followed his gaze and looked at Rudy whose eyes were open wide. Then they looked back to Clay with anticipation. "I drew my weapon and proceeded in the direction of the voice.

"As I got closer, I could tell that just ahead of me, through the thick brush, there was a struggle going on. Someone or something was huffing and puffing as branches were breaking and a thumping of weight hit the ground. Was it footsteps, paws, or bodies? I couldn't tell. Then, I heard it." Clay looked around at all the people listening intently to his every word, and he slowly lowered his tone and head. He then did his best to give out a deep growl as he raised his head with a fierce look on his face.

One of the ladies listening said out loud, "Oh my Lord!"

With tightened lips, narrowed eyes, and stern features, Clay looked back to Rudy while telling everyone, "I will never forget what I saw next." Closing his eyes and shaking his head, he hesitated for a second. He glanced around at everybody with an expression like it was too horrific to continue.

"What did you see?" one of the outbound passengers asked excitedly, pushing the trooper to continue.

"Just to warn you, what I saw has left a permanent impression of this man deep in my soul." Clay pointed toward Rudy, nodding his head and patting his own chest slowly. He cautiously continued with the story. "With all my senses on high alert, I slowly proceeded forward, parting the branches of the brush, holding my gun up in front of me, waiting for a target to appear." Clay held his hands up as if holding a gun. "I tiptoed forward so as not to make any sounds or sudden movement that would make myself known. I peeked into the opening on the other side of the brush, and there they were!" he exclaimed, and everyone held their breath as Clay's eyes popped wide open and his voice jumped to full excitement. "In complete desperation, Rudy and a grizzly bear were locked together in a battle of…of…" He hesitated this time, trying to compose himself, then exclaimed with excitement, "…of tug-of-war!" Everyone except Rudy and Clay stopped, bewildered in thought.

"What...are you kidding me?" questioned one of the passengers in disbelief. "Tug-of-war?"

"You got it," Clay replied with a big smile. "Rudy was holding on, for dear life, to one end of a small black metal box as his heels dug into the ground while leaning backward. He was yelling at the bear, through clenched teeth, to let go. The bear had his teeth sunk in deep to the other end of the black box, jerking it backward. Rudy was putting up a good fight, but when the grizzly started swinging him around and around like you would do with one of your kids, I lost it!" Clay and Rudy started laughing so hard that it became a roar of noise that no one could resist joining. Everyone now was looking at Rudy, trying to picture in their heads this short, jolly man flying around and around in the air like a rag doll.

Asher piped in, not amused, "What really happened?"

"Just as he told you," Rudy replied, still laughing.

Clay stepped to the side of Rudy, hugging him with one arm. He looked at everyone in the room, attempting to calm down enough to explain the story.

"'Tug' here"—Clay gave Rudy some jerks—"was changing a tire on his truck when the bear came out of the woods. The bear snuck into the cab of the truck because Rudy left the door open, smelled something he liked in the black box, and walked off with it. Rudy saw the bear leave, realized what it had in its mouth, and took off after him."

"You mean Rudy was chasing the bear, not the other way around?" Asher asked.

"That's right."

"But what about the blood on the tire iron? Wasn't Rudy hurt?"

"No," Clay responded, shaking his head. "Tug threw the tire iron at the bear, and it bounced off its rear end. The blood turned out to really be transmission fluid; Rudy had all his tools and motor fluids in the same toolbox in the back of his truck, and the bottle of transmission fluid had leaked onto the tire iron."

"What in the world was in the black box that you would go running after a grizzly for? Gold?" one of the oil workers from the inbound flight asked.

Everyone turned to Rudy and stared bewildered, waiting for the mysterious answer.

Rudy piped up in his jolly, loud voice, "My lunch!" Rudy patted his belly. "The fur ball had my lunch box, and I wasn't going to let him get away with my food!"

"Are you crazy?" the oil worker exclaimed.

"No, I was hungry! I was on my way back home from a round trip to Tok. Kathy at The Tok Café had made me one of her tasty Philly steak sandwiches for the road, and I was not about to let some four-legged beast eat my meal," Rudy finished as he folded his arms on his chest and gave everyone a nod of defiance.

"Okay, Mr. Trooper, back to Rudy flying around in the air," Asher interjected, still not amused (unlike everyone else who giggled again). "What happened?"

Clay shrugged his shoulders and said, "I stood there for a second, not knowing if I should laugh or be concerned for his life. Instantly, the latter came to mind, so I screamed at the bear, raising my arms and jumping in the air. Both of them had been so focused on what they were doing that when I did that, it not only scared the bear but Rudy as well. They both let go of the box at the same time. Rudy went flying back about ten feet onto his butt. The bear just stood there looking at me, not realizing that he had released the box.

"Rudy turned to me, recognizing what and who I was, and without hesitation looked back at the lunch box and jumped on it. He tucked it into his body just like a football player with a fumble. The bear stood there on all fours, looked back at Rudy, swayed his body back and forth and acted like he was trying to make up his mind about what to do next. Then, it gave Rudy a big huff of breath and walked into the woods."

"You're out of your mind, little man," the oil worker told Rudy as everyone looked toward him, wondering if this man was insane.

"No, I'm not; just don't ever mess with my food!" Rudy lashed back at the man as he put his hands on his hips. He then slowly gave a friendly smile, and everyone laughed again. Conversations popped up as the crowd began rehearsing and retelling the story.

The trooper stepped in front of Asher, giving him another pat on the shoulder and said, "You're in for a treat if you're taking a trek with Rudy himself, big man."

While looking at Rudy, Asher leaned over toward the trooper. He peered over his shoulder and whispered, "Are you sure he's in his right mind and safe to be with?"

Clay responded, "Asher, isn't it?"

Asher nodded.

"If there was one person I would want to be in the bush with, it would be Mr. Alaska," he said, pointing his head toward Rudy, giving him validation. "He might be short, loud, and a bit crazy, but pound for pound, there is no smarter, tougher, and all-around great guy in Alaska." Clay looked back, giving Rudy a grin and nod of confidence.

"Okay, enough of this fooling around," Rudy said, taking control of the conversation. "Time is ticking away. We still need to find out where in the world we're going in the BR." Rudy was talking about the Brooks Range. He gave Clay one last hug, exchanged a few more words, and hurriedly walked Asher out the door.

Back at the plane, they picked up Asher's large, backcountry backpack, fully loaded, and Rudy asked, "You got everything in there that was on my list for a two-week trip?"

Asher nodded. "Yes, sir, and a few other things."

"Great! Let's go." They proceeded across the dirt runway, down a path about fifty yards toward the river. There, tied to a boat dock, was Asher's final transportation: an orange, single-engine plane with upper deck wings. It was sitting on two large aluminum torpedo-like floats and softly bobbed up and down with the flow of the river. The Koyukuk River ran parallel to the dirt runway and gently flowed east to west. It was a big river about sixty-five yards wide in places, with grayish clear water that was cold as ice. As they approached the plane, a man was tying a long, silver aluminum canoe upside down to the top of one of the torpedo floats.

Rudy said loudly, "Finally we're here, Steven." The man looked back, stepping off the float onto the dock and replied with little emotion.

"It's about time, Tug. We need to rock and roll. There's a small front coming in later this afternoon, and I'd like to get back before it gets here." Steven then looked at Asher. "Wow, you're a big guy; how much do you weigh?"

Understanding this man was in a hurry, Asher responded, "I'm six four, two forty-five."

"Okay, now your pack totals—hmm…about sixty pounds?" he asked.

"Close. The scale showed fifty-six when I checked it in, in Denver."

Rudy cut in and asked the pilot, "Got everything you need, Steven? We need to hurry back to the Geo Room and decide where we're going."

"Make it quick. I'm fueled and will be ready to go in twenty minutes," he said as he opened a side luggage door of the plane to put Asher's backpack onboard.

They quickly got to one of the twelve small buildings lined up next to the Bettles Lodge and parallel to the runway. Rudy explained five of the buildings were homes for the fourteen people who lived there year-round; two were auto garages containing the plows and graders for the runway; one was a well-stocked store filled with food, clothing, building materials, hunting/fishing equipment, and many other outdoor items; three were hangers for housing smaller aircrafts; and the one they were walking to was an office for official work.

Once in the building, Rudy explained that it was used to monitor all activity coming and going from Bettles, as well as all travel in and out of the Brooks Range. Because the Brooks Range Wilderness is so vast, it is very easy for someone to get lost and never be found. The state required everyone to sign in and out when traveling north of Bettles.

Asher and Rudy headed to a back room titled Geo Room. On the right was a large, sloping architect desk littered with maps, sitting against one wall. The desk was adjacent to a wall fitted with a massive bookshelf that contained rolled-up topography maps in individual cubbies that ran from floor to ceiling. On the wall between those two was a very large geographical map that covered everything from the Arctic Circle up to the Northern Sea—with the Brooks Range plastered right in the middle.

Rudy walked up to the map and explained that this would be a special trip for them both because he didn't typically guide anymore. He told Asher to choose any of the two-week trips he wanted since it was just going to be the two of them. He began to point out several options. Each one would fly them north about a hundred miles, up different valleys to a mid-sized lake large enough for the float plane to land and take off. Then, they would backpack for a few days to another lake, where the plane would have unloaded and stashed the canoe. It would be situated next to one of the rivers that eventually dumped into the main Koyukuk River, which flows past Bettles, and would end the trek.

Each option looked great to Asher as he eyed the map and traced the blue lines representing rivers to the various lakes. He asked Rudy which had the most diversification of terrain and scenery and which one he personally liked best.

Asher decided to take the one Rudy favored, which started at Lost River Lake. From there, they would hike virgin terrain with no trails for about four days to Branch Lake, where the canoe would be waiting for them. They would canoe down the North Fork of the Koyukuk River for the rest of the trip. It flows beside Branch Lake and snakes its way through the mountains and valleys for one hundred and forty-eight miles before eventually dumping into the Koyukuk River, eight miles upstream from Bettles. Rudy told Asher this would take about eight days of continuous canoeing, getting them back to Bettles in about twelve days, weather permitting and if there were no mishaps along the way.

Rudy stepped up to a cubby and grabbed a topographic map that showed the area they were going to travel and put it in a waterproof cylinder.

Going back into the main room, Rudy and Asher walked up to a large, detailed logbook located next to the front door. Grabbing the attached pen, they both signed it and explained where they were going and the expected date of return. While signing, Asher noticed a fairly large photograph on the wall of a 747 airplane parked on a dirt runway.

When he examined it closer, the background looked like it was there in Bettles. When he asked Rudy about the picture, Rudy quickly told him that four years ago a German Airliner had to make an emergency landing. Bettles was the closest airport for five hundred miles that could possibly have been large enough to land at. The Bettles runway was almost a mile long, and the plane normally needed more than a mile to land and take off. They had to take a chance; if they didn't land there, more than likely they would have crash-landed in the vast wilderness, probably losing all lives on board.

As they walked out of the building, Rudy pointed down the runway in the direction the plane landed. He explained how the pilot came in so slow that it looked like the jumbo jet had just dropped out of the sky, perfectly touching down on one edge of the runway. The pilot had done this in order to gain as much runway as possible, in his attempt to stop in time; he didn't want to go over the edge at the other end. During the following two days of repairs, everybody in town did everything they could to lengthen the runway. They trimmed down the vegetation so the plane would not get caught up in the trees and tall brush as it attempted to get airborne. The giant plane just barely made it off the runway. At the last second, it flew off with success but not without blowing down trees and ripping out brush by the roots. The tornado-like funnels of power were exiting the enormous engines as the pilot put the pedal to the metal to sling shot the plane into the air. At the other end of the runway, the 747 left the ground, skimming some brush with its tires.

Rudy looked back at the building behind them and said the buildings shook like they were going to collapse from the vibration and noise of the engines on full throttle. He said this was the wildest thing anyone could ever remember happening to this mosquito-sized town on the Arctic Circle.

When they got back to their float plane, its propellers were already humming loudly and showering the area with a fine mist of water from the river. Steven had started the engine when he saw them walking out of the control office. He leaned toward Rudy, yelling over the noise, "Where are we headed, Tug?"

"Lost River Lake," Rudy shouted.

"Okay, let's get going," Steven shouted back as he opened the backside door. "You guys want to fight over who's sitting in the copilot seat?" Steven cracked a smile as he looked at Rudy, already knowing the answer.

"Get up in there and take that seat, big man. This is your trip," Rudy bellowed over the engine noise. Asher climbed in and buckled his seat belt as he looked at the console in front of him. He peered over the dash to see the river. Steven jumped in, and Rudy followed a few seconds later after he untied the ropes that were securing the plane to the dock. They fastened their seat belts. Steven looked around making sure everything was set and ready to go, and then he said loudly over the engine, "All right, gentlemen, Lost River Lake, here we come!"

Rudy leaned forward and patted Asher on the shoulder, saying with a jovial laugh, "You're in for the ride of your life, my friend. There's nothing like taking off and landing on a moving runway." He leaned back with a smile, looking out his side window.

The engine got a little louder and began to vibrate the plane slightly as Steven slowly pushed forward on the throttle. He maneuvered the plane to the middle of the gentle, waving river and, without hesitating, pushed the throttle forward. The engine roared with immense power. Everything inside the plane was forced backward as the plane propelled forward, rapidly gaining speed.

The spray of water off the pontoons rose higher and louder beside the plane the faster it skimmed on the water. Suddenly, the spray disappeared, and all went silent except for the deep hum of the engine.

Before Asher knew it, they were airborne, gaining altitude fast as the view of the river and land got smaller and smaller. Steven soon banked the plane to the north and leveled out.

The three of them sat quietly for a while, taking in the majestic scenery as the plane began gliding through whispers of clouds and into the grand mountain range. Reaching up high from the sides of the valley floors, the mountains had sharp, jagged summits like a saw.

Two-thirds of the way down the mountains, dark gray, rocky ground moistened by misty rain showers laid next to barren fields accented by rich, colorful vegetation at the lower mountain regions—the same vegetation that flowed down into the lush valley floors.

Their plane looked like a small orange insect flying above the ground. In all directions everything was extremely large and magnificent: the mighty rows of mountains, fingers of wide valleys with full, flowing rivers, and streams that snaked their way to destinations far away. The sky above was filled with clouds, marching their way over the mountaintops, seemingly going on forever.

Rudy broke the silence with his loud voice, almost scaring Asher and making his heart skip a beat. His words brought Asher's mind back inside the plane.

"Look over there, on the side of that mountain." Rudy pointed outside the front windshield between Steven and Asher as he leaned forward as far as his seat belt would let him. "See those white dots just under that ridgeline?"

Asher looked in the direction that he was pointing and soon focused on what had gotten Rudy excited.

"Dall sheep. Have you ever seen one before, Asher?"

"No," he replied shaking his head, staying focused on them. "Are they like Rocky Mountain bighorn sheep? We have those back in Colorado."

"They're in the same family, a little smaller and all white. Maybe we will get lucky and run into some on our hike," he exclaimed.

Asher had no idea why, but instantly his mind went back to the airport in Anchorage and the flight attendant Mia, who said she did not believe in luck. Softly amusing himself, he thought, *I would like to run into her again! Now that would be luck.*

Getting closer to their destination, Steven began to review the itinerary with Rudy, showing him on the map where he would be stashing the canoe at Branch Lake. Rudy confirmed the timeline of when to expect them back in Bettles and asked him if there were any other people in the area. Steven answered, "I dropped off two hunters from California downriver at Nora's place yesterday. But besides that, you guys are on your own. Plus, you're the only ones up in the interior for all I know. It's late in the season."

When he said that, Asher's spirit soared. He dreamed his whole life, especially in recent months, of what it would be like to be the only one for hundreds of square miles. Was it the appeal of primal instincts and the search for prehistoric times? Or was it a man looking for the ultimate adventure and excitement of survival, battling the wild and its elements? Perhaps he was finally going to be able to forget his real life and live in another place for a while—a place that seemed like it belonged in another time with no roads, paths, TVs, cell phone towers, etc. No way out but to walk and canoe, just like Louis and Clark in the lower forty-eight states. Would he truly be able to run away from reality, forgetting the frustrations, pains, and heartaches that have been holding him hostage recently?

As wondrous visions ran around in his head, the plane started a downward approach, and Steven slowly moved the controls forward and backed off on the throttle.

"There she is: Lost River Lake," Steven stated as they peered over the dashboard, surveying the area. The valley floor was naturally mounded up at the lower end, damming up the stream that ran through it to form the lake. This valley was narrower than the ones earlier, and the vegetation had changed during the flight as well. There were no trees or bushes, just low-growing grass and very short shrubs with a mixture of small rocks covered with moss and lichen.

Steven did a low flyover, looking closely at the waves in the water to determine which direction the wind was blowing. He banked the plane hard to turn around and land. Asher's stomach floated up into his chest. He looked out his side window thinking to himself, *What a rush!* He was looking straight down to the ground as if there was nothing to stop him from falling…nothing except for the invisible Gs the plane was pulling as it turned around, locking him into his seat.

The landing was smooth and surprisingly short as the pontoons quickly gripped the water. Steven gently maneuvered the plane to the shoreline and unloaded the backpacks. They thanked him for the ride and told him they would see him in about twelve days.

Asher watched the plane glide away off the lake and into the air. Suddenly a hollowness emerged from deep inside Asher, draining the adventurous man he boasted to himself about. The plane flew higher and higher into the distance and down the valley before finally disappearing over the mountaintops. The hum of the engine went silent.

Asher stood there, knowing that could be the last sign of civilization he might ever see, and he had just wished it farewell.

CHAPTER 3

"We've been hunting for three days now and have hardly seen anything worth killing. I'm starting to get impatient with this woman," Marco whispered to Seth as they followed Nora, walking across another opening between batches of trees in the drizzling rain.

Seth replied quietly, "Take it easy. That's why they call it hunting and not killing. We've got to hunt them first before we can kill them."

Marco responded with the grin of a smart aleck. Then suddenly, like a slapstick movie, he tripped on one of the slippery grass heads called tussocks. They stuck up about six to eight inches off the ground, blanketing the vast arctic clearings. He went down, hitting the ground hard and slamming his face and rifle into a puddle of muddy water.

"Are you kidding me?" Marco was getting madder by the moment and slapped the mud puddle with his hand. He and his friend, Seth, were originally from New Jersey but now lived in Southern California. Good friends and business partners, they worked for a man named Willie (short for William). Willie had a transportation business on the West Coast from Central America all the way to Alaska. He was an avid hunter who filled a large trophy room with many regional and exotic animals.

Last year, Willie was up in the Brooks Range, in this exact area, with the exact same hunting guide. Even though he shot a huge, near-record bull moose, he spotted another trophy much larger and more important to him. So he sent his two associates to come up and get it for him.

Marco was a taller, black-haired, burly Italian man with a fat face that showcased his large, crooked nose. It had seen a few fists in its day. Pride and patience were his enemies, and the lack of intelligence was his friend. Seth watched Marco getting up and started laughing, saying in his northeast accent, "I thought you were a big boy, Marco. What are you doing playing in the mud?"

"Hold my gun, jerk, and help me up," Marco replied, holding his rifle out to Seth. He got up and started to clean himself off by sweeping his hands down his clothes, smearing the mud. "What am I going to do now?" he muttered, looking down at his clothing and hands with disgust.

Quietly, Nora, their guide, walked back to where the men were whispering and said, "Don't worry, your clothes are waterproof. Besides, the rain will wash it off." She then looked each of them in the eyes and continued, "You need to keep quiet. They will hear you. We need to hurry to cover in those trees so they don't see us." She turned and started walking swiftly toward the tree line.

Marco looked at Seth with more fire in his eyes and clenched his teeth. "I better see some blood splatter soon, or I'm going to twist the head off that Eskimo woman."

Between the two of them, Seth, a medium-built man with Frank Sinatra looks, had the brains. He stepped up to Marco and whispered sternly, "You're going to calm down! Do you hear me?" Seth paused to get the appropriate reaction from him. Then he added, "Willie sent us up here to this icebox to do a job, but we have to get a moose first for the plan to work."

Seth came within inches of Marco's face (as he had done so many times before). He did it to get through Marco's thick head that he needed to stop wearing his emotions on his sleeve and start thinking before he spoke. "Keep focused on what we're here for. In a week, you can whine and cry all you want. Until then, stick with the plan. If you screw this up, I will personally make sure it's your body that's never found in this godforsaken place…you got me?"

"Yeah…I gotcha," Marco replied, avoiding Seth's glare as Seth clenched his jaw, staring him down.

"Good, now let's go kill something with four legs," Seth said as he turned and started walking in the direction Nora had gone.

***

Asher and Rudy sat on the ground next to the small butane, single-burner camp stove that cooked their first dinner together. Rudy scooped out a pile of beans, placing it next to the thick steak on Asher's aluminum plate, and put a couple of scoops on his own plate as well. Setting the spoon down, he looked up into the evening sky, raised an arm high and pointed up in the air with the hand sign for love. With boldness, joy, and open eyes, he said out loud, "To the Lord of heaven's armies, may we always glorify You, Jesus, in what we do. Thank You for safe travels and for continuing to protect us as we follow the steps You provide on our journey. Help us to always move forward, even if we can't see clearly where You're taking us. Thank You for this meal, and give us a good night's sleep. Until later on…"

Asher was slightly surprised by the way Rudy prayed out loud without telling him or at least asking if he wanted to be included. He was also surprised by how it was said with absolute purpose and faith. Asher did not comment about it but simply took it all in.

"Enjoy this big dinner, Asher. It's going to be the last full, normal one for a while. I like starting all our treks out with a meal like this because the rest of them are freeze-dried where we just add hot water."

"It looks and smells great. But won't it attract bears?"

Rudy frowned, bobbing his head. "Oh, it might, but they won't eat any of it. Especially since they'll have fresh human meat to fill their bellies." Rudy looked away, trying not to laugh as Asher quickly caught on to his joke.

"I'm not that gullible, Rudy," Asher replied.

"Okay, I guess you're not like most people who come up here since you're from the Rocky Mountains. Which, by the way, some say the BR is the most northern part of the Rockies. But to answer your question, no, we don't have to worry about bears." He knew another question was coming.

"Why not?" Asher asked as he put another piece of steak in his mouth.

"Unlike the lower forty-eight states, southern Alaska, or a small town like Bettles, the grizzlies up north here in the vast wilderness have never smelled or tasted cooked food."

Asher let that settle in for a moment. It added excitement to his purpose for this getaway: to be in a place where few people have ever been and where he could be far away from everyone… except Rudy, who, in half a day of knowing, Asher was quickly beginning to like because he was different than most people.

Asher wasn't completely convinced that what Rudy had said about bears was accurate and calmly challenged him, "Is that really true? Bears eat everything, especially meat. My father and

I bear hunt all the time. Well, at least we did before he died last year." He paused to control his emotions, not wanting Rudy to see that part of him. He took a slow, shallow breath to gain composure and continued, "We would fill our bait barrels full of anything and everything, especially things that would stink the area up. The bears would come in and gorge themselves on whatever we had."

"I understand what you're saying, but these are true wild animals with little to no human contact. And unless they're starving, which they aren't because ripe blueberries and cranberries are everywhere, they won't touch our food. We'll be eating the berries by the handfuls ourselves the entire trip," Rudy stated with a smile, smacking his lips together behind his fluffy, graying beard.

Asher was still not convinced as he went back to eating his dinner.

Spooning up another mouthful of beans, Rudy nodded his head and said, "We'll get our answer tonight."

"What?"

"We're not going to finish all this food, so we'll set it away from the tent, and we'll have our answer in the morning."

Asher glanced around the area next to the lake. It was hilly and open in all directions with no large bushes or trees in sight—only short brush that looked like thin, tan grass scattered here and there between the gray rocks that covered the landscape.

This was why they cooked with the butane burner and not a fire; there was nothing to burn. Skimming the vegetation, he asked, "How does any big-game animal live here, especially bears? There's no cover and hardly any vegetation."

"They roam for miles, smelling the whole way to find food. We're on higher ground right now, but when we get lower in the valley near the river, patches of trees and taller brush will start covering the ground."

"So what kind of gun do you carry for protection?"

"Oh, I don't carry a gun. We'll never need it."

"What! You don't have a gun?" Asher spoke up, surprised.

"Nope, we won't need them, and they're too heavy and bulky for me when I'm carrying a backpack full of food and essentials for a couple of weeks."

For once in a very long time, Asher felt helpless, vulnerable, and a bit naked. He always carried a gun when he was in the outdoors, especially in bear country. He had not brought one, thinking it was normal for the guide to have a weapon, but now he was kicking himself. Mentally going through his supplies, the only weapon he had was his four-inch flip-out blade: an Uncle Henry knife his dad had given him for his birthday some years back. That was not alleviating his concern.

After finishing dinner, they packed things away, put the leftover food about forty yards from the tent, and settled in for the night.

At first light, Asher was ready to begin the trek but waited for Rudy, who appeared to be nestled down in his sleeping bag. Suddenly, the zipper of the tent door went up, startling Asher as Rudy poked his head in, "You awake, Asher? Breakfast is ready."

Asher looked more closely at Rudy's roughed-up, empty sleeping bag and asked, "How long have you been up?"

"Long enough to see the world wake up...especially one bear." Rudy's head backed out of the tent as he laughed. "Oh, watch your step as you get out of the tent. It left you a present," he said, laughing again before going back to the cooking stove.

Asher dressed quickly and did his usual routine while backpacking before leaving the tent. Because of his height, he wanted to spend as little time as possible going in and out, so he rolled up his sleeping bag and put everything in his backpack to be ready to go.

When he finished, he crawled out of the tent into the chilly morning air. He stood up, looking at the ground about five feet away from the tent door and exclaimed, "Wow, is that what I think it is?"

Rudy chuckled as he answered, "You got it! He was marking his territory as he walked around the tent, and he almost stepped on your head!"

Asher stared at a huge pile of bear poop that was about the size of a basketball. He had seen bear scat many times in his life, but nothing this big. *Rudy was right*, he thought, looking closer at the mound. It was filled completely with blueberries and cranberries along with green leaves here and there.

"The berries went right through him," Asher commented. Then it hit him, what else Rudy had said. He looked around at the ground, which was covered with a thin coat of frost. "What do you mean he almost stepped on my head?"

Rudy looked up at Asher from his squatting position as he fixed breakfast. He pointed by moving his gaze down to the side of the tent where Asher had slept. Asher followed the large bear prints on the frosted ground and stopped next to the upper corner where his head had lain. He could not believe his eyes. Thoughts raced through his mind. He turned back to Rudy, stating, "And you didn't bring a gun?"

Rudy, jolly as ever, walked up beside him and put his arm on Asher's broad shoulder. He looked down at what Asher was staring at and added, "That one is for the record books. I've never seen that before. You better get a picture of it, or no one will ever believe you." He patted Asher on the back and laughed again, then returned to cooking breakfast.

Asher stood there bewildered for a long time, then went to his pack, got his camera out, and took a picture. The grizzly had walked around the tent and partially stepped on the corner of it, only about six inches from Asher's head. The print was perfectly captured in the frost covering the tent and ground, and now it was in Asher's camera.

Asher put the camera away, still in disbelief that he was only inches from a full-grown grizzly and hadn't known it. Walking over and squatting down, Rudy handed him a steaming plate of food and commented, "Last night's leftovers are still there."

"No way!" Asher said with a mouthful and stood to walk over to the cold food still in its small, neat pile.

"You're right. Sorry I didn't believe you, Rudy," he said as his eyes followed the bear's prints circling around it a couple of times, never getting close to the food.

***

Nora blew out another deep, groaning bull moose mating call through a wide but short plastic tube. In response, they heard brush and branches raked by antlers in the distance. Then it went silent. "He's coming in. Be ready when he steps out into the open, but don't shoot until he gets broadside and stops."

The three hid from the moose they had been tracking by staying low in a batch of brush across the clearing near some trees. Marco was lying down in the prone position with the rifle lying across a fallen tree branch. Seth knelt next to him, looking through binoculars while Nora watched.

Nora was a special hunting guide in the Gates of the Arctic National Park and Preserve, which lies within the Brooks Range Wilderness. Only Native Americans were allowed by the government to guide there. This was to preserve their rights and to give jobs to the local people, which were few in the Brooks Range Wilderness in comparison to its vast landscape.

Besides having the right to guide hunts, Nora was also allowed to own land and live in the national park as well. She and her husband, Martin, a Caucasian man originally from Anchorage, lived along the North Fork of the Koyukuk River. Since work was extremely limited for him here in the middle of nowhere, he mined for gold on their property—property that Nora and her family had owned for many generations. A small stream flowed, winding its way for a couple of miles through their property. It dumped into the North Fork of the Koyukuk near their house.

"Is your safety off?" Nora asked Marco.

"Yes," Marco replied. He had never shot a big-game animal before.

From the beginning, when the two men arrived, Nora was very aware of the fact that the two men were inexperienced outdoorsmen, at least inexperienced in the extreme hunting environment they were in right now. She wondered why they would come way up here to hunt instead of somewhere closer, more convenient, and with the comforts of civilization. Much of the time, only hardcore, rugged hunters came way up here.

The big bull slowly made his way through the brush and stepped out into the open. He was swaying his massive, broad, paddle-shaped antlers back and forth. Marco's and Seth's hearts were pounding, and their adrenaline was surging. They had never been this close to such a beast, even though it was still about a hundred and fifty yards away.

"Breathe deeply and slowly blow the air out through your mouth," Nora said softly as she observed Marco tensing up and holding his breath.

"I know what I'm doing," Marco replied as his pride took over, especially since he was taking instructions from a woman.

Seth bumped Marco on the side of his leg to remind him to keep calm.

Nora ignored Marco and whispered, "Okay, he's sideways. Wait 'til he stops. Then shoot him low and just back behind the front shoulder. You'll take out both lungs and possibly his heart."

They watched the moose as it took its time getting into the position they desired. From behind them, they heard a sudden loud, deep snap of a broken tree branch that had been lying on the ground. They all flinched, then froze, knowing something enormous had snuck up on them.

Nora slowly moved her head just enough to see out of the corner of her eye. Standing with its head over seven feet high and its antlers another two feet higher, another large bull moose had quietly come in. It had heard the mating call from a different direction.

She could tell the bull didn't know they were there, keeping low to the ground. Its head was up high, looking around for one of its own kind. If this second moose took another couple of steps, it would walk on top of them, and at approximately fifteen hundred pounds, it could severely hurt or potentially kill them.

Nora knew moose were more dangerous and unpredictable than even bears, so she only moved her lips, not verbalizing a word, telling the guys to not move.

Urgently thinking to herself, *I have to protect these guys*, she slowly looked to her other side and saw a cluster of pine trees a short distance away. Then she suddenly jumped up and sprinted to the trees as fast as her forty-nine-year-old legs could move through the brush.

When she got to the opposite side of the trees, she turned. She saw the giant animal swiftly coming at her with its long, stilt-like legs easily rising over the vegetation and its flaring nostrils snorting angrily in her direction.

At the trees, it swayed its head back and forth, looking for a way to get to her. Then it raked its antlers across the tree branches and walked around the trees. Nora mimicked its movement, walking around the trees herself, keeping the trees between her and the bull.

Seeing that it was as big as the one across the clearing, she yelled out, "Shoot it! Shoot it! It's a big one!"

The response she heard was, "Yah, yah…over here, stupid animal!" She glanced toward the guys, only to see Seth standing up and waving his arms. At the same time, out of the corner of her eye, she saw more movement. It was the first bull from the other side of the clearing, quickly trotting its way directly over to the moose chasing her. Even though they were in an extremely dangerous situation, she laughed briefly and smiled at their unique situation.

The bull in front of her on the other side of the trees was getting angry. It ran around the trees and then decided to go through them. It lowered its head and pressed its massive antlers into the six-inch-wide tree trunks, which began to bow over toward Nora before one snapped. It slowly fell over, hitting the ground next to her.

The moose stepped back, looking at its work, and noticed another one of the smaller two-legged creatures standing up and making noise. It turned around slowly and stared the human down like a Brahma bull in a bullfight.

Seth lowered his arms, looking up at the animal, completely shocked at how big it was. He saw in its eyes that its intention was to kill him. Seth wanted to run, but his legs wouldn't move. He opened his mouth to yell, but nothing came out. Then, surprisingly, he felt himself being lifted up over Marco's shoulders. Marco had picked him up and started to run away through the brush to another batch of trees behind them.

The bull started to pursue them, and that was when it heard and saw the other bull moose closing in on him for battle. It twisted its muscular body to face its new opponent just in time to lock antlers. Nora watched the whirlwind of activity going on amidst the peaceful surroundings, smiling as the two beasts fought back and forth, tearing up the ground and vegetation right in front of her.

Getting out of the way, she snuck around the moose, gathering the hunting items the two city boys had left behind, and went to look for them.

Not too far away, she caught up to them hiding behind a couple of larger trees and said, "Wasn't that exciting?" with a big smile, showing a more carefree attitude than her brisk, businesslike demeanor as a serious hunting guide.

"You're crazy, woman!" Marco said, looking past her at the two bulls duking it out.

"I had to protect you, so you're welcome, Marco." Giving him a motherish stare, she turned and handed each guy his own rifle, then looked at the moose fighting. "The problem we have now is that you two have to choose which one you want."

"What?" Seth asked.

"You came all the way up here for two moose," she said as she lifted her arm, pointing at the monsters grunting and groaning, pushing each other back and forth. "There they are."

***

For several days, Rudy and Asher had been walking over rounded hills and through wide open, meandering valleys where they could see forever. In the distance, they saw sharp, jagged mountain peaks touch the sky with many small lakes below sparkling like diamonds in the brief moments of sunlight. Big patches of green trees emerged here and there, like dark stains in the tan, grassy tundra that roamed endlessly.

The expanse of everything was so big, it continually seemed like they were never getting closer to anything. Finally, they rounded a knoll and stepped around the grass tussocks that had started permeating the landscape a couple of hours earlier. A clump of trees was just in reach. The vegetation was changing as they were descending in elevation, getting closer to the North Fork of the Koyukuk River.

Approaching the thin batch of trees, Asher noticed old, whitish-gray moose antlers, both large and small, blanketing the tundra floor. There must have been over a hundred of them dropped all over the place by who knows how many moose over the years. An eerie, uneasy feeling of death came over Asher as though he were looking at a graveyard of bones sticking up out of the ground.

Rudy had Asher get his camera out and take several pictures. It began raining again, and Rudy suggested they hurry to the next area of trees about a half mile away and set up camp for the night. From their view, it appeared to be the beginning of a small forest, and Rudy said, "Branch Lake is just on the other side of those trees. The North Fork, which we'll be canoeing on, is coming out of that valley over there." He pointed above the trees where two mountains sloped down toward each other but never touched.

When they arrived at the small forest, they kept walking. They were looking for a good spot with larger trees where branches hung out farther, offering better shelter. After quickly pitching their tent, Rudy asked Asher to collect some dry wood. Asher found branches under trees or buried under piles of pine needles as Rudy prepared for a fire and unpacked the cooking items.

With his raingear on and his hood keeping his head dry, Asher remembered seeing a lot of dead branches in certain areas on their way in. He backtracked, following their semi-fresh footprints in the mud, and looked around for the precious fuel.

Suddenly, he stopped with his head down, staring in disbelief. His heart skipped a beat, and his breathing froze. Chills went down his body as he slowly lifted his eyes up, looking around for something moving or watching him, but there was nothing. Listening intently beyond the raindrops hitting his hood, he slowly turned in a complete circle. He was searching for whatever had left its large paw prints on top of their boot prints…paw prints that were made only a short time ago.

We're being followed and hunted, he thought to himself. Slowly he worked his hand under his waterproof pants and pulled out his knife. As he flipped out the long silver blade, it made a snapping sound that became a warning to the wolf or wolves that had made the prints in the mud. Asher was ready for battle.

Asher began to hunker down, crouching forward like he would in football just before tackling someone. From behind him, toward the direction of the camp, he heard a couple of steps sloshing in the mud.

Before he could turn around to receive the full force of whatever it was, Rudy's loud voice ripped through the chilling silence, "Asher, what are you doing?" Asher's body flinched. In his position, he did not want to look foolish or frightened to Rudy, so he did not turn around. Instead, he continued his body motion to the ground. He squatted down and looked at the huge wolf prints that were as wide as his hands. Keeping the knife in front of him and quickly flipping the blade safely into its hiding place, he slowly slid it up his sleeve so Rudy couldn't see it.

"Oh, hey, Rudy, look at these wolf prints on top of our footprints. They must be following us," he said, staring down at the ground.

"Yeah, they're just curious. They've been watching us ever since we got into the moose antler burial ground."

"They have?"

"They're always watching and have eyes everywhere. The Eskimos believe they are spiritual animals. You think you seen them—then they're gone before you really know what you're looking at."

Asher turned around. "What?"

"Yeah, that was confusing." Rudy rubbed his chin and then continued, "They're quiet, quick, and can smell, hear, and see you before your own senses can react. It's like they are always one step ahead. That's why I stopped trapping them."

"You trapped wolves?"

"For years, along with other things, but now I only buy the pelts from the trappers and sell them to the fur buyers in Seattle."

Suddenly Asher's picture of him was beginning to broaden. The state trooper did call him Mr. Alaska. *Maybe there's some truth to that?* he thought to himself, looking down at the short, stocky man with the continuously jolly smile.

Peering back down at the large paw prints and then scanning the area, he steadied his voice and asked, "So…are these guys… hunting us?"

57

"If they were, you and I would both be dead by now." Rudy turned and began looking for wood himself. He added, "I'm getting cold, and some of our stuff needs to dry out." Then Rudy started nodding his head, stating, "Now there's a combination that will definitely kill us: being wet and cold. Grab an armload, and let's get this firing going." As he walked away, he turned back to Asher, adding, "There's only one animal we need to be concerned about coming after us." Asher gave him his attention as Rudy said one word firmly, "Moose."

CHAPTER 4

The hunters and Nora trekked back to her lodge, their packs loaded with moose meat. It was late in the evening. Nora's friendly Alaskan malamute, Samson, came running up, barking its hello to everyone. Tired and sore, the hunters dropped the packs to the ground outside the butchering shed. Nora told them, "You two go in, take showers, and get into dry clothes. I'll get the fire blazing in the house and some hot coffee going." She bent down, scratching the dog's fluffy neck, and finished, "Dinner will be ready in about an hour after Samson and I get these packs emptied and the meat put into the freezer. It will probably take several trips the next couple of days, back and forth, to get the rest of the meat and antlers back here."

The two men didn't hesitate with her instructions. They were exhausted from another full day of hunting in dreary weather and walking through soggy vegetation, which was already difficult to walk through, even when it was dry. But today, they had each added fifty pounds of moose meat to their packs, leaving approximately eight hundred pounds to retrieve over the next couple of days.

Marco and Seth shot the two battling moose at the same time. Within a couple of minutes, each bull was down, breathing its last. They were surprisingly excited about their accomplishment as they took pictures of each other with their trophies. At first the two were very cautious in approaching such big animals, even though they were dead. They were even more hesitant to touch them.

Once over their fears, they explored both animals until Nora began to cut the moose up. Watching every movement of her blade, the men stood back, trying not to become sick or feel bad for the dead animals.

Nora had asked them different questions during the hunt, trying to figure them out. They never reacted as seasoned hunters, yet they continually commented that they had hunted all the time. They became offended at her questioning, especially Marco, so she eventually let it go, as if it was none of her business, and just did the job she was hired to do.

That evening, after cleaning up and devouring a satisfying meal, Seth began casually walking around the great room of the house/hunting lodge. He was looking at what appeared to be family photos and started to ask questions. "So, Nora, is this your husband?"

She looked over her shoulder while clearing the table and saw him with a picture in his hand of her and Martin together. They were beside their plane, parked just off the short grass-and-dirt runway behind the house, which she called their backyard. Nora answered, "Yes, it is."

"And these must be your girls?" he said calmly, lifting another picture.

"Yes, they are, but they're grown now."

"And which one is this?" He picked up a photo of a beautiful young woman dressed up in an evening gown with a wide ribbon draped from her shoulder to her hip, imprinted with the words Miss Alaska.

"That's my oldest. She was crowned this year."

Putting the pictures down, he commented, "You have a beautiful family, Nora. Are they out of town…or should I say, in the city?" He gave a friendly, short laugh.

She smiled. "No, the girls live away from home, but Martin, my husband, is out working about a mile up the creek from our place. He has a small portable shed-like house he stays in for several days at a time. He comes home for a night, then goes back."

"Why wouldn't he come back every night if it's just a mile?"

Nora was used to this type of questioning when people from the lower forty-eight came up to hunt, and she repeated the answer she always gave, "He only has about two full months to do what he does because of the weather and the short summer season we have up here. Plus, there is the fuel factor. We have to fly everything in, including gas. And we have to conserve as much as we can, so if he uses it to drive back and forth every day on the ATV, it's just a waste. So he stays up there and continuously works very long hours."

"That's what Willie said," Marco stated, instantly kicking himself for saying it out loud. He looked away, not making eye contact.

"I'm sorry?" Nora asked with a frown, not understanding how he would have that information.

Calmly, Seth butted in, "It's a friend of ours who's always in Alaska. He talked about the short summer season." He shrugged his shoulders, glancing over to Marco to go along with this story.

Recovering from his slipup, Marco barked back, "Yeah, that's what our friend tells us."

"Oh, is he a hunter like you guys?" she asked, though they missed her sarcasm.

"He's a big-time hunter, anything and everything. You name it, he's killed it. Go ahead, name an animal, any animal, and I bet he's killed it," Marco challenged her.

There was an awkward pause, and then Nora asked, slightly surprised, "Oh, you're really asking me?"

Marco nodded his head.

"Well, let's see. How about an African animal?"

"Sure. Go ahead," Marco said, shrugging his shoulders confidently.

"Elephant?"

"He's got a half-body mount, with six-foot-long tusks, coming out of a jungle scene."

Nora rocked her head back and forth as she played along with the game and said, "Giraffe?"

"A complete body mount is in the same jungle scene."

"Okay, back to Alaska. How about a wolverine?"

Marco sat there for a second and then looked to Seth, "What's a wolfring?"

Seth thought for a moment, then said, shrugging his shoulders again, "I think it's like a small bear or something."

Nora had stumped them, so she pointed across the room to a stuffed animal the size of a medium dog that looked like a skunk, bear, and badger combined.

"Oh yeah, a wolfring," Marco replied as if he knew what she was talking about.

"Wolverine, Marco. A wolverine," Seth stated for his stupid friend who was embarrassing them both.

"Whatever," Marco muttered, looking daggers at Seth. Marco then turned to Nora with a more confident grin. "No, I've never seen one of those in his trophy room."

"There you have it. Willie hasn't killed every animal. Enough of that, so when is your husband planning on coming back home?" Seth asked, trying to change the subject.

Nora turned, walking back to the kitchen with her hands full of dishes. "He should be coming home this evening. Maybe you guys will be able to meet him if you're still up or if you get up early in the morning."

With Nora's back to them, Seth and Marco's eyes widened as they looked at each other. Seth replied, "I would like to meet him, probably in the morning. I don't know about Marco, but I'm really tired."

He looked over to Marco as Marco answered, "I'm with Seth. I'm going to get to bed early tonight and probably sleep in since you've had us up really early every morning." He smiled, trying to give her a hard time.

"Whatever you guys want to do. By the way, since both of you are done with your moose hunt so soon, I can radio in and get you two caribou tags if you like. You've got a couple of days left on your trip if you want to spend the extra money to do that. If not, you can fish in the river. You'll catch a lot of graylings."

The guys looked at each other as Seth replied, "Well, we were going to see if you could call for us to be picked up early."

"Oh sure, that could be arranged, but you paid for a full week's trip. I usually don't give refunds on the days you didn't use."

"We weren't expecting a refund. The hunt's been great, especially with what happened today. I can't wait to tell everyone back home about it." Seth looked over for Marco to respond.

"Seth's right. Besides the rain, it's been a lot of fun."

She looked at them, sensing they were making excuses. On the other hand, they were definitely not cut out to be up above the Arctic Circle or even in Alaska, for that matter.

"If that's what you want to do, I'll call into Bettles in the morning and see if there's a pilot and plane available. If there is, would tomorrow late afternoon work or the day after? We still need to get the rest of the meat. But what we don't get while you're here, I'll ship to you."

Seth shrugged his shoulders, "The sooner, the better. I'm ready to get back home. It's farther up here than I thought."

"That's for sure," Marco added.

"Okay, I'll try my best to get someone up here tomorrow. I would take you back in our plane, but Martin said he needed to fix something on the fuel line. He thought he noticed it was leaking."

"We appreciate that, Nora," Seth said, stretching his arms out, flexing his sore muscles and yawning. "The meal was awesome. I'm going to get to bed early tonight. You wore me out."

"You haven't had dessert yet."

"That's okay. One of us has to look out for our figures. Let Marco eat mine. He's past the point of no return."

He laughed as Marco accepted the offer, "You bet I'll take Seth's dessert. No matter how big I get, I'll still be able to take him down. Are we having more of that blueberry pie we had last night?"

Nora smiled. "Yes, and I have another one as backup."

"Yes!" Marco exclaimed, swinging his bent arm up in happiness.

"Don't let him eat the pantry dry because he will if you let him," Seth commented as he walked away, out of sight of Nora and down a hallway while Nora walked back into the kitchen. Then Seth turned to see if he was in direct eyesight of Marco. Marco watched as Seth pointed to his watch and spread his arms outward, nonverbally signaling, *Give me a lot of time.* Seth returned a hand signal as though he would be on a phone and pointed outside. Marco understood.

They had been working together for years, very adept at what they truly did for a living.

***

The fire had been blazing and building a good pile of coals throughout the evening. Asher and Rudy had finished dinner and were now rotating their wet clothes on the makeshift clothesline over the fire. It had stopped raining, and they had warmed up. They were sitting comfortably on dry piles of dug-up pine needles and were leaning up against a large, old log. Hypnotized by the flames dancing to rhythms of the peaceful outdoors, they watched as the glow of the fire permeated the area and the sun disappeared behind the mountain peaks.

Not much conversation was flowing, which wasn't unlike the past few days of their trip. They conversed with small talk here and there about the area but nothing personal. This was very uncommon for Rudy and the people he guided on these treks; he could tell there was something troubling deep in Asher that he might be fighting to suppress.

Rudy decided to finally try to break the ice, which was getting thicker as the days went on. He also felt led by a familiar voice inside him saying, "Asher's spirit is going into hiding because he doesn't truly know Me. He doesn't see that I have safe and prosperous paths for him that could fill his heart's desires."

Rudy handed Asher a candy bar for dessert, saying, "I know who you are."

Asher slowly came out of his trance at the odd statement. "What?"

"You're Asher Collins, the great tight end for Nebraska," he said, smiling as the light of the fire flickered across his face.

Asher looked back into the fire, surprised Rudy knew that about him, and, without expression, replied, "Used to be."

"I watched you all the time, especially when you would play Michigan, my team."

Asher looked around into the dark, vast wilderness and asked in a monotone voice, "And where would you do that?"

"Not up here but back at my house, four hundred miles south of Fairbanks, near Tok. I have a cabin on fifty acres by a lake, and it has a really good satellite dish to watch my favorite sport every time there's a game on. You're big time, Asher. You outran or bashed your way through almost everyone."

There were a few moments of silence as Asher tried to think his way around the conversation but decided to bash his way through this one, which seemed to be all he knew how to do. He looked at Rudy and said, "Was."

"What do you mean?" Rudy questioned, staying focused on Asher's demeanor.

"I was big time. Then, I blew out my knee."

"Everyone knows that, but you came back this year, helping your team go to the Rose Bowl. So who drafted you?" Rudy asked, excited to hear the news firsthand, thinking this would help with what was going on inside him.

Asher stood up and wiped the pine needles off his pants. Then he got his dry clothes off the line and turned to the tent, saying, "I didn't get drafted." Silence overtook their conversation for the rest of the night.

In the morning, they woke up to quiet snowflakes slowly floating down, layering a thin blanket of white all over the area, which changed the appearance of their surroundings.

The two had found a rhythm of getting up together and getting everything packed to quickly move on into the new day. Unzipping the tent and poking his head outside, Rudy exclaimed, "It's going to be a great day, Asher!"

As Asher stepped out of the tent behind Rudy, he thought to himself, *What is so great about it?* Then he said out loud, "Does the weather here ever stop changing?"

"No," Rudy quickly responded, turning around with an energized expression. "That's what makes this place so special. It's always different and hard to predict. The only thing you can predict here is the unpredictable." Looking directly into Asher's eyes, making sure he had his attention, Rudy said as though it was a matter of fact, "Isn't that life? The good life—never boring!"

Asher thought to himself, *I've heard that before.* He looked at the short, jolly man who was smiling at him. He was wearing a puffed-out blue coat with a gray knitted wool hat that had a short brim all the way around. Asher could not help but smirk as though he knew better and said, "Definitely never boring, but I would disagree about the 'good' part."

Suddenly, in the distance, a wolf filled the cold air with a chilling howl, echoing far and wide. It sent an invisible prickling up Asher's spine. There were several responses from two other wolves, which came from the other side of Rudy and Asher, giving them the feeling that they were surrounded. Rudy got excited, dashed to his backpack, and dug out a pair of binoculars.

"Asher, hurry! Let's get our rain gear on. We've got to go," he said urgently.

"What's wrong?"

"They're on the hunt, and their prey is being surrounded."

Asher followed the instructions, and both were quickly ready to go. Looking around the firepit, Asher picked up a couple of the long, strong branches intended for the fire, flipped out his knife, and began to sharpen the ends.

Rudy looked at him and asked, "What are you doing?"

"I'm not going down without a fight!"

Rudy couldn't help it and started to laugh quietly, saying, "You misunderstood me. We aren't their next meal. Come on!" He patted Asher on the shoulder and took off in the direction of the first howler. Soon, they were at the edge of the small forest, looking out at a lake. Staying hidden behind bushes and trees, Rudy brought up the binoculars and started scanning the open area, then stopped. "There they are."

"There's who?"

Rudy scanned in different directions, again stopping to look at something to his right and then to his left.

"What are you looking at?"

Rudy handed the binoculars to Asher. "Look on the other side of the lake."

Asher adjusted himself and then had a look through the binoculars. "It's a couple of moose."

"Yeah, a cow and calf. Now look to the right and left, and you'll see the wolves closing in."

Following his instructions, Asher finally spotted the wolves through the fat snowflakes; they were coming in along the edges of the water. Looking back at the moose, Asher began to sense emotions poking his heart. He watched the mother go back and forth, keeping herself between the incoming wolves and her baby.

Hunting with his dad since he was ten, Asher had never gotten emotional over killing whatever they hunted. But this picture was different, and he did not like it. "What are we going to do?" He handed the binoculars back.

Rudy, slightly surprised at the question, brought the binoculars to his eyes and answered, "Nothing."

"Nothing?" Asher popped his head sideways to look at the old man as though he was enjoying this.

Rudy put the binoculars down while still looking out across the lake and said, "Asher, this is their home, all of theirs. You know this is their natural way of living. I don't have to go into that with you; you're an outdoorsman. You've seen this before."

What Rudy had said was true, all of it. He knew better and was embarrassed that he had spoken out.

"Besides, the wolves won't be eating moose for breakfast this morning, at least not these moose." Rudy smiled at Asher, giving him a bump with his elbow to change his tense mood.

"Why?"

"Mom is going to teach her young one that water is their refuge, a safe place. You just watch."

Rudy and Asher were able to see everything in the distance without the binoculars and stared at the cinematic scene playing in front of them. As the wolves thought they had the moose trapped, the cow gave the calf a few hard bumps on the hindquarters to move out into the deep water.

Soon, the calf's head was the only part of its body poking up out of the lake. The wolves went back and forth along the edge, testing the water, only to quickly jump out as though something was coming after them. The cow stopped, staying between her baby and the wolves as the water came up to the middle of her body.

"That's another life lesson for the calf," Rudy said with a smile. He brought the binoculars to his eyes, scanned the shoreline in a different direction, and added, "And there's our canoe. Well, this was fun. Let's go back, get our things, and get on the river."

***

Seth got to his bedroom and locked the door behind him. He dug through his suitcase, pulled out a satellite phone, and quickly dialed a number. When someone on the other end answered, Seth said, "Everything is going as planned. We both shot our moose today, so we need to move the pickup to tomorrow evening instead."

There was talking on the other end, and Seth replied, "Yes, he's coming to the house tonight."

More instructions were given to him, and he replied, "Don't worry. It's going smoother than we planned."

Again, the person on the other phone said a few things, and Seth finished, "Okay, we'll see you tomorrow." He hung up and hid the satellite phone back in his suitcase. While he had the suitcase opened, he unzipped a side pocket, took out a prescription bottle with sleeping pills, and poured two of them out.

Pulling out a piece of steak from dinner that he had hidden in his pocket, Seth embedded the pills in the steak and squished it tightly into a ball. He turned the room light off and opened the window facing the backyard to peer all around and watch for movement. Not seeing anything, he began to whisper for Samson, the big Alaskan malamute. After making a few kissing sounds to attract the dog, Samson came trotting from around the other side of the house. Seth quietly said, "Good dog, here you go," and reached out with his hand as Samson got a good whiff of the meat. Seth dropped the meat to the ground, and Samson finished it in one gulp. He looked up, wagging his tail as if to ask for more.

Just then, in the distance, Seth heard an ATV and saw headlights bobbing up and down, reflecting off the trees and the low cloud cover. The lights and sounds caught Samson's attention as he excitedly turned and ran across the open runway toward his master coming home.

Seth closed the window and kept the light off. He was thinking about Marco, still in the other room, eating. He went to the door, slowly cracked it open, and looked down the hall. Not able to see Marco, Seth decided to quietly try to get his attention and get him to go to his room. The last thing Seth wanted was for Marco to screw things up when Nora's husband got home.

Slowly creeping down the hall and peeking into the great room, he saw Marco sitting at the table by himself.

"Do you need something, Seth?" Nora spoke up behind him, coming down the hall from her office.

Seth flinched and turned. "Ah yes, um…" He thought quickly for something to say. "I've got heartburn. Do you have anything I can take?" he asked, rubbing his chest.

"Sure I do," she said as she walked to the medicine cabinet in the kitchen. He followed her, and as he passed Marco, he bumped him, giving him the eye and pointing to his room. Seth mouthed, "Go to bed."

Marco wrinkled his face, whispering, "I'm not done with my pie."

Seth looked toward Nora and saw that her back was still turned away from him. He then turned to face Marco, blocking their conversation from Nora. He gave Marco a firm look and whispered, "Her husband is almost here. Get your butt to bed."

Marco altered his behavior. He turned to the large piece of pie and gobbled the rest down. Seth turned to Nora as she walked back to him and handed him some antacids, saying, "I decided to make a radio call to Bettles tonight and got lucky. Someone answered. They've got it set up, and someone will be here tomorrow, midday, to start your trip back home."

She smiled, knowing this would make their day, as Seth replied, "That's great! Thanks, Nora. Well, it looks like you're finished with that pie," he added as he patted Marco on the shoulder.

Wiping his face with a napkin, Marco said, "Yeah, that's the best blueberry pie ever."

"But I cut you another piece, don't you want it?"

"Oh, give it to your husband when he gets home," Marco said as Seth eyed him, hoping he wouldn't slip up.

They both turned and began walking to their rooms as Nora told them, "Sleep well, guys. You did good today. Definitely one hunt that we all will never forget." She laughed to herself, picturing the guys hunting and the moose chasing her.

Before Marco left Seth's side to go to his bedroom, Seth whispered, "It shouldn't take long, but just in case Willie missed something or the miner's setup is different this year, don't let him go back up there until I get back. Do you understand? Distract him!"

"I got it, Seth. I know the plan," he replied with a look of *I'm not stupid*.

"Good," Seth said as he raised his hand for a fist bump.

Martin, Nora's husband, stopped the ATV next to the house and petted Samson. The dog appeared to be slowing down and not feeling well. "What's wrong, big guy? Did you eat something you shouldn't have again? Go sleep it off, buddy. You'll feel better in the morning." As though he understood exactly what was said to him, Samson turned, slowly making his way to his comfortable doghouse, and lay down.

Martin climbed the stairs and opened the door to the warmth and wonderful smells inside. "Where's my sweetheart?" he asked aloud.

Nora came around the corner, shushing him with her finger up to her mouth. "Quiet down. The guys just went to bed."

He wrapped his arms around her, saying, "So soon? I came home a little early to say hi to another group of your clients."

"They got worn out today. You should've seen it." She smiled, getting up on her tiptoes and giving him a kiss. She proceeded to tell the big story of the day as she fixed him some dinner.

A little while later, after Nora and Martin went to their bedroom, Seth waited for them to fall asleep. Then he exited the house through his window, crossing the runway in the dark. When he arrived at the tree line, he slowly felt his way around, looking for the ATV trail. It led up to the area from which Martin had just come down. Finding it, he cautiously walked along the side in the brush so his footprints wouldn't be seen in the mud. After stumbling a few times and running into tree limbs, Seth decided he had had enough; he was far enough away to be able to turn on his small pocket flashlight. Now able to see his way through the vegetation, Seth made good time getting to the shed Martin slept in…the same shed Willie had told him about.

Once there, he put on a pair of latex gloves, carefully making sure every move he made would not leave any sign of an intruder being in or around the shed. He opened the door slowly, pointed the light inside, and surveyed until he spotted what he was looking for. Seth thought to himself, *This is too easy.*

Stepping inside, he walked to the only window and reached over the counter and up onto a ledge. There were three dozen old, small, gray, plastic thirty-five-millimeter film canisters. They were stacked neatly in three rows, one on top of the other and lining the windowsill. Seth picked one up and popped the lid off, then shined the flashlight into it and stated, "Holy cow, it's true!" He was in awe at what he saw as he emptied the canister and filled his cupped hand.

"Gold!" he whispered in the small shack. He stared at what Martin had mined for with a large sluice box and old-style panning skills.

Seth's boss, William, had been here hunting with Nora last year. She had taken him up to see Martin's operation before William had left. Knowing he was a business owner too, Nora thought William would get a kick out of seeing another of Martin's and her businesses. However, Martin was not happy that Nora had brought a man up to see his mining.

After many years of mining for gold, Martin had lost perspective and became addicted; he had gold fever. Gold was his main driving force for how much and how long he worked away from Nora and their home. Martin couldn't get enough. With every panful of gravelly dirt and every bucket dumped into the sluice box, he was continuously giddy with excitement, looking for the next small nugget to show itself, which happened often. They had the best gold claim in the region. He would go without food, water, and sleep just to get another piece of the heavy and shiny, precious metal. The last thing he wanted was for strangers to know about his hidden treasure.

Only Nora, his family, and their close friends knew about Martin's mine and his consequential state of mind. It was common for people in his line of work to fall prey to gold fever, especially if they worked alone. With no one else to talk to, there was no one to bring them back to reality.

Seth poured the gold back into its container and set it on the counter that he was leaning up against. Reaching into his big side coat pocket, he took out an empty, medium-sized leather bag and a full, waterproof plastic bag. The plastic bag had been filled with sand that he had collected the day before from the stream below, where it wandered past the main house. Putting the flashlight into his mouth, Seth shined the light down at the leather pouch and began emptying all the canisters filled with gold. After they were empty, he opened the bag of sand and dipped the canisters into it. He packed each one hard to fill them as tight as he could to represent the weight of gold taken out and then snapped the lids back on. Once done, he wiped the canisters clean and carefully stacked them back up, exactly how he had found them.

Seth had brought more sand than he needed, so he secured the opening of the bag of extra sand and put it back into his outer pocket. The bag of gold, however, was puffed out solid and a little larger than the size of a cantaloupe. It was very heavy and unable to fit into any of his pockets.

Scanning the counter, windowsill, and floor with the flashlight, Seth made sure the area was clean. Then, from the inside pocket of his coat, he retrieved a small, solid box. It had a miniature electronic transmitter the size of two thumbs. He also got out a transceiver, twice the size of the transmitter, with a small amount of explosives attached to it.

At the end of the counter, on the floor, was a tall portable propane tank. It sat on a mount to balance it upright with a hose attached that split in two: one hose was going to a heater next to the bed, and the other hose was going to a cooking burner that sat on the counter.

Seth pushed a small button on the transceiver, and it activated as a green light came on. Then, slightly tipping the propane tank, he slid the transceiver that was attached to the explosives under the tank and leaned it back up. Seth glanced at the other small box, the transmitter, to make sure its green light had come on as well. He put the transmitter back into its protective box and back into his inside coat pocket.

Stepping outside, Seth double-checked his work and closed the door. He quickly made his way back to the edge of the runway, staying off the trail.

With his flashlight put away, he squinted all around into the darkness and across the huge, open backyard of the house, where small planes took off and landed. Everything was silent, and nothing was moving. His heart began to pound with excitement. He pulled out the bag of extra sand and scattered it around the area, blending it in with the ground cover. He put the leather bag of gold into the waterproof bag and looked across the opening, where he spotted the outline of the butchering shed located next to the house.

Knowing the runway before him was perfectly flat, Seth dashed across it as fast as he could while holding the heavy bag filled with gold against his body. At the shed, he slowly opened the heavy metal door with its sliding locks. (It was designed to keep bears out.) Unlocking them and making minimal sounds, he then opened the main door, which made a creaking sound. He stopped. He watched and waited for lights or movement in the house, but nothing happened. He proceeded inside, closing the door behind him. Getting his flashlight back out, he opened the freezer and lifted out a heavy, sealed, waxy cardboard box that had his name written on it. Carefully opening the box, he unfolded a thick, large plastic bag. It was filled with semi-frozen sliced-up moose meat that had been packed in dry ice.

With the gold safely in the leather bag and now inside the airtight plastic bag, Seth pulled out chunks of meat from the box to make room for the gold that he had placed inside. Carefully, he then refolded the large plastic bag filled with meat (and now gold). He resealed the wax box and made a mark, the letter G, with his fingernail on the side to identify it. He then placed the box back into the giant freezer.

Almost done, he thought, cautiously making his way out of the butchering shed, closing the door, and locking it back up. He snuck around the house to where the doghouse was. Next to the dog, he tossed the extra meat that he had pulled out to make room for the gold, though Samson was still sleeping.

CHAPTER 5

Asher had not done much canoeing before but quickly caught on. Sitting in front of the wobbly aluminum vessel, he was the power paddler when Rudy gave out the call. Rudy sat in the back, acting as the rudder. Going downriver was easy until there were big rocks or a log stuck. Blindly going around a bend was especially tricky as there might suddenly be an obstacle in their way.

The canoe could easily roll over, spilling all their gear. Or at least, their gear might get really wet if they were caught sideways, up against one of the obstacles. The current behind them had enough continuous force coming at them that it would easily roll them like a log. They could even be sucked under an obstacle. Their eyes, especially Rudy's, were always watching for upcoming objects. He teased Asher that Asher was always in the way because he was a tall and wide-shouldered guy.

At the end of their first day on the cold water, they had come close to tipping the canoe once. However, Asher was able to reach out at the log jam that was squeezing them and pull the canoe into the flowing water before they completely were rolled over.

Again, the day lacked any real conversation for the most part. Asher did apologize for his quick exit the night before after

Rudy brought up his nonexistent football career. Asher explained the details of what happened and why he had not been drafted.

Bringing the canoe to shore in an area that looked good to camp for the night, they both jumped into their routine duties. While collecting firewood, Asher physically felt the effects of being on the water. He was slightly unbalanced and felt a rocking motion, side to side. Emotionally, he was about the same, though somewhat more relaxed. He was not as edgy as he had been for a long time. He was unsure if unloading his bottled-up emotions to Rudy about his failed football career had made the difference or if escaping high up into Alaska, away from reality, was finally kicking in.

Dropping a large bundle of wood next to the small fire, Rudy spoke up. "Beef stroganoff or chili?" He held out the two different freeze-dried meals.

"Chili sounds good."

"Chili it is. That was a great day on the water, wasn't it? And when you pulled us out of the pile of logs, it felt like the boat had a huge motor jetting us free. Thanks! You saved us from a mess." He gave Asher a nod of appreciation.

"You're welcome, but I screwed us up in the first place; I was daydreaming when you were giving out the calls."

"It's no one's fault, just another experience God got us through." Rudy gave a friendly smile, but something hit Asher wrong, so he turned to do something else and ignored Rudy.

After dinner, they sat in front of the fire, soaking in its warmth. They listened to the sounds of sparks crackling in harmony with the soft swooshing of the river close by. Just as the night before, Rudy was prompted to speak. "Your mother said this trip was a graduation gift from her and your father."

Asher looked up with narrowed eyes, not appearing happy, and asked, "When did you talk with my mother?"

"I called the number you had on your application a couple of weeks ago, and your mother answered your phone. The four others who were supposed to be on this trip canceled, making you the only one on the trek. We have a policy of a minimum of two clients per trip; otherwise, we lose money. Your mother got really upset and said they had been planning this for years and that you really needed to get away," Rudy said, shrugging his shoulders.

He stopped and looked seriously at Asher. "Words echoed in my ears when I heard that, telling me to do this trip." Rudy raked his fingers through his beard with a questionable expression, and he then continued, "Usually I don't listen to voices in my head, but"—he paused, looking up at Asher with a corky grin—"this one voice, I always know who it is." He nodded his head as his grin turned into a large smile. "So I told your mother to forget I ever called; the trip was on!

"I never guide anymore. I have several employees that take care of that for me. We had a very busy and profitable season, and this was the last trip of the year. I let them off early, and you got stuck with me, the old man," he said proudly, pointing his thumb at his chest.

Asher suddenly felt guilty. "I'm sorry, Rudy."

"No, no, don't be sorry. Your mother was very nice, but I could tell in her voice that this trip was very important to you."

"You could say that." Asher looked deeply into the flames that flickered around, keeping his attention.

"So what is it? Why are you really doing this trek way up here in the middle of nowhere? You live in beautiful Colorado.

You could've climbed one of those giant mountains or hiked back into one of the national parks there."

The sound of silence weighed heavily between them again. Asher focused on the flames burning up the firewood—firewood that was transforming into glowing coals and later into cold ash.

Why? Asher asked himself the same question because, so far, not much had changed within him. He was in a different place with the same agonizing issues still gnawing at his insides.

With no response from Asher, Rudy had had enough and changed his tone slightly. He asked boldly, "Asher, it may not be any of my business, but I don't understand. Now, for over three days, you won't engage in casual conversation. You cut me off and ignore me. Is there something I've done or said that has upset you?"

Asher blinked himself awake from the mesmerizing fire. He suddenly realized how rude he had been. He had kept to himself, his thoughts swirling around and around in his mind. The pain and misery of his life had no escape.

Now embarrassed, Asher suddenly felt small compared to this generous, amicable man. Having been challenged to be an adult about the situation, Asher replied, "Sorry again, Rudy. I have no excuses. I just have…" Asher struggled with his words as emotions surprisingly interrupted his thoughts. "I've got a lot on my mind, and I'm having a hard time. I'm trying to deal with it."

Rudy saw the familiar, hidden pain. Pain buried deep in the soul. Pain that grips you so much that a change in any direction is the wrong way. His thought process was a tangle of knots, like a bowl of spaghetti, and any emotion could and would show itself at the wrong time. Understanding what was probably going on within Asher, Rudy didn't say another word and let Asher have his privacy as they sat a couple of feet from each other.

The next morning, they were off early. They had secured their gear in large, waterproof rubber bags that were netted tightly in the middle of the canoe. Before pushing off, and while sitting in the wobbly canoe next to the shore, Rudy prayed out loud, again with excitement and energy and without asking Asher first, as usual. "Lord of lords, King of kings, the One who sits on the throne, I come to You this morning praising Your name. Thank You, Father, for Your many blessings and grace, but most of all for Your love for us.

"I ask that You guide and direct us on our journey. Help us to believe and trust that You will be with us in calm waters, through the rapids, and around any dangerous obstacles in our paths. Strengthen our courage and faith, drawing us closer to You, Jesus, our Savior." As he always did, he raised his arm up, giving the hand signal for love, and finished with, "Until later on."

Grasping his oar and stabbing it into the water to touch the shallow bottom, Rudy pushed them off into the current and said, "It's another great day, Asher!"

Asher hesitated before putting his own oar into the water. He had listened intently to Rudy's emphatic prayer—a prayer that had similarities to the other prayers Rudy had said out of nowhere the last few days. Asher thought, *He sure gets excited talking into thin air.* He turned his head, looking back, and bluntly asked, "Why do you say that?"

"What, a prayer?"

"Yeah, that too, but at the end, you always say, 'Until later on.'"

Happy for the intriguing question and finally providing an opportunity to engage in deeper conversation, Rudy was quick to answer, "I learned long ago that I better not hang up on God."

Looking forward to watching where the canoe was going, Asher joked, "What happens when He hangs up on you?"

"Oh, Asher, that can never happen! It's impossible!"

Stunned by the answer, it only stirred up more questions. In his silence, Rudy knew that Asher was trying to figure out what he had said. Then Rudy explained, "How could God, who created all this"—he pointed out and around him—"the river, mountains, air, trees, animals, sun and moon, everything including man, leave it all alone to survive on its own? To be completely separated without His presence, power, and authority and expect it all to live and function, let alone exist without Him?"

Still looking forward while holding his oar on his lap, Asher was suddenly locked in a mental, spiritual battle.

Rudy continued, "It couldn't, Asher, because He is the One who gives breath and life to everything. So, if He hung up on us, leaving our presence…you and I wouldn't be here."

Asher twisted his body sideways, straddled the bench seat, and looked directly at Rudy. "If all that is true, and in your prayers you call Him Father, the One you say loves us, then why…"—a fuse was just set ablaze inside Asher as he raised his voice, getting louder with each word as it got closer to the dynamite charge within him—"does this Father or"—he brought his fingers up, making quotation marks—"God let the ones He created, that He supposedly loves, get hurt, suffer, and let their hearts be ripped apart? Or even be killed? That doesn't sound like He's around to me! He's nowhere to be seen or heard; He just hangs up on us!"

Pausing, Asher tried to control the anger he was spewing out at the graying, bearded man. He narrowed his eyes and stared him down, saying, "Tell me, Rudy, why didn't I get drafted? Why did my fiancée leave me, and why…" Suddenly, his emotions did a one-eighty. He started breathing heavily, and his chin quivered. Tears swelled up in his eyes, and he attempted, several times, to get words out.

Finally, between breaths, Asher asked slowly and calmly, "Why did God take my dad away from Mom and me?" Asher turned his body around, facing forward, slumping his shoulders, and lowering his head.

Rudy stared at his back as Asher appeared to shrivel up. Rudy gently shook his head, thinking, *Good, the truth has finally come out. Thank You, Lord. Now I know why You put me on this trip.* He looked toward the river's edge and found an easy spot to get out. Softly bringing the canoe parallel with the shore, Rudy got out to pull the canoe up on dry ground, telling Asher to do the same.

"Asher, take however much time you need. I'm going to go find a bush to relieve myself. The coffee from earlier went right through me. When I get back, we're going to talk. No more secrets, no more hiding, and that's for the both of us." Rudy gestured back and forth between them, making sure Asher did not feel he was being ganged up on. "Oh, one more thing. This here"—he pointed around the whole area—"is no accident and was perfectly planned by you-know-who!" Now pointing his finger up to the sky, Rudy turned and walked away from the river.

When he got back, they sat down on a couple of large boulders. Rudy had Asher explain in detail the situations he brought up. After unloading the heartaches that were drowning him, Asher suddenly seemed to be able to breathe easier…for the first time in a long time.

Rudy understood where the young man's pains were coming from. He also understood how Asher was lost in the mourning process and unable to find his way back on the path of his life's journey. "Wow, Asher, that's a heavy load you've packed deep down inside. I'm very sorry for the losses of your father, your girl, and the career you were greatly anticipating. For it all to happen in such a short time makes it even harder."

Rudy looked across the river, pondering, and decided it was time to tell his own story so Asher wouldn't feel alone in his suffering. He also hoped to build confidence in Asher. Rudy fully understood the pain, frustrations, and confusion Asher was experiencing. Rudy also knew that there was hope.

"Thanks for sharing all that with me, big guy. I truthfully know how hard it is to talk about things like these that are going on in our lives. Your questions from earlier are good ones, and most people will ask those same questions in their lives. I know I did, although maybe worded slightly differently. Some might say, 'God, why did You do this to me?' or 'Why did You mess up my plans?' Or maybe, 'Why do You let painful and bad things happen, especially to good people?'"

He stopped talking for a minute to allow Asher's mind to reflect on what he asked earlier, then continued, "I asked…" He changed his tone. "No, I demanded answers from God to these questions thirty-five years ago."

Asher looked at Rudy, still peering across the river.

"I'm from Michigan. Surprised? I'm a Wolverine football fan, remember? My life there was going perfectly, just like I had planned it. I was a high school teacher in my third year of teaching, and I was married to a beautiful woman. To top it all off, we had an incredible eleven-month-old baby girl." He smiled big and proud. "We had just purchased our first home; it was a small, older townhouse, but it was ours. We had been living in it for about six months, and life was great. My wife, Marilyn, was deaf, so it was a little challenging to raise Bonnie, our daughter, because Marilyn always had to have Bonnie in her line of sight.

"One day, Marilyn put Bonnie down for a nap. It was a cold winter day, and Bonnie was wearing a one-piece pajama suit with a hood over her head for extra warmth. Marilyn went into another room to do something and then went to the bathroom. She was only gone for about ten minutes, but when she came back to check on the love of our lives, she found Bonnie discolored and not breathing.

"Bonnie was lying on her back and had scooted up, causing the hood to slide off her head. She had scooted up some more, causing the hood to tuck under her back, which pulled the rest of the pajamas tight around the front of her neck...choking her to death." Rudy stood, picking up a small, smooth, saucer-shaped rock, then skimmed it across the top of the river.

Turning to Asher, he continued, "Obviously, this was tragic for us, especially Marilyn, because she blamed herself. She couldn't think straight, was unable to stay focused on anything, and went into a bad depression. A couple of months later, she was driving down a main road, probably in her normal depressed daze, and went through a stop sign. That's when I lost her too."

He bent down again, throwing another rock across the top of the water. The story affected Asher, who said sincerely, "I'm sorry, Rudy."

Looking back at Asher, he said, "Thanks, but I'm not done." Rudy walked back to his rock and sat down. "That's when I lost it. I was in the same state of mind or living, however you want to look at it, as you are now. I soon lost my job because of my performance and constant absences, which led to losing the only piece I had left of Marilyn: our home.

"I had to move back in with my parents for a short time, but they didn't know how to deal with me. My mother, bless her soul, had a brother in Alaska who owned a fish cannery and sent me up here to work. It was literally the bottom of the fish barrel for me. I worked extremely long hours, and it was filthy and stunk like nothing else in this world. But…" Rudy finally returned to his jolly self, his big smile showing as he lifted a finger, "there was this one man, a fisherman who always brought his catch to my uncle's cannery. He saw right through me and understood what I was going through. He took me under his wing, so to speak.

"He helped me clear my head and heart and that's"—he paused with warm, jubilant emotions swelling inside while staying composed—"when I got lost in the wonderful cloud and never turned back."

Taken aback a little, Asher thought to himself, *What is it with these people and their excitement about clouds?* He stood up and picked up a rock, imitating what Rudy had done, skimming it across the top of the moving water. Asher then asked, "What do you mean 'lost in the cloud'?"

Rudy, reenergized by Asher's interest after opening his painful past, answered, "You're an avid outdoorsman, a hunter, and backpacker, right?"

"Yes."

"So haven't you experienced heavy fog or maybe a snowstorm? You're on a narrow trail through the mountains, and it was so thick that you could only see a few feet in front of you, if that?"

"Many times!"

"Good, then you know the only way to safely continue walking is to concentrate only on the trail at your feet, taking one step at a time."

Asher nodded his head.

"Why is that?"

"So you don't wander off the trail and get lost."

Hesitating, Rudy looked at Asher, communicating with his eyes, *You've just answered your own question.* Then he said aloud, "The cloud analogy represents living life in and with the Spirit of God." Rudy quickly brought his finger up, saying firmly, "Before you shut your brain off because I'm talking about God stuff, first hear what I have to say."

Rudy looked around with his hands spread outward. "There's no rush to get anywhere or be anywhere. That's what you wanted, right? To be in the middle of nowhere, hiding from the world and your painful problems?"

He paused now, kindly looking deep into Asher's eyes and tapped him on the chest. "Like I said earlier, you and I being here right now is no accident."

Asher gave Rudy a half smile, shrugging his shoulders and said, "Where would I go without Mr. Alaska? I have no idea where we are way up here except for what the map says."

Rudy picked up another rock and said, "I guess sharing each other's painful wounds levels out the playing field."

Agreeing with a nod, Asher confirmed, "I think it does."

"Good. Now, back to the cloud." He tossed the rock and continued, "I'm going to guess," Rudy brought his fingers up next to his eye, pinching his forefinger and thumb together, leaving very little space, "that you're probably a religious guy or once were. You've gone to church, or maybe you're still going. Am I right?"

Nodding again, Asher said, "My parents always went to church, dragging me along when I was a kid. Then, after my dad's funeral, which was in their church, I never stepped back into one."

"Got it. I played this subconscious religious game too; it was how I was brought up. You probably have the fundamentals of this God thing. Like He created everything, and you know the big names that come up once in a while: Noah and the flood, Moses wandering through the desert for forty years, and then there's the boy David who killed a giant named Goliath and became a great king.

"Then we jump to the New Testament, and Jesus comes along. He's a man like you and me but born from a virgin. He lived a perfect life, calling Himself the Son of God." Rudy paused to get some reaction from Asher, making sure he was listening. Asher looked back up into Rudy's eyes, awaiting his next words, which gave Rudy his answer. "Jesus gave man instructions on how to have a relationship with Him and how to get to heaven. Then He was put to death, crucified on a cross. After that, He came back to life, which we celebrate as Easter, and then He went up to heaven. But before He went away, He left the Spirit of God here on earth. Am I close, Asher, or am I in left field somewhere? Oh, sorry, you're a football player; how about out of bounds?"

"No, you pretty much have a touchdown," he said, giving Rudy a slight grin.

Rudy sighed with relief, talking to God in his head. *You did it again by putting this together*. "Great. So you've heard the statement 'God the Father, God the Son, and God the Holy Spirit'?"

Again, Asher nodded.

"Good. I want you to imagine God truly as the Holy Spirit, being this pure white cloud all around us, like I mentioned earlier, walking on a trail. In the Bible, we're told that if we believe and follow Jesus, we will be filled with His Spirit. Picture this, Asher, not only envisioning the Spirit of God out of our bodies but also experiencing Him on the inside with every breath we take. Got that?"

Asher tilted his head, indicating he was going along with the story, but thought to himself, *This guy's been up here way too long.*

"Excellent, keep up with me here because this one is going to blindside you. Hopefully, it won't give you a concussion." Rudy smiled proudly at his football analogies before he asked slowly, "Why does God the Holy Spirit live inside us?"

Asher's mind went blank. After a few moments, with no answer coming to him, he became frustrated, stood up, and walked past Rudy to the canoe. He turned around and said in an aggressive tone, "Rudy, what does any of this mumbo jumbo have to do with the things that happened to you and me?"

Rudy stepped forward next to Asher at the canoe, answering, "Nothing but yet…everything!"

Looking toward the water, Rudy changed the subject. "It's time to get back on the river."

Asher flinched, and his hands went outward into the air. Surprised, he looked down at the older man. "You didn't answer my question!"

"Patience." Rudy patted him on the shoulder. "It will get answered. One thing at a time." Rudy pushed the canoe into the water, prodding Asher to get in and digest what he had just said and asked.

They had been canoeing for an hour or so, making great time, as it was now midmorning. Rudy purposely put the discussion to the side and let Asher focus on the river and the surroundings, understanding he needed to have the Alaska experience, not a lecture.

This also gave Rudy a lot of time to pray quietly that God would work on Asher, healing his wounds and suffering, and help him to turn around and stop walking backward and staring at the past. Rudy wanted Asher to finally start walking forward boldly in the wonderful cloud of Jesus and begin a fresh, new, clearer relationship with Him.

Asher peered over the edge of the canoe through the clear, cold water. He looked for fish since they were on a smooth stretch of the river. Suddenly, Rudy whispered with caution and urgency, "Asher, quickly lean forward to hide your body as much as you can. We need to look like a floating log."

Asher looked up, saw what Rudy had spotted, and dropped as low as he could. Rudy softly spoke again, "If she thinks her calf is in danger, she won't hesitate to stomp us to death or drown us."

Asher slowly peeked up over the rim of the canoe, looking at a large cow moose with her calf crossing the river. They were just ahead of them, coming up quickly. They were on a collision course, but then, Asher felt the canoe sway gently to the side. He realized that Rudy had used his oar as a rudder, doing his best to not make any noise or waves to change their direction.

The cow suddenly halted, stomped her front leg, and splashed the water twice. She was giving a signal of danger. Both Asher and Rudy tensed up; it appeared the canoe was going to barely miss her. They kept their eyes glued upward on her as their heads were down. Asher held his breath as he floated past the huge head, which was about seven feet high and tilted sideways. Her dark eyes pierced right through him. Her nostrils flared out, taking a deep smell of the odd thing floating up next to her. Suddenly, she snorted and bounced her head up and down. Rudy spouted,

"Asher, row hard and fast!" Rudy knew the cow's next move as she leaned back and raised a front leg.

Asher was used to instructions being yelled out to him, so he responded with lightning speed. He dove his oar into the water, and the canoe surged forward.

Swiftly repeating the motion, he heard loud sounds coming from Rudy, but this time it was of pain. Not stopping the oar, he looked back out of the corner of his eye and saw the leg of the moose lifting out of the canoe. With all his strength, Asher paddled over and over, splashing water everywhere as the boat seemingly skimmed on water.

Not hearing or feeling anything around or in the canoe anymore, Asher turned back again, this time taking in a full view of the scene. He was shocked at what he saw.

"Rudy! Rudy! Say something!" Asher looked past Rudy, out in the river, just in time to see the cow moose and calf. They walked up the bank, out of the river, and disappeared into the forest.

CHAPTER 6

Asher rowed powerfully to shore, jumping out and dragging the whole canoe onto dry ground. He yelled out again, "Rudy, say something!" As he knelt next to Rudy, Rudy's body slumped forward, unconscious, and blood flowed from his head and down his face. Asher looked him over, glanced around at where they were, and spotted a good place to lay Rudy down.

Cradling him up out of the canoe, Asher carried Rudy a short distance and laid him under a tree. Quickly, he went back and unpacked the big waterproof bag and found his backpack to retrieve his first aid bag and a small bath towel, then returned to Rudy.

Taking both Rudy's and his own life jacket off, he put them behind Rudy's head and shoulders to elevate him. Asher then calmly began to survey the wound, blotting the seeping blood with the towel to see exactly where it was coming from. Asher found a large gash on the top of Rudy's head, going down the side of his skull. The moose's hoof had cut him like a knife.

Applying pressure directly on the cut with the towel, Asher began to think everything through: the severity of the wound, their situation, and where they were geographically. Asher knew he needed to stop the bleeding and get Rudy to a hospital ASAP. However, they were still over eight days away from Bettles, and now there was only one person who could paddle.

If there was one thing Asher was extremely prepared for, it was outdoor survival and wilderness first aid. Besides becoming an Eagle Scout, Asher's father had made him attend several wilderness survival training camps in Colorado growing up.

Opening his first aid bag, he took out a couple of large square gauze pads, a large roll of gauze, medical tape, two small antiseptic wipe packets, tweezers, and a packet of blood clotting powder. Looking deep into the six-inch-long cut beginning at the crown of Rudy's head, Asher folded back Rudy's hair. He opened one antiseptic packet and wiped down his own hands and the tweezers. With the other antiseptic wipe, he cleaned the fringe of the opened wound, which smeared the blood.

He found a few chunks of debris from the moose's hoof scattered within the muscle and fat. He took the tweezers and removed everything foreign. Knowing the oozing of blood would help purify the laceration, he decided not to wash it out anymore.

Opening the blood clotting powder packet, he poured it into the deep cut from one end to the other. Next, he opened the two square pads of gauze and positioned them to fully cover the cut.

Asher looked back into his backpack for something long, narrow, solid, and slightly curved to match the curvature of Rudy's wound. Not finding what he was looking for, he turned to the ground and spotted a fallen tree branch about the diameter of a dime. At a faintly curved section of the branch, he broke it to the length of the injury. He then laid the branch on the gauze already on Rudy's head.

He then tightly coiled the roll of gauze around Rudy's head a couple of times, pressing the stick hard against the square gauze pads that ran the length of the cut. This forced pressure downward, directly onto the wound, to help stop the bleeding. Finally, he wrapped medical tape several times over the coiled gauze to secure the bandage.

Asher looked Rudy over to make sure he was not hurt anywhere else when he noticed that Rudy's pants were ripped at the thigh on the same side as the head wound, and a faint hoof print of watery mud was left behind.

Asher pulled Rudy's pants down to his knees and saw a giant black and blue spot forming, making the thigh look crooked. Asher looked back at Rudy's face and thought, *That's not good. His femur is probably broken, and a blood clot could easily be forming, especially at his age.*

Glancing at Rudy's clothes, he saw that his shirt and pants were drenched in blood. With the bleeding somewhat under control, he decided to take all of Rudy's clothes off and clean him up. Looking out into the forest, he remembered Rudy saying that grizzlies up here would not eat human food, but he did not say anything about them not liking human blood; he was not going to take any chances.

After taking Rudy's clothes off and retrieving his belt and everything out of his pockets, Asher threw the clothes into the woods. Getting a fresh pair of pants and shirt back on him, he then unrolled Rudy's sleeping bag and put him inside it.

He took one of the oars and strapped it to the side of Rudy's leg as a splint. He wanted to secure the bend of the leg firmly where the break was. He used Rudy's belt and some rope from the canoe. Once the leg was locked in place, Asher put Rudy's life vest back on him and zipped up the sleeping bag. Taking the small towel, he wiped out the blood in the canoe and then washed it in the river. He then repacked the center of the canoe, making a bed out of their stuff, but kept his first aid bag out and at the ready.

Asher cradled Rudy up again and placed him in the middle of the canoe, facing backward on his new lounging seat. Rudy's head was propped up on the front seat so that Asher could see his face when he regained consciousness. Asher peered around and made sure he had everything packed except for the blood-soaked clothing that he had thrown in the woods. He pushed the canoe into the river and took the rudder position.

For some reason, his arms didn't seem to want to dip the oar into the water, and he thought he heard a faint whisper. He looked down at Rudy, but his eyes were still closed, and he was not moving. Asher shook it off and again went to paddle, but it was as if his arms had a mind of their own. He heard the voice again, this time much clearer, saying, "Talk to Me."

Asher twisted his head around to see who was talking to him. He wasn't frightened because the words were spoken calmly, though powerfully. Not seeing anyone, he instantly had an overwhelming sense of peace move through his body. He could not help himself and asked out loud, "God?"

"Talk to Me."

Sitting in Rudy's seat, he pictured Rudy praying every morning before they left camp and realized he was being asked to do the same. Understanding that he was now in charge of the trip and the fact that he wanted to respect Rudy, he proceeded to do his duty. Clearing his throat and taking a deep breath, Asher tried to think of what to say. The only thing that came to mind was the picture of thick, pure, white clouds, the old grandma on his flight from Seattle, and Rudy talking about the cloud.

Trying to look past the cloud to find words, he was only able to repeat hesitantly what Rudy had said that morning, "God, guide and direct us on our journey. Help us to believe and trust that You will be with us in calm waters, through the rapids, and around any obstacles in our paths." He stopped his conversation with God, thinking about what he had said, and thought in a joking tone, *Well, that prayer went right over Your head today, considering the run-in with the moose, didn't it...* He laughed out loud, finishing sarcastically, "All-knowing God."

An eerie silence instantly surrounded him as if he had gone deaf. Even the sound of the water slapping against the canoe vanished. In the distance, down the river, slowly coming up through the valley, a fog billowed forward mystically, smothering the postcard scenery of northern Alaska.

Stunned at the irony of what he was seeing, though still not hearing anything, the strong, tough athlete began to wither helplessly as worry and loneliness consumed him. Still staring forward, a flutter caught his eye off to one side. A small bird perched itself on the tip of the bow of the canoe. It twisted rapidly and turned around while chirping. Seeing the innocent and lively bird, a memory of a Bible story that he had heard as a child came to mind. It was about sparrows. Thinking back, he recalled something about not worrying about clothes, food, and water and that human life was far more important to God than the sparrows. Also, the sparrows themselves don't worry about anything because God takes care of them.

"Asher, you are more treasured to Me than that little bird. Yet, look how joyful it is and full of life. I'm waiting for you, son." Asher had no doubt who the words came from and knew he had to respond but didn't know what to say. He lifted his arm up and gave the hand signal of love as Rudy had always done.

Then it struck him; Rudy was probably signing because the wife he lost was deaf. They must have signed to each other all the time. But Asher couldn't correlate why Rudy was doing it now.

The bird flew away, appearing to have pushed the front of the canoe out into the current. The canoe was bobbing into the water and taking off as Asher ended with, "Until later on."

As the canoe entered the thick, oncoming fog, Asher was unable to see more than a canoe's length ahead of him and began to have second thoughts about whether he should just wait it out. He looked toward Rudy and saw that the gauze was slowly becoming red around his head. He knew that he had no choice but to continue.

The river didn't have many powerful, high rushing rapids, but obstacles were constantly and suddenly appearing through the fog. Asher had to work hard not to run directly into rocks protruding out of the water. He didn't want to get wedged sideways; this would flip the canoe and dump them and everything they had into the water to float away downstream.

Rarely did he have a moment to rest as he was continually correcting his angle on the water, paddling hard this way and that. To his surprise, despite his strength and physique, his shoulders and arms were beginning to tire and ache. He gave Rudy respect for doing this all day long.

The dense fog remained constant as time and miles went by. Asher became more and more concerned as Rudy continued to lay lifeless. He thought Rudy would have woken up by now with being bumped and jostled as they worked their way down the river. Each time the aluminum canoe collided into a boulder, a loud banging sound would ring through the air, at which point Asher looked hopefully at Rudy, but he only lay still.

Later in the afternoon, Rudy blinked his eyes open without Asher noticing. Glancing around, he tried to understand what was going on. Suddenly, excruciating pain ripped through him, and he began screaming. He reached down and grasped his leg within the sleeping bag.

He nearly knocked Asher backward and out of the canoe, but Asher found his bearings and assured him, "You're okay, Rudy. You're going to be okay!" He pressed onward through the fog to one side of the river. He was hoping for a good, flat shoreline and got his wish. With several bushes in the way, Asher jumped out once the front hit ground and pulled the canoe up onto land. Rudy was shrieking in pain.

Asher grasped under the sleeping bag and gently lifted Rudy. He laid him onto the flat ground. Looking Rudy in the eyes and trying to get his full attention to calm him down, Asher firmly said, "Rudy! Rudy! Look at me! Look at me!"

Rudy quieted down and squinted his eyes closed to fight back the pain. Then he mumbled, "What happened? What's wrong with me?"

Asher answered as he unzipped the sleeping bag, "You were attacked by a moose a long way back. It split your head open, and I think it broke your leg." Asher turned to the canoe and grabbed his first aid bag and a bottle of water.

Kneeling next to Rudy's head, Asher said, "From your degree of pain, I'm now convinced that your femur is broken. I'm going to give you something for the pain, but first, I need to change this bandage. The bleeding has finally stopped, thanks to the clotting powder, but you still look like a cherry popsicle up top."

"What's wrong with my head?" Rudy questioned, still confused, and lifted his hand to touch the dried, bloody gauze Asher was unraveling.

"The moose hit you with its front hoof, cutting you pretty badly."

Attempting humor in the dire situation, Rudy said through gritted teeth, "Besides my leg killing me, I've got a busting headache."

Asher laughed, saying, "I bet you do."

Replacing the bandage, Asher asked, "Are you on any medications?"

"Nothing besides stuff for arthritis and an aspirin a day."

"Are you allergic to anything?"

"Just penicillin…and it appears moose as well." He let out a fake laugh through the pain.

"So you want to be funny?" Asher smiled, also trying to lighten the mood, and added, "Now I've got something funny for you. Since you were knocked out, I've been in that cloud you talked about."

Rudy wrinkled his face, trying to understand.

"Look around if you can," Asher said, turning and pointing outward.

Rudy peered up at the sky and to the sides, seeing the world in a blinding white fog and gave out a true chuckle. "Oh, that is funny. Now, how about something for the pain?"

Asher placed two pain pills in Rudy's hand and gave him the bottle of water. Moving down to Rudy's splinted leg, he checked how tightly the oar was securing Rudy's leg. Satisfied, he zipped up the sleeping bag, packed up the first aid supplies, and said, "We need to get back on the river and get you to a doctor."

Rudy closed his eyes, still swirling in pain. "I'm not feeling like it right now. Let's just make camp here."

Asher looked up and did his best to read the light of the sun through the thick cloud cover. "We don't have much choice. With the amount of blood you've lost and your injuries, an infection or blood clot could come at any time.

"We're also not moving as fast with just me rowing. There's probably another couple of hours or so before it gets dark. Plus, we have so many days to go until we get you to a hospital. There's no time to waste."

Rudy frowned through the pain and questioned, "What do you mean another couple of hours?"

Asher realized Rudy was really out of it. He tried again to explain what had happened, how bad Rudy's injuries were, and how long they had been on the river before he woke up.

Rudy raised his eyebrows, and his eyes grew wide. He tried to remember the river and where they might be. "How long did you say we've been floating downriver?"

Asher shrugged his shoulders. "Maybe five hours or so?"

"So what did you do at the waterfall?"

"What waterfall?"

"From where the moose probably attacked me, downriver about two hours, there's a fault line in the ground. It goes for miles, cutting straight across the river. Years ago, we had an earthquake up here, and part of the ground slid up, and the other part went down, forming a waterfall about thirteen feet high."

They stared at each other, waiting for the other to answer. Asher raised his eyebrows and shoulders like he didn't know what Rudy was talking about.

Rudy added, "There's no way you could've missed it. We would've gone over the falls and tipped the canoe straight over, dropping down onto rocks, smashing everything."

Asher still had the same expression.

Adjusting his body and attempting to relieve some pain, Rudy explained again, thinking Asher didn't understand him. "You have to get out of the water and walk the canoe and gear around the waterfall."

"Rudy, the fog came on right after you were attacked. I haven't been able to see more than a canoe's length in front of us. We've been on the river for most of the day, and we didn't go over any high waterfall."

Rudy lay there, stumped, as a thought came to him. "Okay, I haven't been up this far for several years, so maybe the raised fault line disappeared somehow. I don't know. But what I do know is we don't have to be on the river for very much longer." Thinking quickly as he grimaced in agony, he added, "If you're right, we're only about an hour or so away from some friends of mine that live up here."

"What? You never said anything about anyone living out here. I thought we were alone."

"Asher, this area is so huge that you would never find them. Besides, their home is back off the river, and you would've never known they were there."

This rubbed Asher the wrong way. "Are there more people living around here that I don't know about?"

"No one else," Rudy answered. "This is a special situation. Only native Indians can live and own property up here. Oh, that reminds me—you did know someone else was up here. Remember Steve, the pilot told us that he had dropped off two hunters at Nora's place?"

"Yeah."

"This will be Nora's place with her husband, Martin."

"That's great, but that doesn't get us closer to a doctor unless one of them is."

"Yes, it does. They have a plane and a runway in their backyard."

Asher didn't hesitate; he stood up, cradling Rudy, and confirmed, "We've got a new plan. Let's do it and get you there before it gets dark." After nestling Rudy back into his place in the middle of the canoe, Asher pushed it into the water, stepped in, and took off.

All Rudy could do was watch as Asher frantically switched sides, paddling and steering, doing his best to steer the canoe around rocks and logs. The thick, low clouds blinded any distant view, and Rudy was getting tired just watching Asher constantly move the oar back and forth.

Rudy passed the time by telling Asher all about Nora, Martin, and what they do. However, he kept interrupting his own story to remind Asher about the waterfall, just in case Asher was off on his timing and their location. Rudy was still not convinced they had passed it. "Listen for the waterfall. If you hear it, get to the left shore as fast as you can."

Asher would just nod in agreement. He could tell the strong pain pills were taking effect, but it also appeared that Rudy was slowly going into shock. He was very weak from losing a lot of blood, and he kept drifting off to sleep.

After a while, Asher thought he might be getting close to Nora's place, per the time frame Rudy had given. He had Rudy repeat to him what he was looking for since he needed to find the spot along the river to stop. Rudy mumbled descriptions of a small clearing with a wide bench made of logs. Behind the bench was a wide walking trail between the trees, which led up to the house, about fifty yards or so behind it.

Looking ahead intently, Asher thought he started to see spots of blue sky peeking through the cloud cover. To his surprise, he also heard a faint humming sound. At first, the falls Rudy warned him about came to mind, but it was different than splashing water. The closer the humming noise came, the more the clouds dissipated.

***

Mia was paying close attention, peering through the windshield of her small prop plane. She looked through the low, thin cloud cover as she followed the North Fork of the Koyukuk River from Bettles to her parents' home. She had been delayed in Bettles for most of the day, waiting for this uncommonly thick fog to go away. She had flown in early this morning from Fairbanks to refuel when it rolled in, swallowing up any visibility to take off again.

While she was waiting, the lodgekeeper told her that her mom had called in on the radio last night. She was asking for someone to pick up her clients a couple of days early. As soon as the fog came in, it ruined the schedule for the day. By the time the fog finally lifted, the pilot and plane scheduled to pick them up would have to fly to another location that had been scheduled before theirs.

As the day dragged on, the lodgekeeper asked if she would do him a favor when the weather cleared. He needed her to bring the hunters back. They would pay for her fuel and then some.

Mia had no problem taking the offer. She had been doing these kinds of trips for years before she moved away from home to go to college and start her own career.

Recognizing the bend in the river where her parents' house was located, she made the turn, did a flyover, and then looped around and landed. When she parked her plane next to her parents' place, three people came out of the house to greet her, but Samson, the big Alaskan malamute, got to her first, uncontrollably excited to see his favorite family member.

Nora gave her daughter a hug and introduced her to the two men waiting for their ride to Bettles. "Mia, this is Seth and Marco."

Seth stuck out his hand and said, "Nice to meet you, Mia. We're sure glad you're willing to take us back to Bettles. We're definitely ready to go."

"Nice to meet you two. It sounds like you guys had a, um… how would you put it, a unique hunt?"

Seth laughed. "You definitely can say that." He nudged Marco to say something.

Marco couldn't help himself from staring at Mia but was able to finally get out, "It will be one hunt we'll never forget."

Hoping to get into the air quickly, Seth added, "So can we get going? We have a flight waiting for us to get back to California."

"You do?" Mia asked, having inside knowledge of the scheduled commercial flights in and out of Bettles.

"Yep," Marco replied.

"I just came from there, and there's nothing waiting or scheduled until tomorrow."

Caught off guard, Marco spouted, "Willie is flying in to get us."

Seth looked at Marco and couldn't believe he had given out that information. He calmly turned back to Nora and Mia, noticed their confused looks, and said, "Yeah, our friend is flying in to pick us up. He's been in Fairbanks on his own hunting trip."

Bewildered, Nora asked, "How does he know to pick you up two days early?"

Playing it off as if it was no big deal, Seth replied, "I called him from our satellite phone."

"Oh…okay, I didn't know you had one."

"Willie had extras and let us borrow one," Marco answered.

Seth was becoming impatient and wanted to keep Marco out of this conversation, so he interjected, "So we need to get going. If Willie's not there by now waiting, he'll be there soon. Can we start loading everything?"

Mia glanced at her mother with an inquisitive expression as if to say, *Are these guys for real?*

She turned to the men and said, "Well, let's not waste any more time. Go get your bags. Mom and I will retrieve the meat out of the freezer."

Seth turned to Marco, requesting, "Get my bags out of my room; I'll help them with the boxes."

"Oh, you don't have to do that. We can get it," Nora said.

"No, I insist. They're heavy. I think Marco can handle the light suitcases while we handle the heavy things." Seth smiled at her and then toward Marco to make fun of him.

Understanding he was being teased, Marco grinned as he turned to the house. "That's fine with me. Gives me a chance to steal another piece of blueberry pie."

"Food… Does he ever think about anything else?" Nora joked.

"Nope, that's usually the only thing on his mind," Seth said as they walked to the butchering shed.

They packed the plane and quickly filled it to weight capacity. Unfortunately, Mia's plane was smaller than most and couldn't take all the gear, meat, antlers, two grown men, and herself. Nora suggested, "The boxes of meat take up a lot of the weight, and we know"—she smiled attempting not to embarrass the guys—"antlers are the real reason most hunters come up here. So take your trophies now, and we'll send the boxes on our next trip."

"No, no. We'll leave the antlers and even some of our gear if we have to, but we're taking the meat with us now," Seth demanded.

Again, Nora and Mia were surprised, so Mia said questioningly, "Okay...?" She turned and unloaded the heavy, bulky antlers. She felt the weight of a couple of suitcases and asked, "How about these two large ones?"

"Yes, those work."

"Wait. Both of those are mine," Marco said.

Seth laughed. "That's why I said yes."

"Whatever. They're just filled with wet hunting boots and clothes."

After unloading the two suitcases, Mia stepped away from the passenger door to let the guys in and said, "If you're ready, let's go. I want to get back and spend as much time with my parents as I can."

Seth and Marco looked at each other, both knowing what the other one was thinking as they climbed inside. Seth looked behind in the direction of the mining shed, where Martin had returned late that morning. Seth wanted to get away as far and as fast as he could.

Mia started the plane and made sure the two guys' seat belts were fastened. Looking out the windows, Seth and Marco saw Nora waving goodbye as she stepped back onto the front porch. They waved back while Mia slowly throttled forward, coasting toward the far end of the runway. At the end of the runway, she turned the plane around and throttled firmly forward. The engine roared to life, shaking the body of the plane and everyone in it. Jetting the aircraft forward only about twenty feet, she suddenly pulled back on the throttle, coming to the idle position. The airplane's dashboard was large, so she raised herself up in the pilot's seat; she needed a better look at the runway.

"What are you doing? What's wrong?" Seth asked.

"There's something or someone that just walked onto the end of the runway."

"You can get this plane up before hitting it."

Mia turned back, looking at Marco as if he were crazy, and said, "Are you serious?"

"No, he's kidding. We're just anxious to leave," Seth commented, trying to keep a lid on everything.

Mia had had about enough. She was doing them a favor, and she was not in the mood for this. "Why? Do you have some big emergency?" she persisted.

"Just homesick for warm Southern California, sweetie."

After looking back and forth between them, she peered forward, letting go of the brakes. She coasted back to where they had started, next to the house.

As they got closer, they saw a man holding something big in his arms. Mia shut the engine down and stopped in front of him in the middle of the runway. She stepped out and ducked under the wing support bracket. Standing up straight, she couldn't believe her eyes as she said, "23C?"

"Mia, what's wrong? Who is that?" Nora yelled as she quickly came toward them.

Mia walked up to Asher as he cradled a sleeping bag with Rudy in it, and their eyes met.

"Mia?" Asher said, shocked to see her. He knelt, gently lowering an unconscious Rudy to the ground. They both looked at Rudy. "He's badly hurt. You know him, right?"

"Rudy!" Nora shouted as she knelt down, looking closely at his face. "What happened?"

"We were canoeing down the river this morning when a moose and her calf crossed in front of us. She beat him up pretty badly."

"A moose did that?" Marco asked as he and Seth came walking up.

"Yeah, we need to get him to a hospital. He's lost a lot of blood from the deep cut on his head, and his femur is broken."

Mia looked up at her mom. "This is Asher. We met on one of my flights earlier in the week. This is my mom—"

"Nora," Asher interrupted, holding his hand out.

They shook hands, and she asked, "How do you know my name?"

"Before Rudy lost consciousness the second time, he told me about you and Martin and how to find your place. But he didn't tell me about your daughter." Asher smiled wide, looking at Mia. "This is definitely a surprise."

Nora looked from Rudy to Seth and then to Marco. "Sorry for the change of plans, guys, but you'll have to wait one more day before flying out of here." Her gaze shifted to the sky to determine how much light was left. "Rudy needs the plane now." She turned back to Asher. "You made it just in time; another few seconds and Mia would have been gone."

Seth could not control himself. "I don't think so. Our stuff is already packed." Seth looked down at Nora and then turned to Mia. "Girly, you can come back and get him. Right now, we have a flight waiting for us."

The three kneeling beside Rudy looked at one another and couldn't believe what this man had just said. Looking up to Seth again, Nora asked, "How could you even think of doing such a thing?"

Marco took a half step forward, putting his hands up to his hips, and told her, "You're going to do exactly what he says."

CHAPTER 7

"If this is another joke, it's not funny," Mia stated.

"No joke, pretty thing. We've paid for a flight out of here, so let's get going," Marco responded without emotion.

Mia stood up boldly in their faces. "Are you out of your minds? Rudy is hurt, and if he doesn't get help soon, he could die. You're crazy!" The guys held their ground as Mia continued arguing with them.

Without anyone noticing, Samson had walked up next to Mia. He lowered his head with his ears pinned back when he heard the angry tone coming from his favorite master.

Still kneeling, Asher and Nora were concealed from the two guys by Mia and Samson. Asher leaned over to Nora, whispering, "Do you know how to fly that plane?"

Nora nodded yes.

As quietly as he could, he added, "Good. If this goes bad, I'm going to take on both guys. You get Rudy in that plane and get him help."

Nora whispered urgently, "No! Mia needs to leave."

Asher paused and listened to the escalating argument between the other three. "I have a feeling it's too late for her. There was a state trooper who flew in with me several days ago. He's a friend of Rudy's. Get him up here."

"Hey, what are you two talking about?" Seth asked, moving closer to Asher. Asher turned his head toward Rudy to divert from his conversation with Nora.

"Dude, Rudy's getting worse. I don't know why you're doing this, but he needs help and now."

Seth grasped Mia by the arm. "It's time to go."

Samson bared his teeth and gave a deep growl.

While talking to Nora, Asher had adjusted his kneeling position into more of a crouch, similar to a low football stance. He looked at Nora, giving her a firm shake of his head, and then said to Mia, "The last time someone touched a flight attendant…" He hesitated to let her think and then added, "23C showed up!"

Mia's eyes widened, knowing something physical was about to happen. She stepped quickly to one side while Seth was still holding her arm. This opened a path directly to the two men.

Asher looked past the two guys and said heatedly, "What's that down the runway?" Everyone turned; his distraction had worked. He exploded like his days on the line and tackled both men to the ground.

"Now, Nora! Mia, help your mom!"

Samson began barking and jumping in all directions, confused about what was going on. He didn't know who to protect and who to attack.

After a split second to understand what was going on herself, Mia grabbed Rudy in his sleeping bag. With her mom's help, they each took an end of the sleeping bag and carried him to the plane. They slid him into the back of the plane with the boxes of meat.

To make more room, Mia threw out the rest of the suitcases and the two rifle cases. She then jumped out of the plane, leaving Nora and Rudy in the plane together.

"What the—" Seth started to say before Asher planted a fist to the side of his face.

Marco recovered, got on his knees, and growled, "You picked the wrong man to do that to, boy." Asher slugged him just like he had done to Seth, except he did not get the same result. Marco slowly turned his head back, looking at Asher with vengeance in his eyes. He grabbed Asher's arm, pulling him down to the side as he pulled himself upright. Marco's weight tilted Asher off balance and forced him to the ground, but Asher quickly rolled back up to his feet.

The two men, looking like ferocious bulls, stared at each other, gaining their bearings and examining their opponent. The plane roared to life, which caught Marco's attention. This gave Asher another opportunity to rush at Marco. This time Asher came in low and pushed upward. This lifted Marco and slammed him hard into the ground, causing him to hit the back of his head.

The plane revved up to speed down the field as Seth yelled out, "No!" He stumbled to his feet and ran after the plane as it soared away.

When the plane cleared the runway, Seth was left standing in the field as anger consumed him. He pulled out a handgun hidden in the back of his pants. He took several shots at the plane, hitting the tail end once but missing with the rest.

Mia screamed, "Don't shoot!" Seth turned to Mia and pointed the gun at her. He stepped up and grabbed her again, but this time it was around her throat. While holding onto her, he turned back to the airborne plane as it circled. He raised the gun up, firing a couple more shots. Mia struggled to redirect his aim so he would miss each shot. He put the gun to her head, gritting his teeth, and stared hard at her. "All you had to do was fly us out of here! You messed everything up! I'm going to kill you!"

Asher looked in their direction and stepped back from Marco, demanding, "Let her go. She had nothing to do with this."

Seth pointed the gun at Asher. "You're right. It's your fault. First the fog, then you. This was supposed to be a quick in-and-out job."

Asher suddenly couldn't help but think about the thick, pure clouds Rudy had talked about and why God allowed them to show up in our lives.

"In and out for what?" Mia squeaked with Seth's arm still tightly around her throat. "You were on a hunting trip. You got your animals. You got what you paid for."

"Are you kidding me? No, we didn't!" He wrinkled his face at her naiveté. "We didn't come all the way up here for some stupid animals." Both Mia's and Asher's eyes went to the two sets of antlers lying next to the suitcases. "We came up here for something of real value."

Marco stood up quietly behind Asher and said, "Yeah, your father's gold!" Asher turned just in time to receive a solid punch to the face that knocked him to the ground, dazed.

"What are we going to do now?" Marco asked Seth.

"Radio! The plane's got a radio." Seth jerked Mia around, walking her to the house, and told Marco, "Get him up and follow me." Seth leaned over, putting his face up against Asher's, and said, "I will not hesitate to kill her…and you if Nora doesn't come back."

They walked into the house, and Mia showed them the radio in the office. Seth told her to call Nora as he pressed the gun barrel against her head again.

Bringing the handset to her mouth and pressing the side button, she said, "North Koyukuk Adventures calling Nora. Come in, Nora."

"Nora here. Mia, are you okay?"

"No, we're—"

Seth grabbed the handset from her and screamed, "Nora, turn the plane around now!"

She replied, "I've got to get Rudy to the hospital. I'll come back right away for you."

"Listen to me, woman. Turn around…" He paused as a thought came to his mind. "Nora, look back to where your husband works up on the stream." There was a pause as he gave the gun to Marco and pulled out the small transmitter box from his pocket.

Asher and Mia looked at each other, trying to figure out what he was doing. As the box came out, everyone saw a green light blinking. Seth said calmly into the handset, "Nora, you will turn around now, or this will happen to your daughter."

He smiled at Mia and pushed the button. Marco laughed, saying, "This is going to be good!"

Silence reigned for a few seconds, and then the soundwave of an explosion hit the house. Mia screamed for her dad and slipped away from Seth's grasp. She ran to the window in the office, looking out on the property. An explosion of fire and debris had erupted into the air. Asher was stunned, thinking to himself, *This can't be real. Things like this only happen in the movies.*

Mia shriveled her body inward, collapsing to the floor, crying. Asher knelt beside her. He then looked up as blood dripped down his chin from a split lip. "You didn't have to do that."

"Yes, we did!" Seth shot back, looking deep into his eyes. "Now you know we mean business. We won't hesitate to kill everyone else if you try to stop us or don't help us to get out of here."

Asher stared back into Seth's eyes without saying a word and thought, *What do I care? I don't have anything else to lose.*

Shortly thereafter, they heard the plane land as they looked out the window again. "Now we're getting somewhere," Seth said, pulling on Mia's arm to get her up. "Let's go."

They walked out to the plane parked close to the other side of the runway. It was next to the trail leading up to Martin's shed. As they got to the plane, the door was open, but Nora was not there. "Where is that Eskimo woman?" Marco asked, looking around.

"Where do you think?" Mia yelled out, still crying. "You killed my dad!"

"We don't need her. We've got you. Get in there." He pushed her hard toward the plane's door.

Before they left the house earlier, Asher had anticipated what was going to happen; he understood that this could be a live or die, kill or be killed situation. He had slowly retrieved the knife from its sheath on his belt while he was being pushed around in the house. He hid it in his large, closed fist. Not having flipped the blade out yet, he now moved his thumb to fold out the long, sharp blade.

Suddenly, from the corner of his eye, he saw a large animal racing full speed toward them, growling viciously. Samson leaped at the man who pushed Mia, taking him down flat onto his back.

"Marco, help! Get it off me! Get it off me!" Seth screamed at the shock of the animal thrashing him around. He was like a toy, his arm in a vice grip of large, sharp teeth.

The gun flew out of Seth's hand and bounced a couple of times on the ground, catching Marco's attention. As Marco went to pick it up, Asher kicked the gun out of his hand and gave him a stunning punch to the center of the face. Blood splattered out of Marco's nose.

Looking at Mia, Asher ordered, "Get out of here. Save Rudy. I'll take care of your mom."

"No, I'm not leaving," she responded in the whirlwind of emotions.

"Get on the plane!" he yelled, looking back at the two guys on the ground. He turned to her and grabbed her face to get her full attention. "I'll take care of this. You go do what you need to do."

They both had déjà vu for a second back to when he had said the same thing on the plane to Anchorage, coming to her rescue. As she was clearing her mind, he caught her off guard by quickly kissing her on the lips and then backing away. He asked, "What's your dog's name again?"

"Samson."

"Okay, now get out of here with Rudy…" While Asher was speaking, Marco tackled him from behind, and they began wrestling under the wing of the plane.

Mia jumped into the plane and started it. Seth grabbed his own arm after he was able to kick the malamute in the side, sending Samson yelping away. He yelled out painfully, "Marco, stop the girl! Stop her!"

Marco hit Asher in the stomach, knocking the air out of him. He then looked up at the plane moving away and reached out for the cockpit door handle.

Mia saw Marco and pressed forward on the throttle, blaring the engine alive and causing a powerful blast of air to blind him. Seth rolled over onto his knees and wobbled, standing up as blood dripped down his arm and through his jacket.

Glancing around, Seth spotted the gun. He looked over toward Asher as Asher looked back at him. Both had the same thought, and both dashed toward the gun. Like recovering a fumble, Asher bent down and at a full sprint, he picked it up first. He kept running like he was headed for a touchdown. Before disappearing down the trail, he yelled out, "Samson!"

Mia headed straight toward Bettles, quickly gaining altitude to get over the mountains. She needed to have a clear radio path to Bettles. She called out, "Mayday! Mayday! This is Mia to Bettles Lodge. Roger, are you there?"

"Mia, it's Roger. What's wrong?"

"They killed my dad! The hunters killed my dad!" she cried out.

"Did I hear you correctly? Hunters killed Martin?"

"Yes." Shock was creeping in as she started to lose control of her emotions.

"I'm so sorry, Mia. Hunting accidents happen…"

"No, no, it was no accident." Tears began to flow. "They murdered him. They blew him up in his shed!"

"Mia, what's your location?"

"I'm just getting over the mountains, heading to you." She wiped her eyes and sniffled deeply. "I've got…" She looked back at Rudy lying down. "I've got Rudy with me."

"Rudy?" he responded, surprised. "Let me talk with him."

"No, you don't understand. He's badly hurt. We need to get him to a hospital."

"They hurt him too? But he was supposed to be on a trip with some other guy up the river."

"The guy, 23C...I mean, Asher brought him to our place. Rudy was attacked by a moose."

"What in the world is going on up there? Why did they kill your father?"

"They were stealing his gold and said someone was flying in today to pick them up."

"No one is scheduled to fly in until tomorrow."

"That's what I told them, but they have a satellite phone and said someone named Willie was picking them up. Roger, you've got to get help!"

"Where's your mother?"

"She ran up to Dad's shed." Mia painfully shut her eyes, trying to erase the horrifying images, then rapidly blinked them back open and started crying again.

"Where's this other guy, Asher?"

"He told me to leave and get Rudy help. He was fighting the two guys behind the house on the runway."

"Okay, Mia, you come on in, and I'll make some calls."

***

Nora knelt on the ground next to Martin. She had her cheek up against his, crying.

Ever since he had returned to the shed that morning, he had not gone into it. He dove into his work, so frustrated with himself. He had wasted time by staying too long at home, eating breakfast, and talking with the two hunters. He had tried to pull away from their conversation, but they kept talking and asking questions. Then, after leaving the two men, he walked out to the ATV parked on the side of the house. He was going to ride back up the creek when he noticed it had a flat tire. It had to be fixed, wasting more time.

When the explosion happened, Martin was standing next to the sluice box, about forty yards downstream. The percussion hit him and the sluice box, forcing them back a few yards and knocking him out. Martin was splintered all over with small wood shrapnel, and the sluice box had fallen over and landed on his foot. When Nora got to him, it appeared he was dead.

"Martin, please come back to me," Nora cried out as she lay across his chest. That was when she heard his heartbeat and felt him breathing. Reaching into the stream, she cupped some cold water in her hand and dripped it onto his face, hoping this would wake him. He coughed and blinked rapidly. "Thank You, Lord! Thank You!" was all she could say.

"What happened?" Martin asked, bewildered as he put his hands up to his ringing ears. He tried to reach for his foot and flinched in agonizing pain.

"Your shed exploded and knocked you out." She sat back on her heels as he sat up and tried to lift the heavy, metal gold-sifter off his foot.

"Get this off of me!" he said rather louder than normal because he had gone temporarily deaf.

Standing for more leverage, Nora struggled a moment, but eventually, the heavy mining box gave way and tipped over into the creek.

Martin groaned, "Ah, that's better."

She knelt next to him as he lay back down. "Are you hurt anywhere else?"

Before answering her question, he suddenly realized what she had said moments ago, and he burst out, "What do you mean the shed exploded?" He moved his head to the side to see where the shed once stood. He screamed out, "No, no, not my gold!" He crawled up and got on his feet, not putting any weight on his injured foot. He waved his arms around in a panic, saying over and over, "My gold, my gold!"

"Martin! Martin!" Nora tried to get his attention, but he was obsessed with the gold and couldn't focus on anything else. She stood up in front of him, grabbed both his arms, and shouted into his face, "Look at me, Martin. Mia is in danger!"

His hearing was slowly recovering, and it took a few seconds for her words to sink in. He replied, "Mia? What's wrong with her?"

"Those two guys, the hunters…they did all this."

"What do you mean?"

"I don't know…" Nora was flustered. "They're bad men. You heard how urgently they wanted to leave this morning. They're hiding something."

"They definitely didn't seem right," he replied, coming to his senses and what was important.

"Mia flew in for a visit and was going to fly them to Bettles, but then a young man Mia knows brought Rudy to the house from the river. Rudy's badly hurt."

"Rudy's hurt?" The story was getting more complex.

"A moose attacked him, and now Rudy is unconscious and has a broken leg."

Just then, Samson came running up the trail. "Samson, where have you been?" Nora cooed, bending down to pet him.

"Saving Mia," Asher said as he slowed down from running behind the dog. He bent over, exhausted, breathing heavily and holding a gun in his hand. Blood still oozed from his cut lip.

Martin turned around, looking for something, and picked up a shovel. He started to swing at Asher. Nora stepped in front of him, saying, "No, he's the young man; this is Asher. He's Mia's friend who brought Rudy to the house."

"Wow! You're alive?" Asher goggled. "We all thought you were dead…"

"Where's Mia?"

Asher stood up tall, pulling his shoulders back as both Martin and Nora took a step back. They were looking up at this big and powerful young man.

"She's fine. She's flying back to Bettles with Rudy," he said between breaths, pointing up into the sky in the direction that her plane went.

"Where are the two guys?"

Asher looked back down the path, answering, "Not sure. We beat up on each other, and Samson here tore up the short guy's arm. After Mia got the plane down the runway, I grabbed their gun and ran up this trail to find you."

"That's their gun?" Martin asked.

"Yeah, the short one shot at you, Nora, when you were taking off." Nora's mouth dropped open, shocked at what these strangers were doing.

"So they're heading this way?" Martin asked, raising the shovel back up.

"I don't know."

"I don't understand. Why are they doing all this?" Nora questioned, not knowing if she should be angry or scared.

"They said something about gold when they had us in the house and were talking to you on the radio."

"Gold? They're after my gold?" Martin looked back at where his shed used to be.

"From the way they were acting, it seemed like they already had it and were trying to get away."

"But how? How would they know I have gold up here?" Martin turned angrily, directly into Nora's face as he hobbled, using the shovel as a crutch. "Did you say something to them, Nora?"

"No, I didn't say a word about the mine or gold. They saw pictures of our family and asked where you were. I said you were working up on the property, that's all." Then something came to mind and changed her demeanor. "You know, the bigger guy, Marco, said something after dinner last night. What was it?" She looked off to the side, thinking. "Oh, yeah. He replied to a comment Seth made, saying, 'That's what Willie said.'"

"What?" Martin asked.

"After I said you were working up on the property, they asked me how often you would come home. I said every few nights. That's when Marco said, 'That's what Willie said.' Seth then immediately changed the subject, like Marco was talking about something else."

"Who's Willie?" Asher asked.

Nora shrugged her shoulders, saying, "I don't know."

"So if the gold isn't here, where is it?" Martin asked, still completely enthralled only with the gold.

"The frozen meat boxes!" Nora blurted out. "That's why Seth wanted to help with carrying the boxes to the plane. Then, when the plane was overweight, they said to leave behind the antlers and—"

"The antlers?" Martin interrupted. "That's crazy; no hunter leaves behind the antlers." Martin hesitated, his eyes moving back and forth, figuring out what was happening, then stated, "They were stalling me!"

"What?" Nora asked.

"That's what they were doing this morning at breakfast, stalling me from coming up here. They didn't want me to find the gold missing. They even flattened the tire on my ATV to slow me down. They must have snuck up here last night after I got to the house. They took the gold and set all this up." He looked around, distraught at everything blown to pieces.

"So they're not really hunters?" Asher said, puzzled. "It was just a decoy to steal your gold?" He was putting the puzzle together with Martin. "You've never seen these guys before?"

Nora answered, "No, this was their first trip up here."

"How did they know about the gold and exactly where to go to steal it?"

"Good question," Martin replied.

There was silence for a moment between them as their minds went in different directions. Eventually Asher spoke up, "We have an advantage. They think you're dead, Martin."

He paused to think an idea through and continued, "Keeping you two safe is our first priority…"

"No, it's not. Getting the gold back is!" Martin interrupted passionately.

"You're no good dead to either Nora or Mia, Martin. These guys already tried to kill you once. They won't hesitate to kill everyone up here."

"I worked hard for that gold, and it's mine!"

"Seriously? We're going to have an argument about this?" Asher was taken aback at the selfishness.

Nora stepped in, turning to face Asher, and put her hand up to his chest to stop him. She whispered, "I'll handle this. Martin has gold fever. Could you give us some privacy?" She twisted around to Martin, gently grabbing his hand. Asher walked a few steps away, and after a minute or so, Nora called over to Asher. He had been keeping watch down the trail for the guys to show up as he petted Samson.

Nora had a short but direct talk with Martin. He grimaced, frustrated like a child whose mother was taking away his favorite toy, but finally dropped his shoulders in defeat.

Nora stepped up to Asher and said, "We all now understand the priorities here. Our safety comes first."

Asher looked at Martin, trying to help bring him further back to reality, and said, "You need some medical attention, Martin. Your ear is bleeding. The percussion must have ruptured your eardrum." He then pointed up and down Martin's body, saying, "Look at all the small pieces of shrapnel from the explosion. It's all over you. Are you sure you're okay?"

"Have you looked in the mirror, young man? You don't look that good yourself," Martin replied, trying to save any dignity he had left.

"I'm fine. I'm used to being beat up in football."

"Football, that's it! I knew I'd seen your face somewhere. You're…um, you're Asher Collins with Nebraska! You're one of the biggest and best tight ends in college football!"

Asher was stunned, just like when Rudy knew who he was. "How would you know that?"

"Are you two kidding right now?" Nora tried to interrupt the budding bromance.

Martin answered, "Watching football with Rudy is my favorite thing to do when the mining season is over."

"At Rudy's place?"

"No, at the house. We have satellite TV. Rudy flies in and spends several weeks up here with us in the fall. We watch football and the sports channel day and night."

"Stop with the football, you two. There are murderers coming after us." Nora was getting anxious. "Do you have a plan, Asher?"

He thought for a moment and said, "Well, again, they don't know Martin is alive, and we do have the gold."

Martin wrinkled his face in confusion. "We do?"

"It's in the meat boxes, as Nora said, which are on the plane with Mia."

Martin's demeanor relaxed as Asher continued, "But Mia doesn't know any of this." He racked his brain for a strategy and game plan to work this out, but curiosity overcame him. "So how much gold is there? It must be a lot for those guys to go to all this trouble."

Martin dropped back into gold fever mode. "It's none of your business, boy!" Martin hobbled up into Asher's face. His gray overalls were slightly ripped here and there, and he was covered in dirt smudges. "How do we know you're not in on this with those guys?" Martin barked. "Did you hurt Rudy and blame a moose?"

Shocked at the accusation, Asher looked down, eye to eye with the older man. "I was wrong. That explosion messed with your head. That's not blood flowing from your ear but trickles of any brains you've got left." His entire life, Asher had been good at quick responses to mess with other guys' heads. He used it to distract his opponents during football games.

This fired up Martin as he shoved Asher in the chest, but it was like pushing a brick wall. Asher was ready for any physical action. He had balanced himself before Martin's last comment and barely moved.

Samson stood quickly, hackles raised as he growled, baring his teeth at both men. Everyone looked down and couldn't tell if he was upset with Asher or Martin.

"Martin, how dare you!" Nora said. "Asher had nothing to do with this. He's trying to help us."

Martin looked back up at Asher, scowling, "You better not have."

Moving nothing but his lips, Asher said, "I came up here to get away from the crap in my life. In the few days I've been here, that's all I've gotten, and it's starting to really stink!" Asher returned the scowl, lifting his nose as if he was smelling Martin.

"What is it with you two? You're like schoolchildren." The men looked at Nora. "If Mia has the gold, those guys are going to go after her. Mia is in danger! To answer your question, Asher, Martin has about—"

"Nora!" Martin blurted out, trying to stop her.

She ignored him and continued, "Martin always has about four hundred and fifty ounces of gold by this time of year."

Asher stood there with a blank look, not quite understanding the significance of what was said.

Seeing his response, Martin could tell he didn't have any knowledge about precious metals. This relieved Martin and gave him a good feeling about the newcomer. "Gold right now is around two thousand dollars an ounce." Asher calculated in his head, grateful for the frame of reference. "They took about nine hundred thousand dollars in gold from me."

"Wow, that's a lot of gold!" Asher chuckled to himself, lifting his clenched fist to his lips to hide his expression.

"So you see why I need it back…"

Asher composed himself and nodded, saying, "Sounds like we're going to kill two birds with one stone. The gold for you"—he paused and smiled—"and Mia for me."

"What?" both Martin and Nora said at the same time.

"She owes me a kiss."

CHAPTER 8

"I'm going to kill him," said Marco.

"Forget him for now. We need to contact Willie. That girl's got the gold, and she's heading straight toward him." Marco bent down, opening one of the suitcases to get out the satellite phone. "Grab our rifle cases, head to the house, and load up the rifles."

"Now you're talking," Marco replied with excitement.

When they got to the house, Seth went into the office to listen to the radio. He wanted to know if Mia was talking to anyone. He only heard the last part of a staticky conversation between her and Roger in Bettles. She was too far away, over the mountains. Seth began to feel concerned; it wasn't what they would do but what Willie, his boss, would do to him and Marco. This was one of the simpler jobs they had been planning for almost a year.

Seth made the dreaded call. "Willie, it's Seth. We have a problem."

"What did you guys do to screw this up?" Willie responded.

"Nothing, Willie. Heavy fog came in, and, at first, no one could pick us up. Then, when a plane finally got here, this guy showed up out of nowhere with someone needing a doctor."

"So where's the gold?"

"It's with a girl flying the plane with the injured guy on their way to Bettles."

"You don't have it with you? You two are idiots!" Willie yelled into the phone.

"Willie, we tried to make her take us, but a new guy suddenly showed up, and he's ripped. He even flattened Marco to the ground."

"Hey! Why did you say that? You know I can take him!" Marco yelled, trying to recover from his humiliation.

"I don't care about that guy. Take him out of the picture."

"We lost him."

"What do you mean you lost him?"

"He got away and ran up toward the shed that I blew up."

"You blew up the shed before you left? Was the miner there?"

"Yeah, he was."

"So you killed him, and we don't even have the gold? Nice work… I should've done this myself." He paused to think, then added, "I'm just outside of Bettles. I'll land and wait for the girl to show up."

"What about us? How are we getting back?"

"I'll think of something. But for now, I'm thinking of leaving you screwups there."

"Willie, you come and get—" There was silence on the phone and then a dial tone.

***

"Bettles Lodge to Mia. Come in, Mia."

"Mia here. Is someone coming to help us?" she asked with hope in her voice.

"Mia, listen carefully. I need you to divert to Evansville and land on the Hickel Highway."

"What? Why?"

"Someone unannounced just landed and is getting fuel. I think it's the person you were talking about, and I don't want you near this place. I'll radio Chester and let him know you're coming over there. His place is along the highway, and he keeps his plane in his garage. I'll have him take Rudy into Fairbanks."

"I've never landed on the highway before."

"It's easy; Chester does it all the time. Come in from the east, and it's a perfect straight landing area. They just graded it last week. I'll tell Chester to hide your plane in his garage, and you can stay put until this is all over."

"No, I have to get back. My mom and Asher need help!"

"Mia, I've called State Trooper Clay. He's over in Wiseman dealing with a mining dispute and said he'll head this way as soon as he can. He told me he would call in for some help. Very soon, we'll have reinforcements. For now, we need to take care of ourselves, so you stay there at Chester's until I call you. Okay?"

"Fine, Roger. Mia out!" Mia finished unhappily.

***

Willie had parked his plane next to the above-ground fuel tank. He was exiting when a man came out of the hangar behind him. "Hello, you needing fuel?"

"Yes, thank you. Has another plane landed recently?"

The mechanic smiled, saying, "Nothing has been on the runway in the past hour or so. You looking for someone?"

"You could say that," Willie said as he scanned the sky, hearing the distant humming of an engine. He soon saw the wing lights of a small plane in the late evening sky. Watching it approach, he ran through many scenarios of how he was going to handle this situation. Suddenly, the plane banked a hard left and circled back, flying low. Then, it was out of sight, nowhere near the runway.

"Where did that plane go?" Willie asked.

The mechanic, who was not paying any attention, continued to fuel the plane and, as he looked up, said, "What plane?"

"Hello there," said someone approaching from the lodge.

"Hey, Roger," the mechanic replied.

"Hey, George, how's it going?"

"Good, just fueling this fancy plane for this man who just flew in."

As Roger walked up to the men, he put his hand out, saying, "Hello there, friend. We weren't expecting anyone this evening. I apologize. Did we miss your call in?"

Willie shook Roger's hand, answering, "No, you didn't. I had no idea I needed clearance way up here above the Arctic Circle. You guys have that much traffic?"

George, excited to see a new face and have a conversation, beat Roger to the answer, "You would be surprised. We average about six ins and outs a day. Even more if you include the planes using the river."

"Wow! Much more than I would have expected. How about that runway over there?" Willie pointed over to where the plane disappeared to the east.

George, again, butted in, "There's no runway over there. It's—"

Roger quickly cut George off, trying to take control of the conversation. "There's no runway in that direction for several hundred miles."

"But I just saw a plane land about a mile away."

"Unless someone crashed, there's no place to land a plane over there. Besides, I would have heard someone call in if they were making a landing anywhere around here."

Watching Roger's body language closely, the con man could easily tell that Roger was lying, but he played along. "Okay, I must have been seeing things. I have been flying for a while," he said, stretching out his back.

"Roger, it must be Chester. He lands on the highway next to his house when he doesn't need fuel," George innocently stated.

Roger smiled, chuckling awkwardly and pointing to his head. "Oh yeah, that's right. Things slip past me sometimes."

"Hey, look, there he is." George pointed out on the horizon as a small plane gained altitude, going in the opposite direction it came in. "I wonder where he's going this late in the day."

"I don't know, maybe to Fairbanks to visit his mother in the old folk's home." Roger pretended to be oblivious to what was going on.

"I don't think so," George said. "He just got back two days ago from there."

"Maybe she took a turn for the worse," Roger replied, trying hard to keep this distraction going even though George kept interrupting.

As they all watched the plane disappear to the south, something else caught their attention: another plane.

"Whose plane is that?" Willie asked, twisting his head toward George because he knew he was the clueless one.

"I don't know," George answered, looking hard for plane identification, but with the low light, he could not even make out the color.

"What's in that direction?" Willie asked as it took off the opposite way than the other plane had gone.

George had just finished fueling the plane, but Roger stepped in before George could answer. "So how much fuel did we get there, George?"

"It took on a hundred and fifteen gallons."

"We can take care of the payment inside. Follow me, friend," Roger said as he turned and walked toward the lodge, waving for the customer to follow him.

"Sounds good." Willie stayed on Roger's heels all the way into the building. Roger went behind a counter to fill out a receipt while Willie stood on the customer's side and gazed around. They were the only ones inside.

"For a hundred and fifteen gallons at seven twenty-five a gallon, it comes to eight hundred thirty-three dollars and seventy-five cents total."

"Wow, you would think fuel would be cheaper up here with the Alaska pipeline just over the mountains," Willie joked.

"You would think that, wouldn't you?" Roger smiled as he watched Willie pull out his credit card from his wallet. It fumbled out of his hands, dropping onto the floor at Roger's feet. Roger bent down and picked it up, but as he raised his head, Willie reached over and grabbed Roger's head with both hands. He slammed Roger's forehead down on the hard countertop, causing him to fall to the floor, unconscious.

Willie walked around, picked up his credit card, and dragged Roger's body to the office behind the counter. Once there, Willie went to the airport radio, reached behind it, and tore the long cord out of the wall. He then rolled Roger's body over, pulled his hands and feet together behind his back, and tied him up with the cord. Getting up, Willie went over to the miniature grocery store on the other side of the lodge and picked up a box of gel sleeping pills.

He returned to Roger and rolled him back over so he could pour the liquid from four broken pills into his mouth under his tongue. Once that was done, he looked on the desk and found a roll of scotch tape, which he wrapped around Roger's head a dozen times, covering his mouth and taping it shut.

Satisfied with his work, he dragged Roger's lifeless body to the men's bathroom floor. Roger's arms and legs stuck up in the air, tied tightly together. Turning on the light and fan, Willie locked the door behind Roger so everyone would think the bathroom was occupied. He scanned the lodge for anything out of place. Pleased with his work, Willie hurried back to his twin-engine prop plane. He took off quickly, catching up with Mia's slow-moving, single-engine bush plane.

***

"We need to get back to the house," Nora commented as she finished doctoring her husband the best she could, with little to nothing around. She meticulously removed the small pieces of splintered wood that had stabbed him all over. Fortunately, nothing went in deep or was too big, which would have required stitches. They used frayed bedding materials as bandages, but as for his foot, there wasn't much they could do. Asher and Nora thought that one of the smaller bones might be broken, but it wasn't life-threatening; it was just painful as the foot swelled up. Next, Nora moved over to Asher to work on his face.

"Not sure if going to the house is a good idea. The guys haven't shown up here, so they're probably in our kitchen, eating my blueberry pies and waiting for you two to come back," Martin gruffly stated.

"We can't stay out here and do nothing. With the shed gone, it's going to get cold tonight," Nora replied.

"We could go to one of our safety lockers. You've got them filled with necessities," Martin reminded her.

"That's a good idea, but each one is over a mile away in different directions from the house. You can't walk through the thick marsh with that bad foot."

Asher nonchalantly stepped into the conversation. He looked up and down at the slender, middle-aged man who stood about five feet, nine inches tall. "I can carry him. What are these lockers?"

"Since there's no one around for a hundred miles, we built metal lockers in different directions and filled them with emergency supplies," Nora explained. "Food, water, tents, sleeping bags, fire starters, and first aid items, just in case one of my hunters got hurt or lost. I give each one a map of the area so that they always know where they are. The lockers are also grizzly bear-proof. The shed here was considered the fourth safety locker, even though it wasn't bear-proof."

Asher looked around, asking, "Is there anything here we need to take with us?"

They all looked around, and Nora spoke up first. "The only things worth anything now are the heavy mining tools, but we'll leave them here for Martin to use next year." She gave Martin a smile to let him know there was hope for the future.

He gave her a friendly smile and said, "What about the ATV?"

"Take the key out and hide it under the front tire. That's what my dad and I used to do when we parked them to go hunting."

"Good idea, Asher." Nora pulled the key out and did just that.

"All right, Martin. It sounds like we have a ways to go. How would you like me to carry you? The fastest way is to let me throw you over my shoulder."

"You're not carrying me. I'll hobble along; just let me use you as a crutch." Martin's bushman pride was not going to give in.

"Suit yourself, but it's getting dark fast," Asher said as he holstered the gun around his back and inside his pants.

Martin had to reach far to get his hand draped up over Asher's opposite shoulder. Asher was tall, and it was difficult to hold on. They walked clumsily away from the explosion, weaving through the brush and trees, slowly following Nora. Before they progressed more than a couple hundred yards, Asher was already growing impatient. Their progress was very slow, and his back was beginning to hurt from bending over so Martin could keep hold.

"That's it! We're not doing this," Asher said as he bent down to wrap his arms behind Martin and scooped him up, cradling him like a baby. Asher straightened his back. "Oh, much better," he said in relief.

"Put me down!" Martin ordered.

"No, we need to get to the locker sooner rather than later. You limping along will take us all night."

"Listen to me, boy. I don't know how your daddy raised you, but around here, we do as we're told!"

Asher stopped walking, and everything racing around in his head went blank. A sudden mental flashback of his father looking down at him, yelling, "What is your problem, boy? I've told you over and over—do what I tell you!"

Only seconds passed, and he was left standing in silence, holding Martin in the dark. Then an inner voice came to him calmly and peacefully: "Asher, I wove you in your mother's womb. I know everything in your life. I know your heart's desires; I put them there. Come into My Cloud of Glory, and your heart's desires will be fulfilled."

"Put me down!" Martin repeated forcefully.

Asher looked toward this other voice, the one yelling in his ear. He bent over, letting Martin down.

"Martin, what is your problem?" Nora stepped back to the guys. "He's just trying to help and make things easier for you."

Martin hopped weakly on his good foot, losing his balance. He started to fall over, but Asher caught him.

Letting go of Martin's arm, Asher stepped within inches of Martin's face. He hovered over him and said in a deep, slow voice, "Don't you ever…talk about my father again!" Asher stared at Martin through the darkness as Martin and Nora clearly heard and felt a hard, threatening tone come from this stranger.

Suddenly, Samson gave an excited, low bark. They looked down at him, thinking he was disciplining the two men again. However, to their surprise, he took off running in the direction of the house, disappearing into the late evening.

In a moment of confused silence between the three, a distant buzzing could be heard. They all looked in different directions, trying to locate where it was coming from. Asher and Nora scattered in the sporadic, dense forest, trying to find openings between the trees so they could scan the sky.

"That's Mia's plane. I recognize the high pitch of her small engine. Samson knows it too; he's going to her. Those two are inseparable. He would do anything for her," Martin said.

"What's she doing coming back here?" Asher exclaimed.

They were stunned as a multitude of thoughts raced through their minds.

Asher, extremely worried, burst out as he turned to leave, "I've got to get back to the runway. Those guys will be waiting for her!"

"Wait!" Nora shouted.

"No, I'm not waiting. I've got to get to her!"

"No, no, there's another plane—listen." They all stopped and tilted their heads to listen hard to the night sky.

Martin commented, "That's a much stronger-sounding plane, probably a twin engine."

"Here, take this." Asher drew the gun from his back and handed it to Nora. "You'll need this more than I will out here." In the darkness, he turned and worked his way through the maze of vegetation. Nora shouted out, "Asher, hide in the Cloud of Glory! God will be with you and always guide your steps; just ask Him!"

Asher heard Nora, but his only response was to file away her words into the growing mound of cloud talk…the same cloud talk that had been storming in his brain over the past week.

***

Mia tried several times to reach someone on the radio at her parents' house. She got over the mountains and descended into the valley, but no one ever answered. She had landed in the dark many times, but it was more difficult on shorter runways like the one her parents had.

Even though it was dark, the glow of the rising moon and the clear skies lit the outline of the landscape and defined the silhouettes of the river, trees, and the structures of the buildings on the homestead. Carefully slowing the plane down as she got nearer to the ground, Mia relied on her instruments. They gave her the exact elevation rather than her trying to watch her weak landing lights. She slowly dropped the plane onto the flat, grassy surface, bounced a couple of times, and came to a stop as quickly as she could.

As her plane coasted to a halt just before the end of the shaved line in the forest, a loud voice came over her radio and jolted her with surprise, yelling, "Get out of my way, girl! I'm landing right behind you!"

In disbelief, Mia twisted her head to look out the window behind her. All she could make out was a blinking red light from the end of a left wing, heading right at her. She pressed forward on the throttle and forced the plane to move hard to the left. She got it out of the way just in time as the roar of the twin-turbo plane rolled past her.

Before she completed a one-hundred-and-eighty-degree turn, she felt her right wing bump up against something, stopping her altogether. "No! My plane! Oh no, no, no!" she cried out, knowing she had gotten too close to the edge of the runway. She had hit a tree. She turned off the engine and grabbed the flashlight that was secured to the floor next to her seat.

Jumping out of the plane, she walked to the end of the wing to view the damage. With a sigh of relief, she saw that only the tip, where the light was, had bumped against a branch and cracked the light cover.

She heard the other plane turn around and come back her way. Its bright landing lights were sweeping across the area. Fury suddenly overtook her. "What in the world is this person doing?" she blurted out, stepping away from her plane. She raised her hands in the air while screaming and looked toward the windows of the cockpit, "What is your problem? You almost killed us both!"

"Almost killed you, girly." Words came from the darkness near her, at which she pointed her flashlight to see who it was.

"You!" she spat out as she saw the two guys stepping up to her.

Seth grabbed the flashlight out of her hand and pointed it into her eyes, blinding her.

"Get that out of my face." She swatted at him, trying to move the light away from her eyes, but missed Marco's strong fist coming across her face. She was knocked to the ground.

Looking down at the unconscious young woman, Seth said, "You should've stayed away, but lucky for us you brought the gold back, sweetheart."

"Well, well, my two headaches," Willie said as he walked up, the flashlight still beaming down on Mia. "What have you guys gotten us into?"

"Willie, please let us explain. It wasn't our fault."

"Marco, shut up and dump the boxes out of the plane," Seth responded.

Marco leaned his rifle against one of the tires and stepped into Mia's plane. He began throwing the meat boxes out as Willie stared down at Mia. "That's one beautiful woman you got there, Seth. What are we going to do with her, or should I say to her?"

"She is, or was, Miss Alaska. We saw pictures of her in the house," Seth said as they both admired an unconscious Mia. He then turned his attention toward Willie's plane. "Let's just get out of here."

"I don't think so. Way too many eyes have seen you guys, and now me, in Bettles. We need to clean up this mess while we can."

"Which box is the gold in, Seth?" Marco was cutting into his second box, searching for the bag.

"I scratched a G on the end of the box. It's the heavier one."

"Give me the flashlight," Marco said, taking it from Seth. He shined it at the end of each box until he spotted what he was looking for. "Got it." He handed the flashlight back and cut the box open. He dug his hand in, bringing out the heavy, cold bag. He handed the freezing bag of gold to Willie. "Here you go, boss."

"Finally," Willie said as he weighed the heavy bag in his hands. "That should be somewhere near a million dollars, boys."

After they celebrated momentarily, Willie walked down the wing of Mia's plane and had Seth shine the flashlight up into the tree. He saw the damage, and an idea came to him. He yelled back, "Marco, put the boxes back into the plane and put her in her seat. Strap her seat belt back on. We'll make this look like an accident."

Marco loaded the boxes back in, then lifted a still unconscious Mia over his shoulder. As he turned around, Marco's eyes widened, and his mouth shot open as he tried to get words out, but it was too late. Samson appeared out of nowhere, bursting from the darkness and bearing fangs. He was running full force and lunged at Marco's throat. Marco fell back, hitting the ground hard and consequently tossing Mia to the side. The beast of a dog rapidly whipped its head back and forth, tearing apart Marco's throat.

Marco could not speak and quickly lost any strength he had as Samson shredded through his windpipe and vocal cords.

The other two guys, standing at the end of the wing, heard the heavy thumping of bodies as they hit the ground. There was savage growling and gnashing of teeth from the big animal as it killed its prey.

"What the heck is that?" Willie blurted out as he turned around.

"The stupid dog is back!" Seth answered fearfully. They both stepped back, not wanting to be attacked.

Seeing the carnage, Willie yelled, "It's killing Marco!"

Seth spotted the rifle leaning against the tire and ran to it as his flashlight fell. He pointed the rifle from his hip at the wild beast that was fiercely thrashing a now-lifeless body, and he shouted, "Die, devil dog!" and then pulled the trigger. The bullet hit the dog, and a puff of fur exploded, filling the air and causing Samson to land partially on Mia.

Samson yelped high-pitched squeals of pain. He stood back up, wiggled his head, and then ran away, disappearing into the dark in that same ghostly manner that he had arrived. The bullet had hit him in the meaty part of his neck, going all the way through without expanding or hitting anything vital.

The two could not believe what they saw: Marco lay there dead with a gaping hole in his throat.

"Marco, Marco..." Seth moaned as he knelt next to his friend. "We should've stayed in Jersey. It was safer there."

"Don't get sentimental now. We still have work to do," Willie said with little remorse.

***

Asher made his way as fast as he could with light from the night sky somewhat helping. He stumbled here and there, tripping over hidden ground cover as extended tree limbs slapped him in the face every so often.

Thinking he was getting close, he suddenly heard a rifle shot echo out in front of him. It was to his right, away from the house. Following the explosive sound, he heard painful cries from an animal.

"Samson," he whispered, waiting for more noise, but nothing else came. Stepping out into the runway clearing, he saw a flashlight shining toward the ground. It was next to the outline of two planes about ninety yards away. He snuck in toward the right to get to the closest plane between him and the flashlight. He then sprinted across the open clearing. Slowly he bent down under the plane and next to the landing gear, straining his eyes as he tried to see what was going on.

He saw two dark figures leaning over and grabbing the arms of one of the mounds lying on the ground. Realizing that they were dragging a body directly in his direction, Asher tensed up. With their backs turned, Asher crept back to the tire behind him to be better concealed. As the two came closer, Asher sighed quietly with relief. The person being dragged was much larger than a slender female. *Thank You. It's not Mia.* He paused for a moment and thought to himself, *Who am I thanking?*

Once they had stopped next to the door of the plane that Asher was hiding under, the men let go of the dead man. Then, one of the guys placed an object on the chest of the limp body.

The men walked back to the other plane and picked up the second lifeless mound, which Asher thought must be Mia. They put her in the plane and strapped her in loosely. "Oh Mia…I'm so sorry. I didn't get here in time to save you," Asher whispered sorrowfully. His heart heaved and filled with more hopelessness to add to the hurt that had been piling up in his life.

Still watching, he saw one of the men get into the plane with Mia and start it up. As the engine started, Asher heard a tree branch break as the plane bobbled back and forth and slowly rolled down the side of the runway.

To his surprise, the man jumped out, rolling to the ground, and left the plane to head down the long, grassy backyard. *They're going to make it look like she crashed!* he shouted in his head. Thinking quickly, he reached for his knife and stabbed the side of the tire he was leaning against, and it started to hiss. Then, he crawled on his knees to the body lying in front of him. He lifted up the heavy football-sized object that was on the chest, confirming his suspicion. *It's too heavy for it to be anything else... It's got to be Martin's gold!*

Hidden by the darkness, Asher stood and sprinted as fast as he could toward the plane, all while holding the leather bag at his side. He spotted the black silhouette of a person standing in the open. Lit only by the moonlight, they turned to walk back. They were directly in Asher's path, so he cradled the leather bag like a gold football in front of him with both arms and lowered his shoulders. He proceeded to blast the guy in the middle of his chest as he ran at full speed.

Willie, completely taken by surprise, flew backward. His head snapped forward, and the air was completely knocked out of him. Hitting the ground hard, he lay on his back and saw stars moving around in his head. He then began squirming frantically and held his arms in front of his throat. He thought he was being attacked by the giant dog just like Marco had been.

Seth could not see or hear anything going on with Willie when he jumped from Mia's plane. As he walked back to Willie's plane, he struggled to load Marco's heavy body. After a few moments, he heard Willie yelling his name, "Seth, get the rifle! Help me!"

CHAPTER 9

Seth grabbed the rifle along with his flashlight and ran toward Willie, who continued yelling. Seth quickly got to him, shined the light, glanced all around, and then asked, "What's wrong?"

"Something big just plowed me over."

"What?"

Willie looked up at the moving plane, barely seeing the outline of it in the darkness as it hummed away from them. "I don't know. I jumped out of the plane, and when I stood up, I was bulldozed by something really strong."

"That guy! I told you about the big guy that showed up with a hurt old man. He slammed Marco and me to the ground a couple times."

"If it was him, he hit me from that direction." He pointed toward his plane. "He must have seen what I was doing and ran after the girl." They both looked back toward the moving plane just in time to hear a crash. It ran into the trees, and the engine whined at a high pitch. Sparks flew, and flames exploded in every direction, lighting up the end of the runway. Seth and Willie quickly hunched down in a knee-jerk reaction to the explosion. Watching the ball of flames flicker, Willie saw someone run off the runway next to a building, carrying something big in their arms.

"He's got the girl!" He pointed out.

Seth looked in the direction Willie was pointing. "What did you see?"

"He ran off over there, near that building."

"He's going into the house. Let's get him!" Seth marched forward with the rifle in hand.

"Forget him. This is just getting worse. We've got what we want. Let's get out of here," Willie decided, turning back to his plane.

When they got to the plane, Willie asked, "Where's Marco?"

"I already put him in the back."

"Good," Willie said, stepping in. "Where's the bag?"

Seth froze for a second as he realized it wasn't sitting on Marco's chest like it had been when he loaded him in. "He's got the gold!"

"What?" Willie said dangerously.

"You said he came from this direction. He must have been watching us, then picked up the bag and went running for the girl. You were in the way. That's why he hit you."

"You've got to be kidding…" Willie stopped talking as he tilted his head and asked, "Do you hear that?"

The door of the plane was still open as Seth replied, "It's coming from outside." They both got out of the plane and walked directly to the high-pitched hissing sound. Looking down, Seth shined the flashlight at the almost flat tire. Willie began rambling rapidly under his breath until rage erupted. He was yelling and screaming profanities as he threatened revenge in a multitude of ways. He wanted to kill someone. He started hitting the side wall of the plane to release his anger. In an attempt to calm himself down, he stepped back and breathed deeply, nostrils flaring.

"Whoever this guy is, I am going to hunt him down and hurt him...hurt him bad. He's going to suffer for stepping into our business."

***

After blasting through the man, Asher kept running until he caught up to Mia's plane. Dropping the bag of gold, he grabbed the handle to the door, swung it open, and stepped on the foot peg above the tire. Leaning over, he unbuckled Mia's seat belt and shoved one hand behind her back and the other under her legs. Looking up and seeing the shallow light from the night disappearing behind a black wall of trees, he pulled her toward him. He then curled her up to his chest and jumped backward, rolling them both onto the ground.

Asher stood quickly and adjusted Mia's limp body in his arms. Then he walked away as the plane crashed into the forest, its engine screaming in its last dying moments. When the explosion came, it radiated heat and fiery light at his back, exposing the bag left on the ground. He bent down and grabbed it. With Mia still in his arms, he ran toward the house. Looking down the dark runway he had first approached, he remembered the two men and changed plans. He slowed to a quick walk and decided to get himself and Mia as far away as he could. The only way he knew how, at the moment, was to get back on the river. Squinting into the night, he looked for the trail that would lead him back to Rudy's canoe.

After a short time, he reached the river and the canoe. He fumbled around while laying Mia in the exact bed he had made for Rudy. As he looked at her more intently, his heart jumped for joy that she was not dead but only unconscious.

Pulling the canoe into the water, he heard someone screaming angrily in the distance. He thought to himself, *I guess he found out I have the gold or that his plane has a flat tire. Either way, he's madder than a hornet.*

Looking into the dark night and onto the river, Asher could hear more than he could see. He suddenly realized how difficult and dangerous it was going to be floating blindly on the moving water, but he had to leave the shore. Asher sat down, bottoming the canoe out in the shallows. He hesitated before pushing off, remembering Nora's voice earlier, "Asher, hide in the Cloud of Glory. God will be with you and will always guide your steps; just ask Him!"

He thought about it and tilted his head upward, skeptically speaking out loud and looking into the vast universe of stars. "This will be the second time I've talked to You on this river. For some reason, the cloud thing keeps coming up, and I don't completely understand it. I'm assuming You are trying to tell me something to help me." Asher paused, thinking about what to say and how to say it before crying out, "Hide us in this cloud they're calling 'Glory,' which I think must mean You.

"I can't see what's ahead in the darkness on the river, but if You're the God they say You are, You can see everything in our way." Asher's heart began to beat faster as his breathing accelerated, and his stomach fluttered with anxiety. This was extremely uncommon for him. Just then, the face of the elderly woman from the plane to Anchorage came to mind when she had excitedly explained, "To be honest, I love being in the thick clouds, not knowing what's coming in front of me or knowing where I am. It's mysterious and exciting, almost dangerous."

Asher continued aloud, "If she can go through life like that, unafraid, then so can I." He raised his hand in the air, giving the signal for love, and finished with, "God protect us and guide this canoe safely downriver. Until later on."

Before shoving off into the darkness of the river, an idea came to him. Lifting the heavy bag of gold sitting at his feet, he opened it and sifted his fingers through the wealth of pebbles. Thinking it over, he concluded it was a great idea and carried out his plans confidently. He raised the bag and poured its contents into the shallow water near the shoreline. Then he stashed the empty bag with the rest of the gear, still tightly fastened. He took hold of his oar and pressed down on the shallow river bottom, pushing himself and Mia into the deep, swift current.

***

Seth found the other rifle on the ground where he had grabbed the flashlight from Mia. He passed it to Willie as they walked where Asher had been last seen going into the woods next to the house.

Turning the flashlight off to hide their presence, they stopped at another airplane parked next to the house. "What's this?" Willie questioned. "You had another plane here that could have taken you to Bettles?" He began to flare back up.

"No, Nora said it was broken. Her husband said something about a leak somewhere in the fuel line."

"But it works?"

"I guess," Seth said, shrugging his shoulders.

"Okay, so we still have a way out." He looked toward the house. "I remember from last year's hunt—the house has three exterior doors, right?"

"Yes, the one straight out the back here, the side one on the big porch, and then the one on the other side, facing the river."

"Good, you go in from the porch, and I'll go to the other side. If you can help it, don't kill him; I want him to suffer. If they try to escape, they'll come out this door onto the open runway. Maybe we'll get a shot at them."

The guys split up and quietly made their way into the house. Every time they walked into a new room, they flipped the light on and searched around, under, and behind everything until every light was lit.

When they came together in the main living room, Willie impatiently asked, "Where are they?"

"I don't know. Maybe they went into the butchering shed or the big greenhouse," Seth said as he marched outside toward the butchering shed. They didn't see anyone, so both he and Willie checked the greenhouse on the river side of the house. But they still found no one.

Willie stepped out of the greenhouse and into the dark, saying, "I feel sorry for those two if I have to track them down in the woods. They will not get away from me out there.

"I'll only prolong their suffering for messing everything up and putting us through this." He looked at Seth with a cunning smile and added, "That's where I do my best work!"

Seth chuckled, saying, "You're the best tracker and hunter I know, Willie. You've got more dead animals hanging up in your trophy room than the history museum." Changing his tone and frowning, he said, "Wait a second, the big guy...when he showed up on the runway carrying the hurt old man, he said he was attacked on the river. They must have been in a canoe!" He shined the flashlight toward the river and saw a trail. He started running, telling Willie to follow him. When they arrived at the water's edge, there was nothing there but a small beach with the water rushing by.

"Shine the light down here," Willie said, staring at the ground. "Look, fresh footprints and a scrape mark in the sand. He pushed the canoe back into the water right here." He looked out through the darkness and listened closely to the rushing water. "We're probably not going to have to kill them. The river's going to do it for us. It's suicide to canoe this river at night."

They stood there for a few moments, figuring out their next steps. Then Seth asked, "What do you want to do, Willie?"

"Let's get back to my plane. I need to make a couple of phone calls. We're going to need some help getting that tire fixed. Then we'll get some sleep, and at first light, I'll take a look at that plane of theirs that has a fuel leak. If I can fix it, we'll take a quick flight and hopefully locate them still alive on the river."

***

Asher had been intensely battling the unknowns on the river with some slight help from the faint moonlight. He guessed it had been a couple of hours. Feeling worn out, mentally and physically, he realized he had neither slept nor eaten in a long time. The day had held a surplus of crazy and unexpected events, keeping his adrenaline flowing at high capacity. Now he had completely run out of energy.

He coasted the canoe to his right, the opposite side of the river from the house. They bumped against rocks and sand as they met land. Asher jumped out and pulled the canoe a safe distance from the water up onto a grassy and shrubby open area. He knelt next to Mia, who was still unconscious, and checked her vitals. He thought it would be best to let her wake up on her own in this situation.

Gently digging under her, he retrieved his sleeping bag and coat. Unraveling the bag from its case, he draped it over her, only leaving her head exposed. He put on his coat, sat on the ground, and leaned against the canoe next to Mia. Despite the looming threat, he fell asleep instantly, exhausted.

Morning came with low cloud cover moving in, trapping the cold night air in the valley, which left a layer of frost on the ground. Mia moaned, rolling her head and blinking her eyes open. She tried focusing her blurred vision, but the bright white clouds made her squint. Reaching up to the side of her face and then to her neck, she tried to rub the pain away. Suddenly, she had flashes of what happened before she blacked out, and she sat up gasping in surprise.

Mia was disoriented, and her head pounded with a headache. Not seeing anyone around, she lay back down, holding her forehead. She took a few deep breaths and decided to slowly sit back up and try again. Fluttering her eyes and peering around, it finally dawned on her that she was in a canoe, on solid ground, near the river. The sleeping bag flopped off of her, and cold air hit her. She immediately grabbed the sleeping bag back and held it close.

Once the world stopped spinning, she got her bearings, and her eyes became more dependable, so she decided to get out of the canoe. As she draped a leg over the side, the canoe rocked on the ground. Leaning over to stand, she instantly jumped back, surprised that she almost stepped on someone lying on the ground. She leaned back over to get a closer look, hardly making a sound. To her relief and excitement, Mia recognized it to be 23C, Asher.

She glanced around the area to see if anyone else was near and then quietly whispered his name. When she didn't get any reaction, she reached over to touch his jacket and whispered, "Asher, wake up." A terrible thought ran through her mind that he was dead. Trying one more time, this time shaking his shoulder back and forth, she raised her voice and said, "Asher!"

Out of a deep sleep, Asher bolted up, shooting his arms in the air to protect himself. The back of his hand hit Mia on the side of her face. It knocked her back over to the other side of the canoe and onto the ground.

It took a moment for him to remember where he was. Then he stood, peeked into the canoe, and saw that Mia wasn't there. "Mia, where are you?" he asked, looking around. Then he heard a moan from the other side of the canoe as she sat up cautiously.

"I'm right here."

"What are you doing on the ground?"

"You just hit me as I was waking you up."

"I did?"

"Yes, you did," she said, rubbing her already sore face.

"I'm sorry. Wow, you don't look good," he said.

"Well, thank you for the compliment, but look who's talking. You have a fat lip with dried blood down your chin and a bruise on the side of your face."

Brushing it off as nothing, he replied, "I'm used to it. How do you feel? You've been out for a long time."

"I have a headache, my jaw and neck hurt, and I think I have a loose tooth, maybe two," she said as her tongue examined the inside of her mouth. She looked around, asking, "What happened, and where are we?"

Thinking about the recent events, Asher ignored her question and asked, "Why did you fly back?"

She noticed his blatant avoidance of her questions but answered, "To help my parents and you." Suddenly she remembered that her dad was dead, and a rush of heartbreak gushed out. She cried out, "Dad, dad." Her face cringed as she began to cry, dropping to the cold, frosted ground on her back.

Asher stepped over the canoe and kneeled beside her, gently putting his hand on her shoulder. "Mia, listen." She was so consumed with grief that he had to repeat himself to divulge the good news. "Mia, listen. Martin, your father, is fine."

"What?" she squeaked out, looking up to him.

"Your dad is fine. He's alive."

"He is? You saw him?"

Asher smiled wide, then flinched in pain, reaching up to his lip as it cracked open and started to bleed again. "Yes, he was working in the creek, away from the shed, when it exploded."

Mia, relieved and excited, reached up to hug him, but their faces collided. They both backed away and started laughing, sharing the pain on their faces.

"Where are they?"

"I think they're at one of those lockers north of their house."

"Good, Mom always kept them full of supplies. So where are those guys, and where are we?" she asked, looking around at somewhat familiar surroundings.

"For all I know, the guys are at your mom's house, sitting by the fireplace eating breakfast." On cue, his stomach growled as he added, "That sounds like a good idea, don't you think?" He stood up and held his hand out to help her stand.

Out of habit, the first thing he did was roll up the sleeping bag. Then he opened the backpacks to take out the butane stove, cooking utensils, and two freeze-dried breakfasts.

"You didn't answer my questions… Where are we, and what happened?"

Asher explained his side of the story as he prepared breakfast. He assumed she knew the next part of the story, so he asked, "How did the big guy die? Did you kill him?"

"What? No, I didn't kill anyone!" It disturbed her that Asher would even ask her such a thing.

"Okay, don't get your feathers ruffled. I was just asking," he said with a half-smile as he handed her a bag of warm scrambled eggs. "Here you go. I guess one of the other guys shot him."

She took the bag, soaking in its warmth through her hands, and said, "So what's going to happen now?"

"I'm not sure. Did you get ahold of that state trooper I said had flown into Bettles with me?"

"Roger said he talked with Clay and the trooper would head up here as soon as he got back. He was in a town a ways up the Koyukuk River. He was also going to call in for backup."

"Good, it seems like it's all going to work out as long as your parents can stay hidden and we keep traveling downriver."

While finishing breakfast, they suddenly heard a plane coming their way from upriver. Since it was flying very low to the water, its engine noise had been confined by its surroundings. Like something out of the movies, the plane swung around the bend of the river, burst through the thin cloud cover, and flew right past them.

With joyful excitement, Mia shouted, "That's my parents' plane! Asher, they got away and are looking for us!"

The plane turned around and came straight at them. Asher had an uneasy feeling. "That might be your parents' plane, but can anyone else fly it?"

"Yeah, but—" Asher jumped on top of Mia. He thought he had seen something like a rifle sticking out a side window, aimed right at them. He confirmed his instincts; gunshots rang out from the plane as dirt exploded into the air around them.

"That's not your parents unless your dad is still mad at me!" Asher yelled as the plane dove at them with the fat bush tires hovering inches above the foliage.

The plane circled around to make another pass as Asher pulled Mia to her feet. He pointed to the tree line. "We've got to get to those trees." He took off, holding her hand and almost dragging her behind him until she caught up with his pace.

Once safely in the patch of trees, she asked, "Why are they coming after us? They've got the gold. Wouldn't they just want to get away?"

Asher hesitated to answer since he had left out that part of the story earlier. He looked away from her, answering, "They don't have it."

"What?" She thought back to his story and asked, "Why didn't you say anything about the gold?"

He shrugged his shoulders. "I didn't think it was important."

"Not important? They're trying to kill us because of something you think is not important!" Mia changed her stance, squaring up to Asher.

"I was thinking about your dad, and I just reacted when I saw the bag of gold on the dead guy's chest…and I took off with it." Asher turned to her and realized he needed to defend his actions. He eyeballed her and raised his voice. "Just like I ran after you in your plane to save you even though I thought you were dead!"

"Why didn't you say so?" They both ducked down behind the tree. Bullets showered in their direction, whizzing by and hitting trees.

"Again, it wasn't important at the moment, but obviously to you, I made a mistake!" They hunkered down as the plane flew by again to make another pass.

"So when did you plan to tell me you have the gold? Probably never after you got home safely with it!"

Asher stood up, looking down at Mia with a shocked look on his face, and said sternly, "Are you accusing me of lying to you and stealing your dad's gold? You're a crazy woman! And to think I risked my life only to be crucified for something I never even dreamed of doing."

Asher turned away, feeling devastated. He walked into the open toward the canoe without care or caution. He didn't know what to think anymore. Everything he did, every relationship he had, ended in disaster. He thought this time he was going to experience a hero moment by saving everyone and getting the girl in the end. Instead, he was emotionally wiped and didn't care about anything…again.

"I'm not a crazy woman. I'm Miss Alaska!"

"Does everyone in this state have a title?" Asher asked sarcastically. "Rudy is Mr. Alaska, and you're Miss Alaska. Is your mother Mrs. Alaska?"

"But I really am Miss…," Mia shouted. "Oh, never mind!"

Because he was quick with insults, he turned his head as he kept walking and said to her, "You might look like a Miss Alaska, but you don't act like one!"

"You're one to talk!" she yelled from the trees. "The only thing I've seen you do is beat up on people. You think you're so tough. How do we know you're not in with these guys?"

Asher listened to this beautiful woman in the middle of the wilds of Alaska insult him once more, and he marched back to her, saying, "You are crazy, Mia. Listen to yourself!"

Holding her ground, she replied, "How do we really know you weren't the one who hurt Rudy, then suddenly showed up when you did?" Her eyes went back and forth, trying to put the puzzle together. As Asher walked up, towering over her, she poked him boldly in his chest and added, "You're not with them. You're working alone against them. They did the hard part—stealing the gold and maybe killing someone—and then you steal it from them and get away with no one knowing any better." She stepped back, eyes wide, convinced she had just solved a deep, mysterious crime.

The words swept through Asher's mind, and he decided to play along with the outrageous accusations. With an intense look, he replied, "Yep, you solved the crime, Miss Alaska. They'll probably let you keep your crown for life. But since you now know the truth, I'm going to have to kill you," he said as he pointed right back at her.

Mia suddenly realized the situation she was in. She had already seen this man easily take on other men more than once. She took a step back and prepared to turn and run, but Asher grabbed her arm, seeing in her eyes the fear she felt, and knew he had gone too far.

Just then, the plane made a low pass again and shot at them. He pushed her to the ground and laid his body over hers to protect her.

"Get off me! Don't hurt me!" she screamed.

He started laughing at the comical situation, saying, "Will you stop it, Mia? I'm not going to hurt you, and I'm not stealing any gold. Rudy, your father, and your mother know who I—" A deep thump interrupted him as a painful explosion went off in his shoulder.

He rolled off Mia, shouting out in pain and seizing his left shoulder. He lifted his hand, which was covered in blood, and examined his shoulder, noticing that the bullet had not exited the muscular part.

"Asher!" Mia screamed out. "They shot you!"

He squinted his eyes and gritted his teeth, trying to control the pain, but it was no use. He groaned loudly, "Ahhhh! It hurts!"

Mia sat paralyzed and bewildered, not believing that this was all really happening. Her mind told her to believe her made-up story. Her heart, however, said he was a good, honest person, and she had sensed this on the plane and when he came to Rudy's rescue.

"Mia, we need to get going. We can't stay here; we're sitting ducks," Asher blurted out, putting as much pressure as he could on the bullet hole. He rolled over to sit up.

"What should we do?" Mia asked. They sat there, listening for the plane, but couldn't hear it anymore.

"They left, Asher. I don't hear my parents' plane anymore."

"Yeah, but for how long? Let's get into the canoe and go downriver as fast as we can, but first, we need to stop this bleeding." He looked at his shoulder covered with blood and added, "In the canoe, under the back seat, is my first aid bag. I had it out for Rudy."

Mia went for the bag and when she got back, she kneeled down next to him, opening it as he started giving instructions. "Get out a packet of blood clotting powder and pour it directly on the bullet hole." She found a packet and maneuvered his coat off him. She then pulled his shirt off his shoulder, exposing the bleeding hole, and poured the powder directly onto the wound. After that, he had her put a thick wad of gauze over the hole. He pressed down on it, holding the gauze in place, saying, "Good. Now take my belt off."

"What?" she said as she looked toward his waist.

"Take the belt off so we can use it as a tourniquet."

"Got it." She undid the buckle and pulled hard, slapping the belt off. Up at his shoulder, she wrapped the belt around his armpit and over the top of his shoulder, looping it through the buckle and pulling it tight.

Asher watched her, then looked at the ground for something and pointed. "That fat, solid pinecone—get it."

She picked it up and handed it to him. He had her loosen the belt and place the pinecone on top of the thick pad of gauze, telling her, "I want you to tighten the belt as much as you can over the pinecone, understand?"

She did what he told her and held it tight as he groaned in pain at the pressure that was now being focused directly on the bullet hole.

With that done, he reached down and searched for his knife case. It was no longer on his belt and now lay somewhere on the ground. Finding it, he instructed Mia, "Get the blade out and drill a notch where you tightened the belt so it will hold itself."

She did that and poked the metal piece through the new hole in the belt. Asher watched and held his good hand out that was covered in blood. "Good job. Help me up."

Mia looked at his blood-soaked hand and hesitated, thinking she was going to be sick, but grabbed it anyways.

They walked to the canoe, hearing no sound of a plane. They tossed in the cooking supplies, the first aid bag, and Asher's knife. Pulling the canoe into the water, Mia placed one foot into the back when Asher said, "No, let me sit back there. I can steer with one arm; we need your muscles to power us along." Again, she followed his instructions without hardly saying a word, not sure if she was in a state of shock, unable to think for herself and only follow directions. Or was it that Asher was guiding them with such precision through this moment of trauma that she trusted everything he said was right on key?

Asher thought they were making good progress heading downriver without really knowing how much time had gone by. He found himself becoming weaker by the moment. He looked at his shoulder and saw that inside his shirt, he was drenched with blood. The clotting powder was working, and so was the tourniquet, but with him moving around, neither was able to completely do its job. Knowing they were days from a doctor, Asher understood they had to take care of this on their own before he bled out or contracted a deadly infection. Looking ahead, he searched for a spot that would give them good cover from the plane and shelter from bad weather if it came to that.

Steering the canoe to a precise spot that fit his requirements, he told Mia sluggishly, "We have to make camp in a good hiding spot."

She turned around to look at him for the first time since they got in and exclaimed, "Asher, you're white as a ghost!"

The canoe halted as it hit the hard bank of the river. This was not the normal beach landing area he would have chosen, but what lay behind the bank was what he knew they needed. Asher clumsily stepped out of the canoe, tripping over a few rocks until he was up on land. Mia pulled the canoe out of the water, but as Asher tried to help, she told him to head into the trees and rest.

He ignored her order, saying, "We have to pull it completely up into the trees so no one can see it from the air or the water."

Confident they were finally out of sight, he sat down up against a tree. He was exhausted, in pain, and knew that he would be passing out soon. With urgency, he said, "Mia, listen to me carefully…" She kneeled next to him, knowing the predicament they were in, and listened intently.

"I'm probably going to pass out. When I do, you need to take the bullet out."

Shocked at the thought, she replied, "No, I can't do that!"

He reached over with his good hand, taking hers, and looked into her eyes confidently. "Yes, you can. You're a flight attendant and Miss Alaska. You can do it. Besides, we have no choice. The bullet has to come out. We can't wait this out." He struggled, giving her a smile to lighten the mood, and added, "In my first aid bag, there are tweezers, antiseptic, more gauze, and a sewing kit. Clean the tweezers, needle, and thread with the antiseptic. When you get the bullet out, clean the wound as best you can, flushing it out with bottled water. Then smear the antiseptic all over it and sew the hole up. Do you understand?"

She reluctantly nodded her head and swallowed, pulling courage out of places she didn't know she had. As he slowly drifted into unconsciousness, she calmly smiled and said, "I've got this. You go do what you need to do."

CHAPTER 10

Asher slowly opened his eyes, staring up at two long, thin lines crisscrossing each other evenly. There was something hovering at the intersection of the lines. The sky behind the lines was red and seemed to sway softly, like gentle waves on a pond. He was blinking, trying to focus as he searched his clouded mind for answers as to where he was. A refreshing and powerful voice, the one he had been hearing during his trip, spoke again, "Asher, you are worthy to be in My presence because of My cleansing blood I shed for you. Without My Spirit living in you, you will always be lost in man's foolish and doomed knowledge and drown in selfish ambitions. With My Spirit living in you, you will experience My love, peace, and joy overwhelming you beyond your comprehension.

"Believe in Me, your Lord and Savior, Jesus Christ, and follow My Spirit, the Cloud of Glory. I will dwell in your heart and be with you always. I will protect you, guide you, and love you safely through the darkness and sufferings of this world."

Still in a daze and staring straight up at the calming red waves, a sudden large wave whipped across, interrupting the even flow. An army of black spear-headed shadows shot out and crossed at one edge of the blood-red sky before disappearing back where they came.

Lying on his back, Asher narrowed his eyebrows, trying to figure out if he was dreaming. He looked around, realizing he was inside Rudy's red-domed tent. Peering down, Asher saw that his shirt was off, and his left shoulder was heavily bandaged. That was when it all came back to him. He looked at his right arm, only to see Mia cuddled tightly next to him, keeping warm and sleeping as they lay in an unzipped sleeping bag.

Looking back up at the ceiling, Asher now understood he had been watching the crossed seams of the fabric roof. They moved like smooth waves on an ocean with the soft breeze on the outside of the tent.

There was a small flashlight dangling down. It hooked on a loop that was sewn in at the cross section of the seams. The breeze outside was causing the dark shadows of tree branches and pointed leaves to sway in and out of sight.

The gentleness of the moment consumed him with peace. He didn't feel the weight of anything around him—not the temperature of the cold morning air or the pain in his shoulder. It was calm and tranquil, just like the words spoken to him.

Still staring up at the ceiling, something like a vision was revealing itself to him. From his perspective, it appeared the seams represented two different roads coming up from the ground and intersecting. At the crossroads, the flashlight looked like a human body, hanging and glowing red as the sunlight showed through the red material of the tent.

His eyes followed one of the seamed paths down from the intersection. Suddenly, near the bottom, the leaves' shadows from earlier flew across, clashing with the red light. Their dark shadows stole the light with their jagged spearheads. Asher jerked back in fright as he envisioned demons attacking and killing everything on the path.

Quickly bringing his eyes back to the hanging, red body of the flashlight, he noticed it resembled Jesus on the cross. Then his eyes followed the other seam going the opposite direction, and peace swept through him. It was getting brighter and brighter, blinding his vision. The outside sunlight was shining directly from that direction, warming his face.

For some reason, it comforted him to see that path disappear. The bright red light clouded his view of the path, and he didn't know where it was going. But at the same time, he knew everything going down that path into the light was going to be fine. He had complete understanding that he was safe and loved.

Out of nowhere, a loud snap from a tree branch dissolved his vision and train of thought, bringing him back to reality. He felt the sudden weight of everything implode on him. He inhaled deeply and flexed his muscles in defense, which brought throbbing pain to his shoulder and made him lightheaded.

Asher closed his eyes to stop the spinning as he whispered softly in Mia's ear, "Mia, wake up." She continued to sleep soundly, not responding to his faint words. He squeezed her a little while she was wrapped up in his good arm and repeated softly, "Mia, wake up." This caught her attention, and she quickly turned her head to say something. He swiftly moved his right hand up to her mouth, whispering as their eyes met, "Shh, there's someone or something outside the tent." He let go of her mouth and pointed in the direction of the cracked tree branch.

As though it was planned, when he pointed his finger, they heard rustling and a growling moan. The shadow of a big, rounded body swayed toward the tent and leaned slightly on the red fabric walls. Asher slowly and painfully rose, sitting them both up, and mouthed, "Where's my knife?"

Mia twisted her head around and looked on the tent floor. She spotted the sheath, carefully picked it up, and handed it to him, saying in his ear, "Don't do anything. Let it go away on its own."

He nodded in agreement as they both listened helplessly to the shadow walk around them. Time felt like it stood still while they sat in silence, trying not to move. But before they knew it, the creature was gone.

Mia looked up to Asher's face and whispered with caution, "It left, but it will be back. We have to get out of here carefully and quickly."

"Was that a grizzly?"

"Yes, I thought about them last night because of all the blood. I threw everything that was bloody away from the tent."

Asher lifted the sleeping bag, looked down at his legs, and confirmed that he was wearing different pants.

Watching him, she smiled and said, "Don't worry. It was dark. I didn't see your Nebraska football underwear."

He frowned as the tense moment with the bear drifted away. "You look good in Rudy's flannel shirt," he replied. "It adds about forty pounds to you."

In a knee-jerk reaction, she gently punched him in his bare stomach. He flinched at her actions, causing his hurt shoulder to move. He gasped in pain and reached around her, touching the taped pad of gauze.

"Oh, sorry...but don't ever make fun of a woman's weight," she said quietly.

"Okay, I get the message. Now how about getting my pain pills in the bag?"

She reached over to the bag, opened it up, and retrieved several bottles. "Which ones do you want?" she asked, looking at the different labels of prescription pain medications. "What are you doing with these? They're really potent."

"They're leftovers from my knee surgery last year."

"Is that what the two big scars on your knee are from?" She looked up and saw that he was not happy with her question.

Like a ticking time bomb, Asher wanted to blow up just at the thought of someone mentioning what wrecked his career. Then words floated across his mind, "Leave it alone and walk into the Cloud of Glory." An image came alive: himself walking away sluggishly from something dark and heavy. The darkness struggled to hold on, not wanting to release him.

"Did I say something wrong, Asher?"

Mia's words wiped away the vision, forcing him to reply, "Uh, no. You didn't say anything wrong." As he looked down at his knee, he continued, "It's only something that ended my life as I knew it."

Is he being sarcastic? she wondered to herself.

"I'll take two of those"—he pointed to a specific bottle—"and hold off on the hard stuff. I'll use it only if the pain gets worse." He put his hand out for her to pour the pills into, then swallowed them with water from a bottle she had out. "Thank you for doctoring me up. Did the bullet come out all right?"

"Yeah." She hesitated, slightly embarrassed. "But after I dug around for a minute, I threw up all over your chest."

"You threw up on me?"

"It was gross! I've cut up a lot of moose, caribou, and other animals but never a person. You were bleeding, and the muscles were squishy…I was okay until the tweezers touched bone—then I lost it."

He liked where this was going and replied, "So is that why you really threw away my shirt? To get rid of the stinky evidence?"

They both laughed quietly before Mia smiled and said softly, "We need to get out of here. That bear knows we're here and will be back unless…" She moved her head in the direction the bear had left the campsite.

"Unless what?"

"Grizzlies are very smart. Often, if they know food is in an area, they'll hide, wait for the prey to show up, and then take it by surprise."

"They hide? Or do you mean they stalk?"

"Exactly!" she whispered.

"I've hunted black bears most of my life, and for all I know, they don't do that."

"Well, grizzlies do." She turned away and grabbed a shirt that she had taken out of his pack the previous night. She then handed it to him, saying, "Here's a shirt I pulled out for you. I didn't want to put it on you until I knew the bleeding had stopped."

She helped him put it on and buttoned up the front. Then she told him to hold his injured left arm in the sling position. She picked up one of Rudy's long-sleeved shirts she had made into a sling and strapped it on him to hold the weight of his arm. Asher gave her a friendly grin, telling her he was impressed.

Mia was on a mission. She turned around on her knees in the small tent and efficiently packed everything in the heavy backpacks that she had brought into the tent. Asher liked how she operated and did the best he could to help with one arm. Before zipping up the packs, Mia got out some beef jerky and dried fruit. She had them eat quickly and drink the rest of the bottled water.

Once they were done, with nothing else to pack except for the tent, Mia whispered, "Just in case the grizzly is out there waiting for us, we've got to make this quick. Can you carry one of the packs?"

"I can carry them both," he answered, taking hold of one shoulder strap of each pack and lifting them.

"Wow, you *are* strong. Okay, that helps. No sudden movements when we make our way out of the tent, and let's keep our heads down. We don't want to make eye contact with anything. Look for the river. You get the packs into the canoe and pull it into the water. I'll pull the poles out of the tent and wad it up in my arms as I get to the canoe. Then we'll take off."

"Sounds like a plan," Asher said quietly while flipping open his knife. He placed it in his hand that was in the sling.

"Good," she replied, then leaned up and gave him a quick kiss, saying, "I owed you one."

She turned to unzip the tent, but he had frozen for a second, surprised by the tender gesture. Clearing his head, he grabbed the straps firmly in his hand as she stepped out. Asher followed closely behind, gritting his teeth in pain as he headed straight for the canoe.

After placing the packs into the center of the canoe and pulling it into the river, Asher worked his way onto the back seat, bottoming the canoe out as the front lifted up. Holding the oar securely in his good hand, he waited at the ready to push off. He looked over to see Mia almost done with the tent. Slight movement in the forest behind Mia caught his attention while he was watching her. With trees darkening the area and bushes in the way, he couldn't get a clear view. Losing sight of it, he started to feel alarmed and said in a loud whisper, "Hurry, Mia! There's something moving in the shadows behind you." Even though she had heard him, she didn't look back but simply worked faster.

He saw something again, but this time it was closer and bigger, and he knew something wasn't right. Loudly this time, he urged, "Mia, forget the tent and get in the canoe. It's coming!"

Gathering everything in her arms, she turned to the canoe and ran. Asher's heart pounded as the bear came into full view and stood up tall on its hind legs. Seeing something running away and something else making noise in the water, the bear dropped to all fours and bolted toward the one running.

Never having witnessed a giant animal move so quickly, Asher yelled, "It's almost to you! Drop the tent and jump in!" The tone of urgency in his voice reached her in time as she threw everything in her arms up in the air. The tent fluffed open, and the collapsible poles popped out with a snap. Without missing a step, she kept running. Asher pushed off early into the current, just before Mia arrived at the water's edge. She gripped the side rail of the canoe and pushed them firmly into deeper water. She jumped in, rocking the canoe so much that Asher thought it was going to tip over.

He shoved the oar deep into the river and pushed off as hard as he could with one arm. Mia also paddled as hard and as fast as she could with the makeshift oar they had found yesterday, accelerating them further into the current. They both looked toward the shoreline and watched the bear. It ripped apart the tent that had flown up into its face and almost covered its whole body. Asher watched in awe at how quickly and powerfully the bear's arms swung around, shredding Rudy's tent.

Just as quickly as it had started, the encounter ended. The bear looked around, smelling its surroundings. Although it acted like it didn't see them, Mia and Asher understood that the grizzly knew exactly where they were. But in the end, it turned away, walking back into the trees.

***

After the bullet hit Asher, Willie and Seth turned around and flew back to the house in Nora's plane. Their thoughts were consumed with the bag of gold. Parking the plane next to the house, Willie said, "There's definitely something wrong with the fuel line somewhere: it stinks in here, and the fuel gauge was dropping like a rock. We started with almost three-quarters of a tank, and it's already down to a quarter. Good thing you finally hit the guy. I don't know if we would've had enough fuel to make another full pass."

Seth proudly added, "It looked like a good hit. Hopefully I killed him. Who knows? Maybe the bullet went through him and hit the girl too when he laid on top of her to protect her."

"That would be nice. Let's hurry up and pack everything we need for the trip. Did you say Nora's canoe is on the other side of the house?"

Hyped up, Seth replied, "Yeah, it's off to the side of the trail, hidden in the trees just before you get to the river."

"Where does she keep her guns and ammo?"

"They're in her office in the glass rifle case."

Willie orchestrated their preparations for the manhunt. "Okay, I'll take care of the ammo, guns, and food in the house. You go find her backpacks, which should be filled with survival gear, sleeping bags, and a tent. I'll meet you at the canoe."

The two men went their separate ways, gathering what they needed. A short time later, they met at the canoe and pulled it to the water's edge. Seth strapped everything down except for the rifles; he laid them on top of the organized pile in the center of the canoe.

Willie stood, looking back at the house as he talked on the satellite phone. "We're leaving the house now. They're about half a day ahead of us on the river. So do you think you guys will be up here tomorrow morning to fix the flat tire?"

The voice on the other end of the phone answered, "You got it. We'll finish up here and then head your direction, stopping in Fairbanks to top off the tanks, which will give us enough for a round trip. You said your plane is full?"

"Almost, definitely enough to get to Fairbanks," Willie answered.

"Good, let's go over the plan again. We'll drop elevation once we get to the North Fork of the Koyukuk, following it closely to spot the two you're after if they are still alive. Then when you see or hear our plane, you'll turn your phone back on and call us for their location. Then you'll know where to expect to hunt them down and get the gold back.

"Once we're at the house and your plane is repaired, I'll have my guy fly our plane back as I wait there with your plane until you call me again. You said it would take you about five days to float to Bettles?"

Willie rocked his head back and forth. "Yeah, that's my guess, give or take a day."

"Okay, so when you call me to leave the house, you'll be in eyesight of Bettles but upriver. I'll fly in, and by then you should be hidden in the brush and trees at the east end of the runway. I'll turn the plane around, you'll jump in, and then, we're gone."

Anxious to get the show on the road and get his gold back, Willie said, "That's it. People have already seen my plane and can ID it, so they'll never know you were involved."

"Sounds good to me. It seems to be a simple enough plan, but something could go wrong. What if you don't call in because your phone isn't working or something freaky happens to you?"

Willie paused, then answered, "My plane is yours then. It's worth the effort at least, and you get my cut of everything we're doing."

The guy laughed, saying, "We're not going there. This is going to work out, my friend. We have a lot more money to make, and we'll have fun doing it!"

"I hope so. This has been one of the biggest clusters I think we've had our whole careers."

"Sure sounds like it."

Another thought came to Willie as Seth suddenly turned his head at Willie's comment. Willie told Seth they were ready to go and shook his head at Seth, smiling to acknowledge him. Taking a few steps away and facing the house, he whispered the rest of the conversation, "Marco's body is in my plane. Throw it out between Bettles and Fairbanks in the middle of nowhere so that the wolves can get rid of the evidence. And remember, there will only be one"—Willie turned slowly back to look at Seth, who was sitting in the canoe before turning back to the house—"that you'll be picking up in Bettles."

"Got it, Willie. Be careful. Seth catches on quick. He's very smart and very dangerous."

"There's nothing like a surprise and catching someone off guard, is there?"

"True. Still, watch your back. I'll wait for your call when you hear our plane."

"See ya," Willie said, hanging up the phone and turning around, only to see Seth standing next to him with a devious smile on one side of his face.

They stared at each other, waiting for the other to say something. Seth broke the silence, "What are we waiting for? Let's go catch those two off guard." He gave Willie a pat on the shoulder, turned, and pulled the canoe fully into the water. He held the canoe as Willie started to get into the back seat.

Willie paused, not sure how much of the conversation Seth had heard even though he had reacted like he knew nothing. His friend's words repeated in his head, "He's very smart and very dangerous."

Willie then stepped into the canoe as Seth did the same, and they took off into the current. They needed to cover a lot of distance to catch up, so they both paddled at full force.

After a little over an hour, they finally reached the spot where they had shot at Asher and Mia. They got out to look over the area before continuing downriver. With daylight still available, they decided to stay on the river a while longer before making camp. They'd get an early start in the morning.

***

Putting distance between themselves and the bear was calming for Mia and Asher after all the excitement of the morning. It also helped that the pain medicine was taking effect for Asher. The beautiful, serene surroundings helped to swallow the emotional chaos of the past few days as they gently made their way downriver, almost in perfect harmony. The water had a comforting sway to it, rocking Asher and Mia peacefully as they continued to float quietly.

It was Asher's first time at the rudder position when it was not foggy or dark or when he was in excruciating pain. Even with one arm, he maneuvered easily around obstacles as though he had been doing it all his life.

Very little conversation flowed at first as they both mentally reviewed and processed each step of their journey so far. Mia broke the silence, asking as she looked back, "How's your shoulder feeling?"

He looked down at his arm in the sling and said, "It's doing a lot better. Thanks."

She turned forward again and said, "I wasn't sure how to take it when you mentioned the scars on your knee back there. What did you mean 'ended your life as you knew it'?" She turned her head back to look at him and added, "That's if…you want to talk about it." She watched his expression. When it didn't change, she decided to turn back around.

A few moments passed, then he responded, "I got hurt playing football my junior year."

"Let me guess, Nebraska?" she said jokingly.

"You got it. I recovered from two surgeries and even won a bowl game last year. I was supposed to be drafted last spring, but"—he paused, trying to control his anger—"I wasn't. They said I was a medical risk."

Mia turned all the way around to face him, understanding that this was important to him. In a nurturing voice, she replied, "I'm sorry, Asher. Is this a permanent injury? Is there any way a team will ever take you?"

"Probably not."

"You mean you've never even tried since the draft?"

Looking past her, he said reluctantly, "What's the point? I'm damaged goods and always will be. My dad always told me that failure was never an option, and I failed."

"You didn't fail; you just got hurt. You have to try again."

"'Once a failure, always a failure' was Dad's second favorite quote, and he was right."

"Asher, why would you listen to nonsense like that? You're a grown man. Don't you think he ever failed in his life?"

"Don't bring him into this. You don't know him," Asher responded with an abrasive glare, moving his eyes toward her.

"I might not know him, but it sure sounds like he's trying to give himself a second chance at life, living through you because he's a failure. What does he do?"

"Nothing," he said stoically.

"Well, there you go," she boasted like she solved his life's problem.

"He's dead."

Suddenly, Mia didn't know what to say. She was paralyzed by Asher's glare and unable to look away. Her lips moved slightly, but no words came out.

Asher knew he had blindsided her but almost felt good about it. But upon seeing her beautiful face drowning in her own words, he knew he needed to say something. Softening his expression and tone of voice, he said, "You didn't know, and I know you didn't mean it. You were just trying to help."

She soaked in his kind words as tears swelled slowly in her eyes. "Why do you do that? Why do you always come to my rescue?"

Suddenly, Asher felt like he had her in the palm of his hands, but it was very awkward. He couldn't just walk up and give her a hug, and he couldn't just walk away either. He had to use words, which was not one of his best talents. That is, of course, unless an insult was needed, in which case he could deliver it in his next breath if he wanted.

"What is that now—three, four times?" she said between tears.

"How about six?" A sly smile stretched from ear to ear as he let out a little chuckle.

"Nuh-uh?" she disagreed as she wiped her face.

"Yes…" He looked downriver to make sure all was well in front of them. Then he slid his oar into the canoe and lifted his hand to count each episode on his fingers. "On the plane to Anchorage…on your parent's runway with Rudy…in your plane before it crashed…when I covered you and got shot…yelling at you about the grizzly…and just now. Six times, but"—he shrugged his good shoulder and grabbed his oar to adjust the canoe—"who's counting?"

"Okay, fine. Six. But you can't do any more for me until I catch up."

"Oh, so this is a competition now?"

Mia looked away as the word struck her hard: competition. It echoed in her head. Suddenly, she realized that that had been her standard of living for the past year with everything having been a competition as Miss Alaska. She answered, "No, not really. I guess you can say it's been a personal challenge for me lately."

"All right then." He frowned at her, not sure where she was going with this.

She was still bewildered at the sudden thought of her selfish competitiveness ever since she won the crown. She dropped her head into her hands, saying under her breath, "I've been an idiot. I've been walking outside the cloud."

"What did you say?"

"Nothing. I'm just disgusted with myself."

"No, really, what did you just say?"

She looked at him reluctantly and repeated, "I've been walking outside the cloud."

"You too?" Asher shook his head in disbelief and said, "What is it with everyone up here obsessed with the clouds? It's almost comical."

"What do you mean?"

"It started when I first met the old lady who was sitting next to me on the plane. Then it was Rudy, your mom, and now you. Each one has mentioned living in the cloud or clouds. Even God said it to me. At least I think it was God."

Mia paused to think and then commented, "There was no old lady sitting next to you on the plane. There was a guy in a suit in the window seat."

Asher cocked his head, replying, "Yeah, there was. She was a really short, petite grandma-looking type who sat right next to me in the middle seat."

"Asher, I remembered your seat number, 23C. I served you water after you interrupted the guy next to the window. I would've known if there was an old lady sitting in the middle seat between you two."

Something caught Asher's eye. He popped his head up and then yelled out, "Quick, paddle hard!" He had taken his eyes off the river too long, focusing on their conversation. An outcropping of boulders, right in the middle of the river, loomed just ahead. Mia quickly plunged her stiff tree branch paddle into the water and strove to move them out of harm's way.

"We're not going to make it," she shouted.

"Try to push us off and away instead of running directly into them."

She pointed the makeshift oar toward the rocks as the river quickened and became louder with the rushing water splashing around. Her stick hit the rocks, but with the weight in the canoe and the sudden surge of the current, it had little effect. The right front part of the canoe hit hard, bouncing to the left and pushing the craft sideways, instantly smashing the right side of it into the rocks.

They both tried to balance themselves as they dug deep into the water, desperately attempting to paddle themselves out. For a moment, it appeared their efforts were going to work, but the oncoming water continued to press them against the rocks. It forced the canoe to stay in place and then began to roll them under.

At that second, Mia screamed, "Jump out!" They both had the same thought, and Asher was already on his way overboard. They plunged into the water that rushed at them. It instantly pulled them under, pressing their bodies against the rocks. Asher reached up out of the water to the rocks, straining against the pressure. His feet were able to tiptoe on the river bottom below to help push him up.

With the sudden lack of body weight, the canoe bounced up high on the surface of the water. It grasped at the current, went around the rocks, and made it out of the watery trap without its passengers.

Asher crawled out of the river onto a stack of boulders and looked around. The adrenaline coursing through his veins helped dull the pain in his shoulder. The fear of death focused him, for he could not see Mia anywhere. He began to yell her name as his eyes found the canoe heading downriver. He moved his gaze back, looking into the water's undertow and next to the boulders. He lay down and reached into the water, trying to feel for her, but there was nothing. Without hesitation, he jumped back in, feet first. He fought harder than he ever had in his life. He felt around and looked for Mia in the freezing water.

Coming up, gasping for air, he went back down, over and over again, but he couldn't find her. The water was pressing him hard against the rocks. Finally reaching the point of exhaustion, he strained to get out. Once he was on the top of the rocks, he lay on his back, yelling out Mia's name one more time, but heard no reply.

CHAPTER 11

Asher lay sprawled out, vulnerable to the world, with hard rocks poking him in the back. His chest heaved as he tried to get air back into his body. Groaning over and over, he said aloud, "What have I done?" He squinted his eyes closed. "I'm sorry, Mia. I'm so sorry. It was my fault. I wasn't paying attention!" Physically spent and in the middle of the North Fork of the Koyukuk River, he was now emotionally suffocating.

He continued babbling as his mind went back and forth to the past. "It was my fault. It's always my fault." After a while, Asher settled down and peered up into the blue sky as though he were looking up at someone. He began to confess the deep agony that had been buried almost a year ago. "Dad, I'm so sorry. I'm sorry I yelled at you to leave me alone, to mind your own business, and to never come to my games again."

Asher's dad had driven eight hours to watch his team and him play against the University of Oklahoma in Oklahoma. They had lost the game. Afterward, his dad again pressured Asher on what he had done wrong and what to do better, which led to the biggest fight they ever had.

His whole life, his father always pushed him past his limits, and Asher finally had enough. Enough of constantly being criticized for all his weaknesses instead of complimented on his strengths and never being told he performed well at anything.

Nothing he did was ever good enough for his dad. Asher was maturing but was still constantly being forced to do even better by his father. Most of all, Asher's father only wanted Asher to do what he wanted him to do (like football), even though Asher had other interests.

Asher couldn't control himself any longer, and after the Oklahoma game, he told his dad to leave him alone. He never wanted him to come to one of his games again. Stunned at the sudden demand from his son, his dad had turned and left without saying a word.

On his drive back home to Colorado Springs, Asher's dad got into a horrible car accident and died. Ever since then, Asher had hidden his feelings. He blamed himself for his dad's death even though he had struggled with his painful upbringing and the abusive relationship.

"I'm sorry, Dad…it's my fault you died. You just wanted me to be the best I could be. Mom, I'm sorry you're alone. I killed him." Asher kept mumbling sorrowfully to his parents. On top of that, he felt responsible for failing his dad by not being drafted. He cried, emptying out what had been stored up inside. It had been preventing him from living free, so he begged for forgiveness with tears streaming down his face.

After a while, he calmed down, his breathing regained a normal rhythm, and he refocused on his current situation. Rolling his head to the side, he looked upriver at the water rushing toward him and said mournfully, "Mia, I'm sorry I wasn't paying attention to the river. I'm sorry I couldn't save you."

When he rolled his head back and looked up, he saw a few large, white clouds slowly making their way across the wide-open blue sky. "Are You kidding me? 'Live in the Cloud of Glory' is what they all said, including You. That's the dumbest thing I've ever heard. Where is the glory in any of this? Aren't

You supposed to be this wonderful, glorious God protecting us? Why didn't You save my dad? Why didn't You protect Rudy? Why did You let this happen to Mia?"

Asher burst out in frustration, "Lies! All lies! You're a lie!" The fresh healing and the opening of his heart that had happened after his talk with Rudy suddenly slammed shut. He sealed in his dark anger, and it became heavier with each breath.

Sitting up gingerly, he pondered his next move. He spat into the river and said, "What's the use? I came up here to be alone in the first place. So maybe this is how my pathetic life finally ends, and this place will be my grave."

He looked to his side at the flowing water around the island of rocks and continuing down the valley. He surveyed each side of the vast country, noticing the colorful vegetation growing everywhere: the grass, shrubs, and trees stretching out toward the mountains that were shooting up high from the low valleys with jagged and rocky peaks saturated in gray.

There was no one for countless miles, and he was days away from civilization. The feeling of being small and insignificant crept through him. He looked down at his drenched shirt, pants, and boots, which were the only things he could see that he still had. Before bailing out of the canoe, his coat had been draped over his shoulders, with his bad arm in a sling. Now, both his coat and the sling were nowhere to be found. He remembered that he had folded his knife closed and put it back in the sheath on his belt. Feeling around for the hardware, Asher sighed with relief when he found it was still there.

Leaning against a boulder and closing his eyes, he took a few deep breaths and thought about his next move. Alone now, with nothing except the clothes on his back and a knife, he ran through the many scenarios he had learned about wilderness survival. He knew he could survive, but it was not going to be easy, especially with the bullet hole in his shoulder. Prickly whispers began bouncing around in his head, *Do you really want to make it? There's nothing waiting for you back home. What's the use?*

A hollowness in his chest echoed with a surprising loneliness he had never imagined could exist. Drifting off in thought, he unexpectedly heard something different over the rumbling water, which caused his eyes to shoot open. Hearing it again, he sat up, not knowing which direction the sound was coming from. He looked around, and something caught his eye as it moved downriver. Watching closely, it appeared to be walking in his direction. It weaved in and out of bushes and around trees along the shoreline.

As it finally stepped fully out into the open, he heard his name. It was Mia. Completely stunned, his breath got caught in his chest. He waited for a second to make sure he wasn't dreaming and let out an audible exhale. She put her hands together to cup them and yelled out to him again. This time he sprung up and yelled back, waving.

Mia hesitated before realizing it was Asher and excitedly screamed his name as she began to run through the mess of vegetation toward him.

Seeing her and her excitement flooded him with joy, and all he wanted to do was get to her as fast as he could. He looked down at the water on the other side of the pile of boulders and jumped in. He swam with all his might toward the bank. When he got to the shallows, he stood and stumbled through the water as he ran toward her. But before he reached the dry land, she was already splashing her way to him with her arms open wide. Their bodies came together with an explosion of emotion as they held each other tightly. Asher stood tall, lifting her in spite of his pain.

"I thought I lost you!" he exclaimed.

"Me too!" she said, smiling big.

"I dove into the water over and over, but I couldn't find you. What happened?"

"When I jumped out, the current took me under for a second, and when I got back to the surface, I was facing downriver and passing the pile of rocks. The canoe was going away, so I took off after it. I thought that you must be doing the same thing. When I finally caught up to it and got it to shore, I was way downriver." She pointed in that direction, adding, "I couldn't find you. I looked for you farther downriver for a bit and then came back up. And here you are!" She jumped up, grabbing his neck, and hugged him again. She let go, and they stood there, up to their knees in the chilly water, staring into each other's eyes and holding hands. Silence consumed them, both extremely relieved. Moreover, something strong had suddenly developed between them in a very short amount of time.

Asher leaned forward without thinking or asking and slowly placed his lips on hers. Her reaction was one of acceptance as she pressed herself up against him. She reveled in his kiss.

Although he enjoyed everything that was happening, suddenly the reality of his pain forced Asher to step back as he reached up to his shoulder.

Mia looked at the wound and could see that it was bleeding again. "Let me see," she said, prying his hand away.

"The stitches are broken, and the hole ripped back open. We need to get back to the canoe and fix this again." She turned, grabbing at his good hand to walk back, but he didn't move.

He looked deep into her eyes and said, "I really thought you were dead."

"I was beginning to think you were too." She smiled, turning back to him.

The thoughts and conversations Asher had had with himself on the boulders seemed to vanish. The emptiness suddenly filled with peace and joy as he peered into her beautiful face. They looked at each other, knowing the other cared not only for their welfare but for something much greater.

They walked back leisurely, hand in hand, to the canoe, not wanting to let go of the other. The dramatic separation changed their very short acquaintance into a rich, caring relationship, and neither wanted distance between them.

At the canoe, they contemplated their next steps only after Mia did her best to repair Asher's shoulder and apply a fresh bandage. They agreed to put on dry clothes while Mia fretted over wearing Rudy's old man clothes. Her appearance to Asher all of a sudden meant the world to her, but they were able to make light of the situation. In her tall and slender but full female frame, Rudy's short pants looked like she was wearing high waters, and his flannel shirt puffed out like she was pregnant.

Asher joked about her current fashion issues, which made her think about being Miss Alaska. It was then that she decided to open up her life to him. "Last winter, I was crowned Miss Alaska. I was finishing my degree in education at the University of Alaska and graduated in the spring. That's when I was hired by the airlines to be a flight attendant."

"Why didn't you go into teaching?"

"The timing wasn't right. I do a lot of traveling as Miss Alaska. The airlines said they would be flexible with my time until I passed the crown on next year. But I still want to be a teacher one of these days."

"So what else don't I know about you?" Finally, Asher was able to peek into her life after he had exposed his. He liked the redirection of the magnifying glass.

With a stutter, she said apprehensively, "There are a couple of things you need to know that will help you understand me, especially my relationship with God."

He jokingly raised his eyebrows as though a deep secret was being revealed and said mockingly, "Oh yeah, let's hear it."

She rocked her torso back and forth shyly, as though she was ashamed of what she was about to say but was more concerned about how Asher would react. "When I was a junior in high school, I was diagnosed with early-stage ovarian cancer." She paused, watching his response, but he didn't move a muscle, so she continued, "I had to go through chemotherapy..." She lifted her hand, touching her hair as she began to get slightly emotional. "And I lost most of my hair."

Asher saw her pain and took her hand as she dropped it from her head. "Let's sit down," he suggested. They both sat down on an old, smooth, gray log. It was missing its bark and was just a few yards away from the beached canoe. It was in a comfortable open area that didn't obstruct the sun's warmth that shone on them, except when clouds passed by every so often.

Mia thought for a moment about what to say next, then continued, "Everyone was so nice and supportive. They even had a big party for me in Bettles. It was after my last treatment, when the doctor told me that I was cancer-free. People flew in from all around." She giggled, "Roger at the lodge complained because there were so many planes. He was running out of parking spots."

Asher returned a smiled but stayed silent as she continued. She cleared her throat as her eyes watered up. "Early on, when I was first diagnosed with cancer, I was extremely mad. I was sixteen years old and furious at everything and everyone, but most of all, God. I couldn't understand why He would allow this to happen and accused Him of doing it to me, like I was being punished for something. Then when the doctor said I would never have children after the chemo…" She looked back into his eyes again through her tears. Asher didn't flinch as she finished, "That's when my life changed."

She stood up, inhaling the refreshing air deeply as she wiped the tears from her face and walked around the log. She hesitated to tell him her next confession but then said bluntly, "I tried to kill myself."

This time Asher did respond by jerking his head back, surprised. "Whoa…" Having a quick wit, he tried to make light of the situation and added with a corky smile, "Did you succeed?"

Mia didn't think it was funny at all and gave him a stern look, which he immediately understood. He quickly responded, "Sorry."

She tilted her head and grinned. "You know, if I think about it from a different perspective, in a way, the old me did die." He didn't reply this time but simply had a look as if to ask, *what do you mean?*

"It was in the middle of the summer when I attempted suicide, and I hadn't even started chemotherapy yet. I was recovering in the hospital in Fairbanks, and my mother was with me, by herself again." She shook her head in disgust. "My dad was where he can always be found…in the creek, digging for gold." Shaking the thought away, she got a big smile, and her voice suddenly cheered up. "But Rudy showed up!" She looked up into the sky, relishing the thought of what transpired, and explained, "Rudy was the one who helped open my eyes to the truth of life and how to live in the Cloud of Glory." She looked back at Asher. "Do you know what the truth of life is?"

He looked away, searching for an answer. With a frown, he said, "I'm still trying to figure out this cloud thing. But no, I don't." He adjusted his posture and stated, "I thought I did, but with everything that has happened this past year, my life has lost all meaning and purpose. I basically don't care anymore because everything seems to end up being a lie." Asher held his empty hands open, indicating he wasn't holding on to anything in life.

Mia smiled, understanding exactly how he felt, having been in his shoes about seven years ago. Excited to share her experience with him, she said, "When I was in the hospital, Rudy told me his story and how bad it got for him. That's when he explained the truth of life to me." She turned, dropping the conversation, and walked to the backpacks by the canoe. "Are you hungry? I am."

"What? You're going to leave me hanging?" Asher asked. "That's exactly where Rudy left off with me, except for the truth thing. He never mentioned it."

"I concentrate better on a full stomach. Plus, what's the rush? We have a long time to talk until we make it to Bettles."

He stood up. "Okay, I'll eat something."

She dug into Rudy's pack and pulled out a couple of items. "He sure has a lot in here. He's prepared for almost anything."

"Yeah, there's a lot in there, except a gun," Asher replied jokingly.

Mia laughed. "He's that way. He rarely carries one, especially up here."

"We could've used one this morning."

"Could we have?" She stood up next to the pack, turning to him.

"Yes, we could have," he continued. "That bear was going to kill you."

"Well, he didn't. So we didn't need a gun."

"Yeah, but—"

Creating an opening to continue her story, she interrupted by saying, "No buts, we didn't need it, did we?"

He thought about it and conceded, "I guess not."

"No, we didn't, and that's exactly what living in the Cloud of Glory, also known as the Holy Spirit, is all about: Not worrying about anything, even when the situation seems impossible. Leaving fear behind and knowing everything will work out, no matter how prepared or intelligent we think we are. We let go of anger when things don't go the way we planned." She paused, making sure their eyes met to let him know that she was talking about him. "Asher, you have to move forward, leaving the past to God. It's His problem, not yours."

Asher turned from her and picked up a rock. He threw it across the top of the water, just like he and Rudy had done several days earlier. With a variety of emotions and thoughts racing through him, he needed a moment to break away.

Not wanting to let go of her train of thought, Mia continued, "Asher, we will never understand God and why things happen. It's beyond our comprehension. I know; I was where you are right now, exactly where Rudy said he was at one time. Then he explained to me and read out of the Bible about how much God loves us. We are His children and treasure."

Asher thought about the sparrow—the one that had landed on the bow of the canoe a few days ago when God first talked to him. Looking at Mia, Asher shook his head slightly, dismissing it all, and said boldly, "Nice ideas, but in reality? I don't think so."

"That was my first thought when Rudy talked to me about the Truth."

Asher could tell he needed to clarify what he was saying and where he really stood. "The truth is God doesn't care what happens to us, Mia. If He cared about and loved us, His so-called children, then why is there so much pain and suffering?"

"You're there!"

"Where?"

"You are where I was and where a large majority of people are hung up."

Folding his arms in skepticism, he asked, "And where is that, Mia?"

She looked up and pointed. "Living in the worthless open blue sky, frolicking with selfish and minuscule human understanding. This short life we live is just a speck in time compared to living in eternity. We waste it by maybe only believing in God, seeing Him as a religion, and playing church, which is a very shallow way of living. That's how we get to this point with God and why He allows things, even tragic things, to happen. Those events bring us to our last straw, to our knees, to show us that there is more to Him than we see. It's about more than a religion; it's to show us that it's all about a relationship with Him.

"Asher, no matter what happens in life to you or anyone else—sickness, pain, death, and even the good—God is always with us. He wants to walk through these experiences with us, keeping a strong hand out to hold onto ours and experience what we experience." She unfolded his arms and grabbed the good one. "We need to let go of the stuff in our lives and let Him take care of it. We can then move forward and live in the joy of great expectations and what He's going to do with all the brokenness in our lives. Because life will never be perfect or pain-free, but His love for us is perfect!"

"So you're saying to just ignore the stuff and somehow everything will be all right," he retorted.

"Yes, no…" She was getting frustrated and shook her head, trying to explain. He wasn't making it easy. "It's about giving God the stuff—kind of like a gift."

He laughed. "A gift? That's what you've come up with? A gift? Oh sure, here, God, let me give You all these horrible things. How do You like Your present? Welcome to the real world, God. How do You like it?"

Mia sensed Asher letting go of some pressure with that response and said enthusiastically, "Yes, exactly!"

"Girl, that's crazy talk." He let go of her hand.

"Sounds like it, but it's the truth, and that's where the truth of life comes in. It's about Jesus, who He is, what He did for us and is doing for us every day. He takes Himself and every gift we give Him, including our pain, sorrow, anger, love, and joy, to work for the good of those who love Him, according to His purpose. This is so we can see, understand, and experience Him. All this is what living in the Cloud of Glory is about. He takes our past experiences and miraculously works them out for our future good so we can have a close and dependent spiritual relationship with Him."

He sat back down as she finished, with her hands held open and shrugging her shoulders. Asher put his hand to his chin, thinking deeply about what she had just said, and asked, "So how am I supposed to accept everything that happened?"

She smiled, knowing this would be his reaction. "Live in the Cloud of Glory."

Dropping his hand, he slapped it to his side and stood back up. "Of course…put your head in the clouds and hide."

"No, don't put your head in the clouds and hide, but live in the Holy Spirit. There's a difference. With your head in the clouds, you're acting stupid, ignoring your responsibilities, and going nowhere. Again, it's about letting go of all your fear, worry, anger, and worldly understanding and moving forward by letting God take your life and running with it."

He was seriously considering what she said. "Putting all kidding aside," he continued, "I think I know what you're saying. When Rudy got hurt north of your parents' home, we went downriver, and it was extremely foggy. I could only see maybe a canoe's length in front of us. When Rudy came to and asked how I got past the waterfall, I said there hadn't been a waterfall."

"You never went through the falls?" Her eyes got big.

"Nope, never heard one or saw one."

"It's a miracle you're here. You can't miss them!"

"Then when you were knocked out at your parent's house, we went downriver in almost complete darkness. I could barely see anything with the minimal moonlight, but we floated smoothly. Then today, with perfect weather, all the sunlight we needed, and both of us awake, we crashed. It doesn't make sense."

"Yes, it does. All that is, is a perfect example of what we're saying about living in the Cloud of Glory. You went forward, going downriver, even though you couldn't see a thing…trusting what?"

"Luck."

"Oh, please, don't be an idiot, Asher! You know exactly who you trusted or at least wanted to put your trust in: God."

"I know. Don't get all excited." He paused and said, "I agree with your point. Both times I couldn't see, and I prayed first. When we left the bear, I didn't pray, and look what happened."

A smile crept across Mia's face. "You're going in the right direction, but that's definitely not living in the Holy Spirit.

What you did was live by just believing in God from a human standpoint, using Him like a Santa Claus. Just because you didn't pray doesn't mean God wasn't with us. He's always with us, living inside our hearts as the Holy Spirit."

"But we almost drowned in broad daylight."

"But we didn't. Asher, bad and painful things, suffering, are going to happen in our lives, whether we pray about it or not. It might appear wrong or not make sense, but that doesn't mean God isn't with us. He'll love us through these things. He'll always use everything, no matter how tragic, for the good, like I said earlier, if we trust in Him. Time heals all wounds, and hindsight is always twenty-twenty."

Walking up close to him, she continued, "If we didn't hit those rocks"—she paused to make a point—"do you think you and I would be where we are right now in this relationship?"

He looked down with a confused look. "And where would that be?"

She put her arms around his waist, saying, "We're right here, you and me together."

"Oh, this relationship." He smiled, letting her know he was joking, put his good arm around her, and bent over, giving her a kiss.

She prematurely backed away, and he asked, "Did I do something wrong?"

"No, listen. A plane is coming." She stood motionless, her eyes scanning the sky.

He looked toward the sky, listening, and stepped close to the river's edge to get a clearer view. "Yeah, I hear it. It's coming from downriver."

Mia got excited. "It's Trooper Clay and his backup!"

"Do you think?"

"Roger said Trooper Clay would get up here as soon as he could."

"What should we do?" Asher questioned, trying to figure out how this was going to play out.

"Nothing. Just keep moving downriver."

"There it is." Asher pointed upward.

"He sure is flying low. That's strange," she commented as she waved her arms at the plane.

As the plane flew over them, Mia and Asher were briefly able to see the pilots.

"I didn't recognize Clay, did you?" Mia asked as she watched the plane continue upriver.

"Not sure, I don't think so. I only met him once."

"What was that about?" Mia said, slightly confused yet curious as she watched the plane flying away from them.

"What do you mean?"

"He waved." Mia wrinkled her brow and continued to look at the plane shrinking in the distance.

"I don't understand."

"When communicating from the air, to let someone know you see them, you rock the plane back and forth. They did that, but not until they got way up there, almost out of sight. Why didn't they do it when they were looking at us?"

Feeling relieved that help had finally come, it suddenly felt like a good time to get back on the river. Asher's shoulder was patched up again. They had dry clothes on and had eaten, so they gathered everything together without saying a word.

Once everything was secured, Mia stood up in front of Asher and gently held his hands. She looked up into his eyes and said smiling, "I'm glad you came to my rescue, 23C."

He mirrored her smile as he drew her against him, replying, "I couldn't let that man get away with touching you the way he did."

She looked to the side, slightly embarrassed, as Asher leaned in, kissing her on her forehead.

Pulling back, he added, "Now I'm convinced there were two more angels on the plane other than that old lady—you and me coming to each other's rescue."

She glowed as her feelings for him intensified. He had surprised her with the compliment and, at the same time, had revealed more of his heart to her.

Standing in the river next to the canoe, they instinctively ducked as an explosive noise came at them from upriver. They recognized it as a high-powered rifle shot, and a sudden surge of fear and caution pumped through their veins as they looked at the canoe. They heard a high-pitched ping echoing from the vibrating aluminum. They were being shot at, and the bullet had hit the canoe. Hearing another round go off, Asher pushed the canoe into the river, shouting, "Get in!"

Asher didn't like the situation as they paddled hard and searched for a swifter current. His heart was pounding rapidly, and he yelled out to Mia, "This isn't good. We're in the open like sitting ducks, and water is coming in from the bullet hole. It looks like the river curves to the right up ahead. Once we get around the corner, we'll beach the canoe, grab the backpacks, and run!"

"I agree!" Mia yelled back without turning her head. She rowed as fast as she could.

Around the corner and out of sight, Asher angled the canoe to shore. They swiftly jumped out and threw the packs on, Asher using his good shoulder. He adjusted the canoe back into the water and angled it directly downstream, toward the center. The current was strong there, so he shoved it out as hard as he could. They momentarily watched the canoe start to reach its target as Mia said, "Good idea—a distraction, at least long enough for us to get ahead of them." Turning into the forest, they disappeared.

CHAPTER 12

"I told you we should've gone to the shore to shoot them! I can't keep this rifle steady on the water!" Seth told Willie.

"How hard can it be? They're only about two hundred yards away, and you've got a scope."

"Then you do it if you think it's that easy," Seth said, turning around with eyebrows narrowed. "I'm tired of being put down."

"Just shoot at them again. Maybe you'll get lucky like you did from the plane."

Keeping his thoughts to himself, Seth eyed Willie a few seconds more before slowly turning to fire more shots. He was doing the best he could in the uneven flow of the water.

Willie didn't like being eyeballed like that, and a few different thoughts ran through his head. He was trying to plan how he would take care of this whole situation…

"They're taking off!" Seth exclaimed.

"Put the rifle down and paddle hard. We can catch up to them with the big guy hurt."

They rowed briskly as they watched the canoe in front of them disappear around a bend. Shortly, they rounded the corner themselves and caught sight of the silver aluminum canoe floating nimbly ahead of them. The sun hit the canoe just right, and a sharp reflection briefly blinded them; they were unable to see anything in the canoe. As they continued to catch up, it appeared to be floating awkwardly and not drifting in a straight line. It meandered to both sides of the river and even twisted around once. Finally, it stopped against some rocks near the shallows, against the left side of the river's edge. Willie hastily guided their canoe to the shore on the opposite side of the river. They remained a bit upriver to get a clearer and more open view of their targets.

They both bailed out with their rifles and rested against some rocks. Looking through their scopes across the moving water, they could clearly see the canoe was empty. "Did you see them get out?" Willie said quietly under his breath.

"No."

"Look along the shore and carefully in the background for them." They scanned the area for a short time but couldn't see a thing.

"Where did they go?" Seth whispered.

"I don't know, but we need to get over there before they get too far ahead."

They crossed the water but were still upriver from the empty canoe as they carefully and silently picked their way along the water's edge until they were a stone's throw from the canoe. It was still bobbing in the water but trapped by rocks.

"Cover me. I'm going to get close and find their tracks," Willie whispered, stepping forward.

Getting closer, he scanned the area both in and out of the water. He investigated the vegetation away from the river as he moved about. After a while, he lowered his rifle and looked back at Seth, who was standing guard. Willie shrugged his shoulders, mouthing, "They're not here."

Returning to Seth, he said, "I think they pulled a fast one on us. There's no sign of them here, and that canoe has been floating oddly ever since we came around the bend. I bet they got out and ran."

They looked back upriver as Seth asked, "Which side do you think they got out on?"

"I don't know, but we're going to find out." Willie reached into their canoe, pulled out his satellite phone, and called the contacts that were fixing his plane.

"Hey, we've got a problem. How much longer until your guy is ready to fly back?" Willie asked.

There was silence for a few seconds before he relayed, "He's got about another thirty minutes."

"Is there any way you can finish up? I need him now. Those two ditched their canoe and are on the run. We don't know what side of the river they're on or what direction they went." Willie's frustration rose with each passing second, knowing Asher and Mia were lengthening their distance.

"I can take care of this. He'll be above you shortly. Where are you?"

"Downriver, about a mile from where you saw them last. It's also where the river takes a hard right from your direction. Someplace shortly after the curve, they got out. That's the spot I need him to look for them. We're downstream a few hundred yards, past the bend."

"Got it. Keep your phone on, and my guy will call you when he flies over."

Less than thirty minutes later, the plane came around the bend, and the pilot and Willie were talking. Willie told him to search the shoreline for tracks. After flying back and forth over the river a couple of times, the pilot called back. He had spotted an area where it looked like the sand had footprints. It also appeared to have drag marks from a canoe. Willie told him to fly inland from there and try to spot them.

***

Asher and Mia had been hustling their way through the trees and across a couple of clearings in hopes of distancing themselves from the river. Deciding to take a short break and unload the packs, they once again heard a small plane flying over the river.

As it made a few passes in the same area, Mia said, "It's got to be Trooper Clay. He's looking for us!"

Asher shook his head. "I don't think so."

"Why?"

"Because you said he waved the plane's wings not when they saw us but farther upriver. He obviously waved at the guys who shot at us."

"Maybe they didn't see us because we were on the bank. The other guys must've been in plain sight, and possibly they were in the middle of the river in my parents' canoe. Trooper Clay must've thought it was you and me."

Asher shook his head. "No, there's something wrong here. You said they were flying too low."

"Yeah, they were...," Mia admitted.

"Like they were looking for someone. How would the state trooper know to look for us on this part of the river? No one knows we're even on the river except the guys after us. For all the authorities know, we're still at your parents' place."

Mia thought about it and said, "Remember they said they had a satellite phone?"

"That's right!"

"They called for help because you flattened their tire and they couldn't fly the plane out." She shot him a slanted grin.

"You're probably right." He wrinkled his nose and smiled back.

They had lost focus on the plane flying along the river when it suddenly flew over them again. It made a quick turn back toward the river. Both Asher and Mia felt their hearts jump as fear struck them.

"Shoot, they saw us. We should've hidden better, under a tree. Now they know where we are."

"If you hadn't taken the gold, they wouldn't be after us, Asher," Mia reminded him.

"Really? You still want to blame me for trying to help your family out?"

"You know it's true. Those guys would be gone by now, and we wouldn't be running for our lives if you would've just left it alone."

"I guess you're right," Asher replied with sarcasm. "Your head is in the clouds…the clouds known as me, myself, and I. You're so full of yourself, Mia. All you do is blame someone else for everything that goes wrong. You even accused me of stealing your dad's gold. I don't need to take this." He stood up. "I should never have kissed you back on the runway or saved your life by pulling you out of the plane. You're just as screwed up in the head as I am. What was I thinking?" Asher bent down, picked up his backpack, and started walking away.

"Wait up—you're not leaving me here alone." Mia hustled, grabbed her pack, and caught up with him. "Asher, I'm sorry. I really didn't mean—"

He cut her off and kept walking briskly. "Forget it. I just came up here to get away, clear my head, and figure things out. I hadn't planned to get involved with other people's issues. I have enough of my own."

She quickly walked past him and turned, stopping in front of him. She held her hand out toward his chest, saying, "Asher, I'm sorry. I really am." She looked genuinely sorry.

"Oh, no, you don't. First time, shame on you. Second time, shame on me. Well, the second time isn't going to work on me." He stepped around her and started on a stubborn walk with long strides. It took her two or three steps for each one of his to catch up to him.

"Will you slow down so we can talk, please?"

"No."

"Come on. Asher, please."

"No."

She suddenly stopped, stamping her feet, and said, "Fine, run away then."

Asher didn't hesitate and just kept going. He twisted his head back, informing her, "I'm not stopping because there are two guys after us with guns. And now they have the advantage of friends in an airplane to spot us. So, if you want to stop and wait for them, go right ahead. You'll definitely slow them down for me with your whining and complaining." He stopped before adding, "You do it so well that they'll want to kill themselves if they catch up to you. They just need to give you a chance to talk." Asher turned and continued walking. He fumed inside as his mind went over her accusations and the events of the last few hours.

Mia caught up, keeping up with his pace, and didn't say a word. Again, they heard the plane coming their way. Asher grabbed Mia's arm and pulled her down under a low pine tree. It flew by, then turned around to make another pass of the area. Mia whispered, "I don't think they saw us."

They spied through some branches covered in green pine needles and dotted with pinecones. Then they proceeded to wait silently for the plane to go away. Their eyes followed the tail section as they both sighed with relief. But the relief was short-lived as Mia stated, "Oh no! He just waved."

She looked at Asher, who had seen the same thing. "They aren't far behind us for the pilot to wave that close." He looked around where they had been. They were leaving a sporadic foot trail in the soft ground. "He saw our tracks."

Thinking rapidly about what to do, he told Mia, "We need to run. Help me get this strap around my shoulder."

Mia saw his concern and urgency and knew his mind had just switched gears. She helped pull the strap around his bad shoulder as he grimaced in pain. Then he asked her, "Is there anyone or anything around here that you know of that could help us before we get to Bettles?"

"My parents are the only people who live up the North Fork." She thought for a second and said, "The only thing that direction"—she pointed toward Bettles and up the mountain range—"is an old mine, halfway up the mountain. My dad took me to it when I was younger. Sometimes when I'm flying, I'll take a short detour from the flight pattern to look at it."

Surveying their situation, Asher came up with a plan. "We need to head to the river."

"Why? The mine is that way." She pointed again.

"Trust me—there's no time to explain. Come on!" They took off with backpacks bobbing up and down as they changed their course and angled away from their pursuers.

Once they made it to the water, Mia asked, "Now what?"

He looked up and down the river, making sure there was no one along the shore or in a plane watching for them, and said, "We get in and swim downriver."

"You're kidding, right?"

"No, I'm not. We need to get them off our trail and make them think we crossed the river. But we will float down a distance and get out on the same side." Asher turned and pulled Mia's pack off her back, and she did the same for him. He grabbed one shoulder strap of each pack with his good arm and told her, "Hold on to my belt and don't let go, understand?"

She nodded her head.

He walked them into the water, not too far in the swift current but just enough to propel them downstream. He tried to keep them at a depth where he could continue to walk on the bottom and simultaneously hold the packs as high as he could out of the water.

"The water's freezing." Mia's teeth chattered.

"I know. Just keep going for a little longer."

After what seemed like a mile but was only about a hundred yards or so, Mia asked with quivering lips, "How much farther? I can't take much more."

He looked ahead and said, "See that pile of rocks along the shore? We'll get out there. They won't see our footprints on the rocks." Asher kept his mind focused on the task at hand.

Stepping out of the water, dripping wet and shivering, they stumbled but caught their balance on the slippery rocks. Asher dropped the packs. Frowning, he remarked, "I don't know how much longer I could have held them above my head like that."

She gave him an appreciative smile and said, "You did awesome keeping everything dry, but we need to change clothes again. Lucky me, I get to wear short, baggy, old man clothes." Her smile turned into a disgruntled frown.

"Wait until I tell Rudy you complained about having to wear the short, baggy, old man clothes that saved your life."

She nudged him in a friendly way with her shoulder. She had her arms wrapped around herself, and she said, "You better not" in the hopes that they had moved on from the earlier argument.

Giving her a wink, he answered, "Okay, maybe I won't, but changing is going to have to wait. We need to get up the mountain and hide out of sight. Do you think you can find the old mine from here and get us there before dark?"

"I think so. If we can get into an open area, then I can get a good look at the mountains and give you a definite answer."

He scanned the river's edge and didn't see anyone. He pointed with a nod of his head. "Let's get into those trees over there. I need to take some pain pills; my shoulder is throbbing. Then we'll take off." After moving to cover and swallowing a couple of pills, he decided to only shoulder one strap of his pack on his good shoulder. He tightened the hip strap so a majority of the weight would be on his hips, then looked up at Mia and said, "All right, let's go."

***

The pilot instructed Willie over the satellite phone, "Keep moving in the direction you're heading, and you'll see their tracks. I think they dove under a tree about a hundred yards in front of where you are from what I saw when I flew over. I've got to go if I'm going to have enough fuel to make it to Fairbanks."

"Thanks for your help. You made it easy for us."

HIDING IN THE CLOUD

"No problem. See you down the road."

"You got it." Willie hung up the phone and placed it in his jacket pocket. He and Seth took off right away, tracking the culprits who stole their gold. They only had rifles with them, which made it easy. They weren't burdened with the weight of backpacks (unlike Asher and Mia). They arrived at the spot where the pilot thought Asher and Mia had been hiding and began following the trail.

Leading the way, Willie was watching for footprints and any other clues. "It looks like they went back to the river," he concluded.

Once they arrived at the water, they noticed where the couple had gone in. As they looked across the river, Seth said, "I'll get our canoe. It's just up the river a ways."

"Sounds good. This guy seems to know what he's doing, even with a bullet in him. Are you sure they didn't say anything about him at the house?"

"No, he just showed up, carrying this unconscious old man right when we were about to take off. He said the old man was attacked by a moose upriver and needed a doctor. The girl knew him from somewhere. She introduced him to Nora, and that's when this mess started. They knew the injured old guy and were determined to get him on the plane instead of Marco and me."

"You should've put a bullet into all of them," Willie growled with his teeth clenched, still staring across the rushing water.

Seth eyed Willie but didn't reply. They could both feel the tension between them rapidly increasing. Without saying another word, Seth turned and walked up the shoreline. After a while, he was back and guiding the canoe to shore. Climbing in, Willie said, "I think we're being played."

"Why do you say that?"

"They got out of their canoe to get away and purposely pushed it back into the river to get us off their trail. I think they're doing it again…"

Before shoving off into the current to get across the river again, they paused to think it through. "So what should we do?" Seth asked.

"They're heading to Bettles. The fastest way to get there is a straight line and that's from this side of the river. They were spotted by our man flying over them, so they're doing everything to distract us. The big guy is hurt, which is slowing them down, so they're going to try any diversion to slow us down."

"He's pretty smart," Seth commented.

"Yeah, but we're smarter." Willie thought for a moment and said, "I bet they got into the water, drifted down the shallows, and then got back out on this same side. That's what I would've done."

"So what do you want to do?"

"Let's pull the canoe way out of the water. We'll put on the packs and go on a little hike. What do you say?"

Seth looked across the river, then downstream. He nodded his head in agreement. "Let's do it. There's no reason for them to go to the other side. It would just slow them down."

They stashed the canoe and put on the packs, which were full of camping supplies. After double-checking their handguns and boxes of extra bullets, they stowed them away. They then shouldered the rifles and took off along the shoreline, heading downstream in search of tracks.

***

Mia was able to point out the exact spot where the mine was located once they got to an opening. They made good time, reaching the base of the mountains that walled in the wide valley by late afternoon. There was not much conversation since they concentrated on covering their tracks and evading the guys chasing them.

Asher's shoulder ached and was slightly oozing blood through the bandage. Mia made another sling, and Asher soon realized that moving his arm back and forth, with its weight, was not a wise idea. He had pulled open the wound.

They took an unplanned break when Mia suddenly stopped. "Wait a minute, Asher." She had knelt and put her hand into a fresh impression on the ground.

Asher turned around, looking down at Mia. "What's up?"

"Nothing unusual, but something we can definitely do without."

Asher stood over Mia and replied, "That's for sure. I'm not Mr. Alaska, but I guess I need to believe like he does."

Mia looked up, surprised, and asked, "Like living in the Cloud of Glory?"

Asher was surprised himself at what he just said. He didn't really mean it that way, but as he thought about it, he was beginning to understand it more and answered, "We don't have a gun to protect us from the grizzly that made that fresh print that your hand is in. So, if it means not worrying and just staying focused on getting to the mine without a gun to protect us, then I guess so."

Smiling, she said, "You're almost there. If you would've added not worrying about it because God is with us, you would've come full circle. That's what Rudy teaches about God and His Cloud of Glory."

Not wanting to fully submit to the idea, Asher said jokingly, "Right now we've got no choice, so let's put our heads in the cloud and hide."

"That's not what we mean, and you know it," Mia retorted.

Asher ignored her as he looked around and found a fairly straight, long, strong fallen tree branch about two inches in diameter. Getting his knife out, he cut off the unwanted smaller limbs and smoothed the stick out. He sharpened one end, making a spear tip, and said to Mia, "I'm pretty sure God would want us to be wise and protect ourselves. We don't want to become rag doll toys for the bear. What do you think?" He lifted the spear up and jabbed it into the air. He then looked around the area as though the beast were hiding somewhere, watching them.

Understanding Asher's mindset, she added, "As long as we go up against our giants like David did. He was a boy who went into battle with Goliath." She pointed back down at the paw print that was the length of her boot. It included four-inch claws that protruded out farther than the actual print. "This grizzly is probably more than two and a half feet taller than you and most likely weighs about five hundred pounds more."

Suddenly, Asher's strong spear seemed like a toothpick. He looked at Mia. "You sure aren't making this any easier."

"Just bringing some reality to our situation." She turned and started walking away as he followed. She continued, "Asher, David didn't see himself as a young teenager with skinny arms and a small rock, ready to face the giant. But instead, he confronted the giant in complete faith, without doubt or fear. He believed the power of God was always with him. He could conquer anything in his way if he called upon the name of God, even with his skinny arms and only a small stone."

Asher was speechless. Mia's tone was certain, and her words were said with such confidence that there was nothing he could argue with. Looking back at him, she asked, "So do you have the power of God working through you, big man?"

He diverted his eyes as she turned back around and kept walking. Silence fell between them as Asher felt a new and different challenge. He was being asked to rely on a strength that did not lift weights in the gym or do wind sprints on the field. He felt deflated and almost embarrassed about how big he physically was. It was as though everything he had worked so hard for over the years was worthless and a waste of time. Flashes of all the training and the hundreds of games he had played came crashing down like an old brick building being demolished, so much so that he couldn't even recognize what the pile of rubble had been originally.

Mia sensed she had just launched an attack on Asher, mentally and spiritually, and she didn't know if he was hurt or just disoriented. She took charge, looking toward the mountain, and told Asher, "Let's make it up to the mine before it gets dark."

They continued walking quietly and cautiously as this new concept simmered in Asher's thoughts. He had been taught that you're on your own; you don't need to rely on anyone else. It was all about you. It was about being dedicated and working hard. Never quit, or you'll become a failure and never succeed.

This notion that strength had nothing to do with his physicality was challenging to him. He now felt very vulnerable and weak, trying to access strength and power that he couldn't see or touch. He always saw himself as more of a Goliath, walking around big and strong.

Mia was also deep in thought. Completely exhausted, they wearily climbed the mountain one step at a time. It was dusk when they finally reached a ridge on the mountain that flattened out.

"We're here!" Mia cried, looking around. She scanned the view of the valley below. "Wow, it sure is beautiful up here. Isn't it, Asher?"

He took in his surroundings: There were old piles of tailings that had been poured out from the mine. The tailings were over the edge of the flattened bench and extended the mountain out about thirty yards from the edge. A couple of old, unorganized piles of thick lumber rested on the brownish, red earth.

Asher thought that the lumber might have been used to support the walls and ceiling in the mine. They could also have been used as railroad ties, supporting the metal rails for the tailing carts. Several of the old, metal, rusted-out tailing carts were tipped over and left next to the entrance of the mine. The entrance appeared to have had a slight cave-in, with only half of it still open. A beat-up, rusted sign lay on the pile of rocks that said, "Danger, Do Not Enter."

Other debris and rusted items were scattered all over the flattened part of the mountain, which was about fifty yards wide. Then his eyes caught something out of place, and before he turned around to see what Mia was commenting on, he said, "It looks like our big, fury friend knows about this spot too."

She turned around as he pointed to several large scat piles, one of which had fresh colorings of blue, red, and green. This matched the poop piles they had seen before that had contained bits of wild blueberries, cranberries, and leaves.

"Great...," she said reluctantly. "He's been marking his territory. Let's pray he's making his rounds several miles from here."

They both turned around to look at what Mia had been commenting about. "You're right," Asher said. "It's a spectacular view from up here." He scanned the valley below closely, looking for any movement. To their left he saw a good-sized, brown dot in a marshy clearing. It was about a third of a mile away. "Do you think that's a moose?" he asked.

She looked where he was pointing and instantly replied, "Definitely."

"What am I doing? I've got a pair of mini binoculars in my pack." Asher unsnapped the buckles and slid the pack off his good shoulder. "Ah, that's better." He straightened his back up, stretched out his shoulder, and bent down to open the backpack for the binoculars.

Asher sat down on a flat area and dangled his legs over the edge. He began to closely examine the details of the valley and where they had come from, starting at the river. He followed their route, working his way closer to the base of the mountain. Suddenly, he spotted something and took a moment to concentrate on it.

Mia saw him tense up and asked, "What do you see?"

"Not sure. I thought I saw something. There might've been two things moving in the shadows of those trees, but I don't see them anymore."

CHAPTER 13

Asher gazed into the dark opening of the mine. The bright beam from his small LED flashlight moved across the walls and floor, illuminating the inside. It was quiet, except for the echoes of water dripping from the ceiling into puddles scattered here and there. They began walking over the piles of rocks that had fallen from the ceiling over time and were blocking part of the mine opening. Asher asked Mia, "Did you and your dad ever enter this mine?"

She was walking right behind him with her hand on his back, making sure she stayed close. "Yes," she answered. "Dad had one of those old glass lanterns that made a hissing sound. It would get really hot, and he would hold it out in front of him as we explored different tunnels. Our shadows would follow us, so it constantly gave me this eerie feeling that someone was stalking us."

"Did you go way back inside?"

"Oh yeah, it was just as spooky then as it is now. Dad would tease me when the mountain made groaning sounds deep inside. He said it was the spirits of the dead miners killed in here, trying to talk to us."

"Men died in here?" Asher asked, cautiously moving forward.

"Yes, that's why they closed it. They had two different cave-ins, killing many miners, and after the owner's son was buried alive in the second cave-in, he shut it down and never reopened it."

"Stop!" Asher whispered as he halted, seeing something about fifteen yards in front of them. "What is that?"

Mia squinted around his broad shoulder and answered, "It's bones."

"Bones of what?" he asked, frantically shining the light into every nook and cranny of the tunnel. The tunnel was about seven feet high and just as wide, and Asher was beginning to feel claustrophobic. The underground bowels of rock seemed to be giving off a stench of stale death that made his skin prickle with goosebumps.

Returning the flashlight to the white glow of scattered bones, Mia stated, "It's probably from one of the miners left behind. Some of them eventually freed themselves from being buried alive but were too weak to make it all the way out. By then, the rescue crews were gone."

"How could you joke about something like that?"

"Who said I was joking?"

He turned the light toward her face and noticed that she wasn't smiling. Eventually she couldn't help herself and giggled, "Okay, sorry. I guess it was a bad joke, but I had to pay you back for your suicide comment earlier."

After the day's tiring and painful events, Asher didn't feel like joking and continued walking. When they got to a pile of different bones, he asked, "They're probably from a caribou or a smaller moose, don't you think?"

"It looks like it, but because there are so many, it's probably several dead animals. A grizzly or a pack of wolves might have brought them in here." She lifted her head, looking farther into the deep, dark tunnel. "I bet something made this place its home. I wonder if anything is still here."

Asher shined the flashlight down the throat of the mountain again. It appeared to go on forever. He turned the light toward Mia to ask a question. Something on the side wall glistened, catching his eye. She turned to see what he was staring at and said, "Iron pyrite."

"What is it?"

"Iron pyrite. You know, fool's gold."

"Wow, that looks real."

"To the untrained eye," she boasted, knowing her stuff.

He caught his breath as an idea came to him. "That's it! That could be our ticket out of here."

"What are you talking about?"

"I can fill the empty, leather gold bag with fool's gold, and if those guys ever catch up to us, I'll have a bargaining chip. They'd probably never even notice the difference until they're long gone."

"Asher, if those guys catch up to us, just give them my father's gold. It's not worth the risk."

"I can't."

"What do you mean you can't?"

He closed his eyes and inhaled deeply because the pain in his shoulder was increasing. It was a reminder of their real-life situation. With hesitation, he divulged his little secret, "Because I don't have it."

She jerked her head back. "What do you mean you don't have it?"

"I don't have it because it's in the river."

She thought for a second and said, "Oh, it fell out when we jumped out of the canoe this morning? When were you going to tell me?"

"No, that's not what happened to it." He turned the light away from the wall toward her face and saw a confused look. "I dumped it into the river at your parents' place."

"You did what?"

"You were unconscious and lying in the canoe. Just before I shoved off into the night, I dumped it out along the river's edge into the shallow water. I had no idea what we were about to go through."

"Why dump it?"

"Well, it was so heavy, and I didn't want to carry it because it would've slowed us down. Then I thought if we did turn over or crash, it would never be found. Plus, it was a good hiding spot. All your dad has to do is pan right behind the house, and he'll have all his gold back."

This new information stunned her into silence. She suddenly jumped up, giving him a big kiss. Startled and wincing in pain, Asher didn't understand what she was doing.

She let go. "I'm so sorry that I accused you of stealing it." Then, her smile vanished as she asked, "Why didn't you tell me earlier, during our fight about it?"

"I didn't know those guys were going to come after us like this when I dumped the gold out. And I didn't have a plan until now." Looking at her, he felt her relax a little and continued, "Plus, you caught me off guard at how easy it was for you to accuse me of stealing."

Smiling wryly, he added, "Now about that kiss…?"

"Oh, no, don't you get the wrong idea. That was an impulse just because I was so excited." She turned to walk back outside, smiling wide again. Now she knew that Asher really was a very special man. "We've got to build a fire, rebandage your shoulder, and make some dinner."

They made their way back outside the mine, carefully looking for anything that would prove to be unfriendly. When they saw nothing suspicious, Asher suggested, "Let's make camp just a little ways into the mine. It's going to get cold tonight being that we're higher up the mountain. I don't want the light from our fire to be a tip-off out here in the open. Especially with those two down there somewhere hunting us.

"We can make a small wall from a bunch of rocks next to where we're going to sleep by the tunnel wall. The wall will help reflect heat from the fire and keep us warm. We'll need to be close enough to the entrance that fresh air will circulate. That's just in case there are poisonous gases drifting through the mine. I don't know about you, but I'd rather not permanently fall asleep and have someone else find our bones."

"Good idea, me neither," she agreed as she picked up her pack. "Why don't you gather some firewood to last through the night, and I'll get everything set up inside?"

With just a nod of his head, he handed her his flashlight.

Soon they had a small fire crackling, lighting and warming up the inside of the mine. It was situated about fifty yards from the entrance. Mia boiled water in a small aluminum pot on the butane stove from one of the water bottles they had with them. They had decided to split one of the dehydrated meals and start conserving what they had left. It was going to take a lot longer to walk than canoe to Bettles.

Asher couldn't let his guard down; he kept thinking about the two guys possibly still on their trail and the grizzlies that appeared to be so abundant around the area. He didn't want Mia to worry, so he didn't bring them up.

He did, however, have her help him rig an alarm system at the entrance of the mine. In the emergency fishing kit in his pack, there was a small spool of fishing line. He tied one end around a rock about two feet off the ground and threaded it through a hole in the rusted, old metal "Do Not Enter" sign. He then strung it invisibly across the entrance and anchored it between two rocks. With the slightest touch, the line would break away from the rocks and bring the sign clanking down.

While they worked on this, Asher told Mia a story from when he was younger. He and his buddies used to play capture the flag with paintball guns in the mountains of Colorado. They played in a mile-long valley, heavily forested near a medium-sized creek. The creek flowed down the center, separating the two territories. They would play for several days until a team finally won.

One year, on the second day of a game, Asher's friend on the opposing team killed a grouse while they were playing. The friend decided to keep it cool in a deep hole between some rocks that were against the mountain near their tent. He wanted to have it for dinner the next day. Like usual, they put up a fishing line alarm around the perimeter of each of their camps and clamped small bells to the line in different areas in an attempt to catch the opposing team sneaking up on them while they slept. Sometime after midnight, his teammates woke up to the bells jingling. He said they were so tired they all agreed that if the other team had worked this hard into the night to capture their flag, they could have it. When his buddy got up the next morning, the flag was still there. He couldn't understand what had happened until he went to get the grouse out to cook it. The grouse was gone... because a bear had snuck into camp and stolen it!

Asher told her, "This time, if the alarm goes off, we won't sleep through it if that's all right with you."

"If we hear that sign clanking," Mia said, "we're probably going to have real problems, so no, I'm not going to let either of us sleep through it."

On their way back to the fire, they stopped at the vein of iron pyrite on the wall that they had seen earlier. Asher chiseled out enough of the fool's gold to completely fill the leather bag. Feeling the bag in his hands, he said with confidence at his bright idea, "Not as heavy as the real stuff, but someone might not know the difference, so it should be just fine."

When they sat back down next to the fire, Asher looked toward the dark hole that plunged into the belly of the mine and asked, "So how far in did you and your dad go? Is there another way out?"

"We walked much farther in. I was young, so I can't remember exactly how far. I do remember that we got to the point where the main tunnel splits in two different directions. We followed the tunnel to the right until a pile of rocks stopped us. We guessed that that's where the final cave-in occurred."

"You said main tunnel; are there others?"

"Yeah, there was an occasional one here and there. The smaller tunnels went in different directions, only about twenty or thirty yards, and then dead-ended at a solid wall." She paused, thinking of something. "You know, there was a place somewhere back there where the tunnel went left, and light came in from the ceiling. I remember looking up through a small shaft about three feet square. It went a long way up, like it came out at the top of the mountain. Dad said he thought it might have been a breathing hole to help circulate air into the mine. Or it could've been an emergency escape hole."

"Good to know."

As the fire burned down, Asher added several logs and secured everything into their packs. He wanted to be ready for a quick getaway if anything happened during the night. The only items left out or not strapped down were a sleeping bag (which they were discreetly sharing), Asher's and Rudy's flashlights, and Asher's knife. He left the blade of the knife flipped out and resting near his spear, both of which were right next to him. He had Mia climb into the inner part of the sleeping bag while he blocked her in with his good shoulder. He didn't want her bumping into his injured shoulder while they slept. The other half of his body stuck out of the sleeping bag and was covered with Rudy's coat.

After Mia had doctored Asher up, she had hoped to lie in the same positions as the night before. Asher, however, was adamant about being in a position that would make it easy to react quickly in case something happened. Also, he didn't tell her, but she needed to get as much sleep as possible. Asher might need her full strength to help them survive, especially if his health started going downhill.

***

Willie and Seth found the tracks Asher had tried so hard to hide. Even though Asher's diversion didn't completely work, it did slow them down. Following the sporadic trail, Willie commented several times about how the two in front of them were doing a good job of trying to conceal their tracks. But he still boasted about himself, as always, explaining that if he was not an experienced tracker, they probably would have completely lost them by now.

It was almost dark, and suddenly the trail dead-ended at the base of a mountain. There were so many rocks; no visible tracks were left behind. Frustrated, Willie spoke up, "Well, if I was betting on what they were doing, I'd say they were heading to higher ground."

"It makes sense," Seth replied as he looked up the mountain. It was sparse—not many trees or bushes. "I would get as high as I could to be able to see someone coming."

Willie examined the terrain of the mountain in the dim light, thinking out loud, "So do we continue up the mountain in the dark? There's hardly any cover to hide in. Or do we camp here for the night, get up early, and start fresh in the morning?"

Seth ventured, "That's what ordinary people would do, but we're not ordinary."

Willie grinned and laughed. "You got that right. I just want to get the gold and kill those two. Then we can take a rest back home on the beach with a couple of hotties in our arms and cold drinks in our hands."

"That sounds good to me. So what's the plan?"

"Let's split up and search about fifty yards apart. Communicate with flashlights as we climb. They can't be too far ahead, especially since that big guy is hurt, and he's dragging a girl along. They're definitely stopping somewhere for the night."

"Let's do it," Seth agreed, anxious to get this over with.

"We need to maintain our night vision and make sure that we don't give ourselves away. Only click the flashlights on and off three times when we've got something or need the other to come over."

"Got it," Seth replied. As he walked away from Willie, he removed his rifle from his shoulder to securely hold it in his hand while climbing up the rocks. A sinister smile came across Willie's face as he watched Seth walk away.

They slowly made their way up the mountain. Their eyes worked tirelessly for a trace of their targets. They were only able to see the outline of the mountain with the help of a partial moon, which glowed through clouds.

After a long hour and a laborious climb, they were both ready to give up for the night. That is until Seth saw something unique and promising. Above him, the shadow of the mountain suddenly had a perfect, wide, horizontal outline on it. Too perfect. As he inched his way to the lip, he peered onto an area that did not look natural; it was too flat. Ducking back down, he backed up a few steps and retrieved his flashlight. He then pointed it to the side that Willie had been on and clicked it on and off three times. He waited for a few minutes and did it again, but Willie still did not respond. He thought about what he should do next if his partner didn't signal back when he caught a whiff of something. Slowly going back up to the ledge, he peeked over, took a deep breath, and identified what it was. *Smoke! They have a fire going somewhere, but where? I don't see anything*, he thought to himself.

He tried to get his eyes to focus better, but the light of the moon was not much help. The mountain was darker here because it was recessed. The only thing he could tell was that he was at one end of a man-made area. He decided to move over more, toward the center.

However, if he did this, he would be even farther away from Willie. He tried the flashlight a couple more times but still didn't get a response, so he moved.

Stealthily walking just under the ledge, Seth sensed he was getting close. Figuring he had moved over far enough, he turned back and flashed his light three more times where Willie was supposed to be, but, again, nothing. Before peeking over the ledge, he hesitated. He was frustrated that Willie was not responding to him but never considered what might have happened to him. Seth decided to move on without Willie. He looked over the rocky edge, and from this new angle, he scoped out the smoke.

Wrinkling his brow and squinting his eyes, he looked hard into what appeared to be an opening to a cave. A faint yellow and orange glow could be seen far back in its throat. Without seeing it precisely from this position, he never would have seen it at all.

Ducking back down, he continued to move his flashlight up and down the mountain on Willie's side, just in case Willie was moving at a different pace than he was.

He didn't want to give himself away, so he gave up on the flashlight. He glimpsed back over to find it very quiet, except for the weak flickering of the fire. Squinting his eyes, he tried examining the flat area but without much success. It was just too dark.

This is too easy, he thought. *They don't know we're here, and they're probably asleep.* Just like a predator sneaking up on its prey, Seth smoothly made his way onto the flattened part of the mountain. He tiptoed toward the opening and felt his way with every step as his feet stepped cautiously over logs and rocks.

He neared the opening and realized that the fire was much deeper into the cave. He lifted up his rifle and viewed the light of the fire gently bouncing off the rock walls through his scope. It took a second, but he was finally able to see some hazy details. He stopped short when he saw what looked like a backpack.

Lowering the rifle, he looked around outside, trying to see if there was any sign of Willie, but there wasn't. As he turned back to the mine, he whispered under his breath, "Fine, I'll end this thing now and get the gold back." He took one step forward, and an unexpectedly loud metal clanking noise pierced the quiet night. It shocked him so much that he started and jerked the rifle up to protect himself from whatever might be coming at him. Frightened, he loudly stuttered incoherently, which echoed down the mine.

Seth froze. He was frantic and moved his eyes around, trying to understand what had just happened. Suddenly, it was like his heart stopped, and he couldn't breathe. The dim light from the fire, way out in front of him, was gone. He was now staring into complete darkness. He thought it could not get any darker, but when he looked down, he could see neither the rifle nor his hands, and he began to panic.

Seth didn't know if there was someone beside him, behind him, or an arm's length in front of him. What he did know was that someone put out the fire.

He was breathing heavily as he broke out in a sweat. He tried to take a step backward, but it was as if his feet were attached to the ground. Thinking he heard some faint sound down the tunnel, his only instinct was to shoot at it. He aimed the rifle and pulled the trigger, but nothing happened. He was so anxious to protect himself that he jerked on the trigger several more times until he finally remembered the safety. He flipped the safety off and pulled the trigger, setting off an explosion. The bullet left the barrel, lighting up the end of the rifle with a flame. The sudden blast echoed down into the belly of the mine. His ears were ringing as the sound bounced off the solid walls and ceiling and then back at him.

Letting panic take control, Seth pulled the bolt back on the rifle and injected another bullet. He shot again and again until there were no bullets left. He heard the hollow click of the firing pin hitting nothing. Fear engulfed him. He shouted curse words and hurried to get his pack off; he needed more bullets. He retrieved the miniature flashlight from his pants pocket and placed the back end of it into his mouth. He frantically opened a side pocket on the pack and took out a new box of bullets. Fumbling, he kept dropping them. He reloaded, looking back and forth between his hands and the tunnel. The beam of his light flashed all over the place.

Once reloaded, he jumped to his feet and spun around. With the flashlight still in his mouth, he looked forward down the beam of light, only to see a mountain of a man standing inches from his face. Seth recoiled in horror as he felt the man's breath almost searing the skin on his face. His chest burned in sudden fiery pain.

Realizing he could not take another breath, Seth's wide-open eyes slowly looked down and saw the big man holding a pole. It had penetrated Seth's chest and exited out his back. He tried to voice words but only made gargling sounds.

I'm a dead man, Seth thought. He blinked in complete disbelief as the flashlight dropped from his mouth and hit the ground. Within seconds, his limp body collapsed on top of it.

Without emotion, Asher pulled the spear out, knowing what he had done was what he had to do to save them.

Suddenly, there was a deep cracking and popping sound coming from the ceiling as dust and small pebbles fell onto Asher and the dead body. Asher didn't look up or hesitate but swiftly ran out of the way and back into the mine. He moved just in time as the ceiling gave way. It dumped a truckload of boulders, sealing the entrance and burying the dead man.

In the chaos, Asher felt his way until he thought he was getting close and whispered, "Mia."

Just in front of him, he heard her anxious voice. "Asher, I'm here."

"Are you okay?"

"I'm fine. I thought you were buried alive."

"Not me, but one of the two guys is now in his coffin. None of those bullets hit you, did they?" he asked as he slowly worked his way around the small rock firewall toward her.

"No, but they were bouncing off the walls, all over the place."

He set the spear down and blindly reached out to feel for her. When he touched her shoulder, she reacted by clutching his hand. She turned around to give him a big hug before sitting down and asking, "What happened?"

"He ran out of bullets. I ran up to him and put the spear through his chest. Then the entrance caved in, probably from the loud vibrations of the rifle shots."

There was silence, and Mia gently wrapped her arms around him again as they sat down in utter darkness. She tried to understand what might be going through his mind and whispered in his ear, "Thank you for risking your life for me."

The past few minutes ran through Asher's mind over and over again—from the moment he first heard the sign drop on top of the rocks to putting the fire out with the dirt around it and then cautioning Mia to stay low behind the rocks. He had seen the flash of the rifle and dropped to the ground. And he had rolled over to the wall, behind an indent, until he heard the click of the empty rifle.

Then he had quickly gotten up, and because of the moonlight's faint visibility, he was able to make out the shadow of the one shooting at them. When the shadow of a man had turned on a flashlight, he knew that was the moment to make his offensive move. He had to sprint to the man and impale him with his spear before he could reload and get another shot off.

Asher and Mia still held each other. They were grateful that they had not been hurt, but the realization that they were in real danger of being killed reawakened them. Asher was the first to pull away, telling Mia, "We are an easy target if the other guy or even more of them are out there. They aren't that dumb if they were able to find us this fast, especially at night. We've been fooling ourselves, not them."

"What are we going to do?"

He thought for a moment and asked, "Can you remember how far back in the mine the breathing hole in the ceiling was?"

"Not really, but I do remember it was down the tunnel we took to the left."

"Well, we can do one of two things. We can move boulders out of the way to get out the entrance and hope no one is waiting for us on the other side. Or we could try to secretly escape in the opposite direction. That's as long as we can find the hole in the ceiling and it's big enough for us to climb our way out."

Mia was unable to see anything inside the mine. She began to feel like it was their own tomb. She reached out again for Asher. As soon as he felt her soft hand, he held it, saying, "I'll go along with whatever you think is best, Mia. You know this place better than I do."

She paused for a moment, then replied, "I believe God is directing our steps by closing the entrance. He wants us to trust faithfully in His guidance by staying in His Cloud of Glory and go deeper into the bowels of this dungeon."

CHAPTER 14

Here we go again, the Cloud of Glory thing, Asher thought to himself. He clearly understood the predicament they were in and knew he needed to be supportive. The last thing he needed was for her to begin to panic or be afraid, so he went along with it. Feeling around for his small LED flashlight, he switched it on. They both squinted at the sudden brightness. "Let's shed some light on our situation," Asher said slyly.

"Wow, that's blinding, just like the light of God in the darkness of this world."

He could not stop himself. "Are you serious? You're going to preach to me again right now?"

She raised her hand to shade her eyes as they adjusted to the light. "Is that what you think I'm doing? You've got it all wrong. This is how we live—me, my mother, and Rudy. This is what living in the Cloud of Glory is. We don't just discuss it or listen to people preach about it or read about it in the Bible. We live it, think about it, breathe it, and talk about it all the time. This is what God calls us to do: to live by the Spirit always, just as Jesus did."

Asher turned toward the caved-in entrance and shined the flashlight. He then twisted around to the deep, dark tunnel as the beam of the flashlight shined endlessly until it faded away. He said, "Okay, I get it. So God hasn't really given us a choice this time. I guess He wants us to follow His way into the tunnel of doom."

A bit disappointed, Mia didn't comment. She thought he was understanding her but also felt he was poking fun at her. She changed the subject and asked, "So should we get going now or wait until morning?"

"Well, since it'll be almost impossible to find your hole in the mountain until the sun's up, we should get some rest."

"How are we going to know when it's morning? Do you have a watch?" Mia asked.

"Didn't bring one on this so-called vacation, and my phone is dead," he said, knowing it was buried deep in his pack.

She saw his frustration. "I didn't either. I use the clock on my phone too, and I'm guessing that it burned up with my plane."

He prodded at the doused fire and saw remnants of hot coals buried underneath. "Let's stay here and try to get some sleep. From what you've explained about that hole in the ceiling, we're going to need to crawl up and out of it, and that's going to be a workout." He slowly moved his bad shoulder, grimacing in pain and clenching his teeth.

Mia took the flashlight from him and examined the wound. She pulled at his shirt. "It's started to bleed slightly again. The new stitches are holding, but it needs to be cleaned and changed with a new bandage."

He sat motionless while she worked on him, not saying much. When she had finished, he rekindled the fire, brightening up the area. The flickering of the small flames danced on the walls, keeping them company as the warmth soothed their bodies. They had moved the sleeping bag around to use as padding while they sat on the stone floor and leaned against the rock wall. They snuggled up together to keep warm with Rudy's coat draped around them. Asher put his good arm around Mia, and she pressed into him.

His mind calmed down as he watched the hypnotic fire. They had not spoken for a while, and for some reason, he felt the need to say a few words before his eyes shut for the night. "I'm trying to understand your glory thing."

Mia faintly heard his words as she slept shallowly. She didn't know if they were for her or if he was talking to God, so she let go and drifted off to sleep.

***

Mia was the first to wake up, coughing in the dead silence. The sound rattled against the walls and down into the mine. Throughout the night, the fire started to fade several times. One of them would then wake up to the chill and place more wood onto it. But now, the flames had fully dissipated, and the remaining smoke swirled in the darkness. It slithered in ghostly patterns as it made its way to her lungs.

This woke Asher, and he coughed a couple of times, saying, "I've never seen it so dark."

"Me neither. Can you imagine being trapped in here with no flashlights or matches?" Mia said, blinking hard as though she was clearing something out of her eyes to see.

He yawned and, through slurred words, said, "Don't speak so soon. Batteries and matches run out."

"Don't even think about it, Asher."

"If we don't find that hole in the ceiling…"

"Asher…" She grabbed his arm, giving him a pinch.

"Okay, okay. We're going to find that escape route." He switched on the flashlight, and they both squinted. They sat silently for a while until one of them got the fire going again. It illuminated the rocky tunnel and fought off the cool dampness of the mountain. The other fixed breakfast.

Asher happened to look, from a different angle, at the smoke coming off the fire. Before he turned the flashlight off, he said aloud, "Look at that."

"What? What do you see?" She looked in the direction he was facing. She didn't realize he was looking just in front of himself, not into the distance.

"The smoke. It's flowing slowly down into the mine."

"So?"

"So that means it's going somewhere to escape." She still didn't catch on, so he explained further, pointing down into the mountain. "It's going that direction because outside air is coming in by funneling through gaps—gaps in between the fallen rocks at the blocked entrance. And that air is being sucked out, down in the mine somewhere. Since air travels up the side of mountains in the morning, it's finding its way along here and then through an outlet higher than where it came in. Which means your hole in the ceiling deeper in the mountain is higher than the entrance air that's coming in. It proves your opening is still there."

He watched a smile spread across her face, and this time he was prepared. He braced himself for her next move as she leaned over and hugged him. She held his face with both hands and gave him a quick kiss. "I knew it! He always finds a way."

"It's just plain science. I didn't really do anything."

She laughed, "I'm not talking about you, silly."

"Oh yeah, God," Asher said with little enthusiasm.

"That's right."

Looking down the mine, Asher reviewed in his mind how easy it could be to find the exit hole. "Do we have anything in the packs we don't need that can burn for a while?"

They dove into their packs, pulled out several items, and spread them on the floor. Looking over what they had, an old pair of Rudy's camp slippers caught Asher's attention. "There we go." He picked one up, looking at the sole, and said, "This is going to work as long as we can get the rubber to burn."

"Are you sure? We have his socks and...," picking up something lying in the pile with a stick, she finished, "underwear."

"Those will burn up too quickly. The rubber on these slippers will burn or smoke forever with a thick black smoke that's easy to follow."

"You're smart. I'll give you that." She smiled with admiration as she built up his pride, and they repacked everything.

They finished breakfast, but before heading out, Asher put one of the slippers into the fire, sole down, to help it catch a flame. It took a little longer than he anticipated, but it finally caught on fire. The smoke filled the area and began to drift away lazily.

Mia helped Asher put on a new sling that she had made. He flinched in pain. "You need to take something for that," she said, watching his face.

"Yeah, I just don't want to run out of pills before we get to Bettles. And with the climb I think we're going to be making, I'm going to get my butt kicked, big time."

She held onto the flashlight as she helped him settle his pack onto his good shoulder. It was much heavier with the leather pouch now full of fool's gold. Asher put his knife and Rudy's spare flashlight away and grabbed the spear leaning against the wall to poke the end into the foot of the slipper, which was still in the fire. He carefully lifted it up and pointed it down the tunnel as both of their eyes followed the smoke trail.

Mia directed her flashlight down the hollow hole to illuminate the path. At that moment, the bowels of the mountain gave a deep, vibrating groan. They hesitated and looked at each other, feeling helpless and waiting for something to happen. Once it stopped, Asher said, "I guess the spirits of the dead miners don't like us smoking up the place."

"That's not funny. It's still spooky to me," Mia commented, looking down the mine.

"Why don't you just pray about it? Didn't you say with the Cloud of Glory you don't have to fear anything?" He still had a grin on his face, but this time, it was one that challenged her faith. "Do you really walk the walk, or is it all talk?"

She shined the light toward him like a wall of defense and replied, "I can fear things, but that doesn't mean I don't trust God. And by the way, I was going to pray before we left anyways."

He looked at her, not wanting to agitate her any more than he already had. He tilted his head down, raising only his eyebrows, and said, "Okay, then pray."

Her glare softened as she accepted his so-called challenge. Mia prayed out loud for their travels, for their safety, and for Asher's wound to heal. She finished with, "Until later on." She heard a faint echo of the same words coming from Asher and snapped her eyes open. She witnessed his good arm raised and his hand signaling the love sign as he reached toward the ceiling.

He, too, opened his eyes and gently lowered his arm. He gave her a sweet smile and said, "Thank you."

Mia was stunned as joy filled her body. She was temporarily lost for words. She wanted to reach for him and squeeze him tight, but instead, she calmly said, "You're welcome," and then turned to follow the black smoke.

As they walked deeper and deeper into the mountain, a claustrophobic sensation started to suffocate them. The bowels of the earth communicated with soft, eerie moans. It was as if they were forbidden to enter the dark sanctuary of rock and dirt. Sporadic dripping water oozed from the ceiling and walls, forming puddles in the paths of its two uninvited guests.

Piles of rocks, big and small, littered the tunnel's floor, having fallen from the ceiling and walls over time. Their flashlight had begun to weaken, and after creeping along together for a while, they came to a larger, open cavern. Stopping to watch the dark, slithering smoke through the weakening light, they realized that they had come to an intersection of tunnels. Mia happened to look at the ground and noticed, even in the poor lighting, what appeared to be a large puddle directly in front of them. She kicked at the loose pebbles on the floor. She wanted to see if the water would shimmer with the shower of rocks. It didn't, and instead she saw (and heard) nothing at all.

Asher had not noticed the hole and went to take a step. Mia promptly reached up and grabbed his arm, jerking him back, and shrieked, "Stop!"

Her sudden reaction jolted him as her alarming word echoed down the different tunnels. Asher followed Mia's eyes toward the light shining at his feet.

Looking into the deep hole in front of them threw him off balance, causing him to stumble backward in fright. "Thanks. That would've hurt really bad."

Mia stepped back with him and said, "That's number two."

"You got that right. I almost pooped my pants," he said, incorrectly interpreting her meaning.

She laughed, "No, no, that was the second time I've saved your life. I'm catching up!"

"Well, aren't we the competitive one?" he said as he bent down to pick up a rock.

"No, just keeping balance between us. I want to pull my weight too."

He chuckled, joking with her, "All hundred and sixty pounds of you."

"One hundred and twenty-five pounds, smart aleck," she was quick to point out. "Rudy's shirt adds thirty-five pounds."

"Touchy, touchy!"

She dropped her shoulders and sighed, "When you compete against hundreds of other women, many much prettier and in better shape than you are, even one pound is a nightmare that haunts you."

Asher peeked over the edge and into the black hole again. Mia shined the flashlight down into it for him.

"Let's see how far this goes." He tossed a rock, and they waited for what seemed like a long time before it could be heard bouncing off the side walls. It eventually splashed into water, ending its fall.

"Wow, that's really deep. I wonder if it was part of a mine shaft or if it just collapsed on its own."

"I don't remember seeing it before. Maybe my dad did, and we just walked around it."

Mia raised her head, looking down the tunnel to her left. "I knew it. Look at the smoke. It's going into the left tunnel."

Holding the spear up with the smoldering rubber sole of the slipper, he spoke ominously, "You're right. Let's keep following this black spirit demon as it draws us deeper into its chamber." He ended with an evil laugh.

"Stop it, Asher."

"You don't think that's funny? Look where we're at!" He gestured his good arm out. "We couldn't have made a story like this up when we were on the plane together just a week ago. You and I trapped inside a mountain above the Arctic Circle and in the middle of nowhere. Only one person knows where we are, and he happens to be trying to kill us." Listening to himself, the realization of their true situation sounded desperate and final. The smile on his face turned upside down.

"Oh, so you heard yourself," she said, smirking at him.

He started laughing internally but could not control himself and let it out.

"Now what's so funny?" Mia asked.

"If you were in my shoes before this trip and knew my thoughts and intentions, you would think this was either a nightmare or a hilarious dream."

"I heard your story, and I guess it might seem funny…"

"I wanted to escape from the world and hide from everything and everyone. I guess I really have." He sounded sad as he realized the irony of his statement.

The mood dimmed just like the flashlight, which was in desperate need of new batteries. Instead of changing them, they retrieved Rudy's flashlight from the pack. The fresh light from this new flashlight gave them a boost of confidence and pushed them to continue around the pit. Just a little while later, they saw something other than blackness in the distance: a faint mist of soft light began to show itself more the closer they got.

Before long, they found themselves looking up at a decent-sized hole in the ceiling. It appeared to telescope the higher it went until the blue sky was looking down at them like a small blue eyeball.

"So how are we going to do this?" Mia asked, staring up.

"You're going to take your pack off, and I'll lift you up to go first."

"And who's going to lift you up?"

He looked around on the ground. "While you're making your way up, I'll collect the larger rocks lying around to pile them up as high as I can to make a step stool. But you'll also have a parachute cord tied around your waist. There's a cord in each of the packs. When you get to the top, you'll pull up the backpacks using the cords. Then, I'll tie them to me, and you'll help hoist me up."

"There is no way I'm going to be able to lift you!" she said desperately.

"You're not going to be lifting all of me, just enough to relieve me as I climb. Remember I only have one arm." He raised his good arm.

"Once you're up in the hole, press your back against one wall and your feet against the other. Crab-walk your way up, pressing against the walls. I'll do the same; I won't need much of your help until I get to the top."

She stared back up into the hole, watching the black smoke rise as if it were in a chimney. She was envisioning what he had explained and rocked her head back and forth with a cautiously optimistic grin. "I think it'll work. I've done some rock climbing before, so I'm not scared of heights, but it was nothing like this."

Looking up, he added, "It's a good thing we both have fairly long legs. It'll make it much easier to reach across from one wall to the other."

Asher tossed the remains of the smoldering slipper off his stick and back down the tunnel. He dropped his pack to the ground and said, "Could you shine that light into the pack?" He pulled out the long, tightly wound-up parachute cord and told Mia to pull the cord out of Rudy's pack too.

With both cords out, Asher wove them together as one long, strong lifeline. While he worked on this, Mia prepared them a snack.

After eating and sharing a bottle of water, they agreed to reorganize their packs. They would take out any items that weren't essential to make the packs lighter. Mia lifted out a large item in her pack. "Are you sure we can't leave this heavy leather bag of fool's gold behind?"

"No, I want to be prepared for anything."

"Okay, but I hope I'll be able to lift these packs out of here. It's a long way up."

"You will; you're a tough Alaskan girl," Asher said as he nodded his head. He gave her a confident grin, then knelt down to tie one end of the cord around her waist.

Deep in that old, musty mine, the mood was becoming tense as it got closer to the start of the climb. Mia said hesitantly, "I don't know if I can do this."

Asher looked up at the hole and replied, "You can do it. Your legs are longer than the hole is wide." He looked directly into her eyes. "Just keep your lightweight body pressed against the wall." He thought for a second and added, "Did you ever see one of those Jean-Claude Van Damme movies where he would hide from the bad guys? He would be up near the ceiling basically doing the splits."

She sank her body to one side, putting her hands on her hips, and said, "I'm not doing the splits up there."

"I know, but it's the same concept. It's pressure. You'll have to walk or scoot your way up. Ready?"

She looked up as her heart began to beat faster. "Not really. Tell me why we didn't dig ourselves out at the entrance again?"

"The other bad guy, who also has a gun, is waiting for us to dig ourselves out."

"Right..."

Still staring up at the small hole glowing with the blue sky, he knew she was stalling. "Okay, let's get this over with."

Asher bent down for her to step on his back. She wobbled, trying to keep her balance as he stood. Mia reached up, balancing herself, and touched the ceiling. She found herself in the vertical shaft as she released an anxious breath.

She stretched one foot up to a wall and braced herself with her arms. She pressed her back up against the opposite wall and locked her body across the width of the hole as Asher had explained. Then she slowly inched her way up. Asher watched attentively, standing directly below her, ready to catch her if she fell. After several feet, she rested and said, "I think I got it." Just then, a rock in the wall under one of her feet shifted. For a split second, she lost her balance, but she immediately tensed her muscles, which pressed her tighter against the walls. Small pieces of rocks and dirt fell as she called out, "Look out!"

Asher dodged the debris and heard the pieces hit the tunnel floor. "Are you all right?" he called.

"Yeah, just lost my footing for a second."

"You're doing great, Miss Alaska. Just wait until everyone finds out what you've been through. They're going to want their beauty queen to be governor."

She laughed, trying not to be scared, but Asher could hear the fear in her voice. He decided to change the conversation to distract her a bit from the grueling task before her. "You know, I told you about my fiancée, who's no longer in the picture, but you haven't said a word about all the men in your life."

"There's not much to say," she said, keeping her focus on the task at hand.

"Why not? It's obvious any man in his right mind would chase after you."

Mia raised her voice as she climbed higher. "Remember where I grew up. There wasn't a guy my age for two hundred miles."

"When you were in college, didn't you meet anyone?"

Mia paused for a second as she struggled to get around an area that was bulging out. On the side of the protrusion, she was able to sit on it somewhat and take a breather. She resumed with some hesitation, "I met a few guys and dated a bit, but once they found out I had cancer and had attempted suicide…" There was a distinct pause that Asher readily understood as she finished, "They would lose interest and drift away like there was something wrong with me."

Keeping his gaze toward Mia as she looked down, Asher replied, "There is something wrong with you." He paused for dramatic effect and finished, "You're hanging out with me, the crazy one from 23C."

They shared a comfortable laugh with the feeling there was more to come in this new friendship. "Besides," he added, "I'm stuck with you in this mine unless you can make it to the top, Miss Alaska!"

"I'm getting there, and when I do…," this time she paused, finishing, "that will be number three."

"Still keeping count, I see. That's okay. I'll let you win here and there just to keep you in the game." He let out a short laugh.

"Oh, so you're letting me win?"

"You're a lady, and I'm a gentleman. What else am I to do?" He knew that would light her up a little.

Sternly, she replied, "We'll see about that!" She double-timed her speed as she neared the top.

He smiled, watching her distance herself from the dark pit and knowing she needed that little mental boost. Then he remembered that he needed to pile rocks to stand on in order to get himself high enough to start his climb. Scouring the ground for large rocks, Asher used his good arm to roll or lift several into place.

After an exhausting climb, Mia finally crawled out to freedom and stood up. Raising her arms in victory, she looked down, peered into the pit, and yelled, "I made it! You look tiny down there, Asher."

"That won't last long. Once I get up there, I'll be the one looking down on you."

She cupped her hands, saying loudly, "Very funny."

"Okay, lower the loose end of the parachute cord that's tight around your waist. I'll tie one backpack to the cord, and you can pull it up. Don't let it touch the ledge on the edge up there. The rocks could cut it."

She straddled the hole and pulled straight up on the cord. Eventually, the first backpack reached her. Repeating with the second pack, her hands and arms were starting to become extremely tired and sore. Once the second pack was up, she dropped the cord into the hole again, and Asher tied it around his waist.

The only items he still had with him were his knife that was secured in its sheath on his hip, his spear, and Rudy's flashlight. He decided to leave behind the spear. After teetering up onto the pile of rocks, almost half of his body filled the hole. "Okay, pull!" he yelled. Trying not to use his bad shoulder, Asher slowly worked his way into the chimney-like hole. Mia pulled, giving him a little relief from his weight.

He was able to secure himself in the hole and braced himself against the walls. Here he used the strength in his back, core, and legs to steady himself. He took a moment to rest his aching shoulder before shouting up to Mia, "You can stop pulling. I've got it now. Just keep the cord tight so I don't get tangled up in it."

"Okay," she responded. "How's your shoulder doing?"

Not wanting to give her the real answer, he said, "It's okay, but this is going to be a lot harder than I thought."

"Oh, please! If a girl can do it, so can a big, tough guy like you."

They smiled at each other through the dimly lit escape hatch, knowing she was feeding him the same encouragement he gave her.

Because he was larger (and injured), he was quite clumsy at scaling the walls. It was taking Asher longer, and he had only scaled about fifteen feet up the hole when, out of nowhere, he heard Mia. She screamed and cried out, "Let me go!" followed by a man's voice, saying, "Calm down."

Asher's stomach sank. Looking up the hole, which instantly seemed a mile long, he felt completely helpless.

"Hello down there." The man peeked down the hole, trying to see Asher as he weaved his head back and forth.

"Let her go!" Asher yelled up. "You don't need her."

"You're mistaken, my friend. I do need her." The man pulled Mia to him by her hair as she shrieked out in pain.

"Where's the gold, big guy?"

"If I tell you, will you let her go?" Asher quickly replied.

"Of course. What do I need from a beautiful woman like this?" He leaned over, smelled her hair, and gave her a kiss on the forehead.

Asher thought he was going to be sick. Tension and fear distracted him momentarily in the cramped opening. He knew that it was his idea that had gotten her into this situation. A rush of anger overcame him as he roared, "Get your hands off her!"

"My friend, you are in no position to be making demands."

"Let her go, and I'll tell you where the gold is."

"Don't play any games." He let Mia go, pulled out his handgun, and pointed it at her.

"No, please don't shoot her!"

"It's up to you. Where's the gold?"

Asher was painfully tired as he continued to brace himself against the walls, but he looked up the hole and said, "It's in my backpack!"

"Get it out for me, Miss Alaska. Yeah, I know who you are." Mia looked at him, surprised. She reached for the leather bag in the pack and showed it to him. "Open it up, and let me see."

Apprehensively, she untied the heavy bag and opened the top. She showed the shining gold-colored rocks to him, trying to keep her distance. She didn't want him to examine it too closely.

"There it is! You know, both of you have wasted a lot of my time and really screwed things up. And a couple of my people are dead because of you." Willie paused and inhaled deeply. He thought out loud, "What am I supposed to do with you now?" He spat, raising his voice.

"You've got the gold. Just leave us alone!" Asher yelled up.

"It's not that easy. You see, I can't trust you two now that you've seen me and my plane."

It just occurred to Mia as she cried, "You! You're the guy who almost hit my plane and then crashed it!"

"Yeah, well, you were supposed to have burned up with it, but that guy messed everything up and came to your rescue," he said, pointing the gun down the hole.

Now Mia was getting angry. She retied the leather bag tightly and stepped forward, slamming it into the guy's chest. She looked him squarely in the face and said, "Get out of here."

Willie backhanded her across the face and sent her tumbling to the ground. She flinched in pain. Her face already ached from when she was hit previously.

"Leave her alone, or I'm going to—" Asher was interrupted mid-sentence.

"Or you're going to do what? Say goodbye to your girlfriend because you're not leaving your grave. Oh, by the way, thanks for the black smoke coming out of the ground here. I almost gave up on you and started walking away down below, but then I saw your smoke signal."

He picked up a heavy basketball-sized rock and dropped it down the hole as Mia screamed, "Look out, Asher!"

Asher watched everything happening in slow motion. The little bit of light from above was growing fainter as a black object fell rapidly toward him. He didn't want the rock to smash directly down on top of him, so he let go of the wall. He caught the oversized rock mid-fall like a human catcher's mitt. His body twisted around in midair and smashed down on the rock pile below. The rock in his arms hit first, then one side of his midsection. He cracked a couple of ribs, and his head bounced off a rock.

He bellowed in excruciating pain and rolled onto his back, trying to catch his breath. His brain was scrambling around as it tried to refocus. The echo of his painful cry finally dissipated through the mine when he heard Mia yelling, "No! Get your hands off of me!"

He could tell there was a struggle going on between them as Willie told her, "Calm down and stop fighting me. This is going to happen, no matter what." The tone of her scream changed to true horror. Willie's voice mimicked her fear, but it wasn't because of her; it was because of something else.

The roar of a giant animal overwhelmed all sounds as Asher lay helpless, imagining what was happening. Gunshots rang out, and screams made their way hauntingly down into the dark tomb of the mountain…to Asher.

CHAPTER 15

Asher painfully inched himself off the pile of rocks and onto the floor while his head was spinning frantically. He lay on his back, looking up into the narrow passageway that was supposed to lead to freedom. He called out helplessly, over and over again, for Mia. But the stabbing agony of his broken ribs and the throbbing pain in his shoulder kept the volume of his voice to barely more than a whisper.

After a while, he found himself just listening and watching for something, anything, good or bad, but nothing revealed itself. It was so quiet that he couldn't tell if anyone, including himself, was still alive. There was no movement or sounds of any kind, so he asked himself, *Am I dead? Are we all dead?*

As Asher cleared his thoughts and released all reasoning, his physical pain mysteriously disappeared, including his broken ribs and the bullet hole in his shoulder. Even the hard dirt and rocky floor he rested on were no longer painful. He wasn't hot or cold, and his body seemed to be weightless. Only the slow rhythmic motion of his chest rising and falling with each shallow breath was evidence that there was still life inside him.

Asher didn't know exactly when, but he eventually fell asleep in this peaceful state. Being unconscious opened a photo album in his mind, and he had a view of the past couple of years. It started with the crushing tackle that injured his knee and the two surgeries that followed.

His dad's angry face appeared after Asher hurt himself. He heard the lectures that followed: if he had run a different way, it wouldn't have happened. His mind moved on in time. During physical therapy, he did not heal fast enough. Again, his dad demanded that Asher put more effort into it to get back onto the field as quickly as possible.

The scene and atmosphere suddenly changed. He saw a collage of dozens of pictures. They were the faces of all the doctors, nurses, and physical therapists who had helped him. They all spoke at once, their voices jumbled but seemed to be saying, "You're going to be all right, Asher. We'll help you get back on your feet, and you'll be better than ever." The impression of these smiling faces and kind words filled him up like helium in a balloon.

Switching now to his dad's funeral, he watched the preacher talk about his father. Asher couldn't hear a word the preacher was saying while he sat in the front row of the sanctuary, only a few feet from his deceased father. Suddenly, his dad sat up in the coffin, dressed in a suit, his hair neatly combed and makeup all over his face. He twisted his head sideways and looked directly at Asher, saying, "Look what you've done! You messed up and failed again. This time you got Mia killed."

Lying on the ground of the cool, damp mine, Asher awoke from his nightmare with a shocking inhale. He opened his eyes, looking around, but was unable to move his head. Soon, his eyes focused up into the hole in the ceiling. The hole now looked white as clouds passed over in the sky. Hypnotized by the small light from the opening above, his inner ear awakened to a soothing and loving voice. "Asher, My son, My way is simple and full of riches, more than you could ever imagine. You must choose one of two paths in your life. One leads to darkness, pain, and loneliness. But more importantly, you will be separated from Me and My love, which will echo for eternity.

"The other path is the Light and Truth of this world. It's the only path that gives comfort, rest, hope, and My endless love. Down this path, life's pain and suffering will be viewed by you through Me, giving you courage, peace, hope, and understanding. If you go down this path, the true desires of your heart will be revealed as I walk with you. If you do not choose this path, our relationship will be one of no consequence because you will always have another god before Me. That god will be you and your selfishness."

Asher didn't push against the voice but questioned peacefully in thought, *If you're really God, what am I doing wrong?*

"You must stop walking backward in life."

I don't understand.

"You are constantly looking at your past."

But my past is my life? Asher wondered, puzzled.

"It is not your whole life, and you have wrongly made it your future. You are allowing your painful past to define and influence who you are today. You will never grow, and you will continue to live in the misery you created in your mind and heart. Let go, turn around, and move forward from the past."

Asher responded with frustration. He was still thinking through the conversation as he lay on his back. *How am I supposed to let go and move forward with everything that has happened, especially now that Mia is dead?*

"I will take care of it for you. All you must do is accept My Son, Jesus, as your Lord and Savior. Tell Him you are sorry for the wrong things you have done. He died to take care of them for you. Then openly turn away from your past and face Him, the

Light and Truth of this world, and He will fill you with His glory, the Holy Spirit."

The past relationship with his dad was painful, but he felt a responsibility to hang on to it.

The profound and comforting voice continued, "I am not asking you to forget your dad but to turn around and let Me be your Father. I made you; I know you better than you know yourself. Follow My Son, Jesus, and you will finally experience peace, hope, joy, and true fatherly love."

Asher took a few moments to reflect on his life and everything that God had just said. It was the total opposite of what his life had been, what his life was, and what direction it was going. He knew he didn't have peace or hope in anything, let alone joy or memories of a loving father.

Asher knew he was lost, having been gravely entombed in all these areas of his life. Depleted of energy, fight, and ambition, he finally surrendered all of himself—mind, body, and soul—to God and decided to follow the new path presented to him.

Just then, an image from a couple of mornings ago made complete sense. He had been lying in the red tent, looking up at a depiction of two different roads crossing each other. A sensation of peace he had never felt before swept through his body as the Spirit of Jesus now permeated Asher's heart like brilliant beams of sunlight. He breathed deeper, and his mind and muscles relaxed. The light coming from the hole above him had darkened. Storm clouds formed, and raindrops started falling on him.

Asher lifted his arm to block the rain that was coming in from the hole, but it didn't help. He spoke up, "Are You serious? I turn to follow Your path, and now it's raining?"

"Mia is alive, but she needs your help." The tone was one of urgency, and the words took Asher by surprise.

With a surge of energy, Asher lifted his head and gingerly moved his body out of the way of the rain. He groaned and grimaced as he leaned up against the rock wall, repeating, "She's alive. She's alive."

His ribs, shoulder, and forehead were screaming in pain as he looked around for his spear. Spotting it, he awkwardly stood up, grabbed it, and rested his weight on it. He checked his pocket for Rudy's small flashlight, pulled it out, and turned it on. He spoke into the now lit-up tunnel, "Oh, thank You. It's not broken." This time he knew exactly who those words were for.

He surveyed the area and looked back up the hole. Asher concluded that he would not be able to make it up this chimney. He had to go back to the main entrance and dig his way out.

He shined the light back down the black tunnel from where he and Mia had come. He continued to lean on his spear with one hand for support. He was hunched over at an angle, holding his ribs with his other hand. He was physically broken and weaker than he had ever been in his life, but it didn't matter. Asher no longer had his backpack full of survival gear; his food, water, and tools had gone up through the hole to Mia. This made him even more vulnerable and helpless than ever, but it never crossed his mind. There was something different about him. All he could think about was getting to Mia.

He also felt intense relief. The heavy and invisible anchor he had been dragging around from the past was much lighter. He was feeling freedom for the first time. He was free from the burden of pleasing his dad, free from the demoralizing way his dad talked to him, and free from those words being stuck in his head. But most of all, he felt released to finally dream for himself. It gave him energy and excitement to remember the smiling faces and encouraging words of the doctors, nurses, and therapists. How they had helped him physically and mentally recover kept dancing around in his mind's eye.

Asher worked his way back through the mine, slowly moving himself around obstacles. His mind kept him busy with this new, profound reality. He remembered the different visions and conversations he had had with Rudy and Mia over the past few days that had led him to where he was right now.

As Mia came to mind, he sped up, knowing he had to get to her. He went through scenarios of what might have happened and cringed at the sounds of her last screams. They echoed in his head, and he knew full well that she had been hurt. It made him sick to think that he had put her in danger. Burning the slipper's rubber sole to find an exit had been his idea…

Right now, though, he was on a mission to get to her, so he didn't dwell too much on it. He had no perception of time, but it seemed to take forever to finally get back to their dead fire. Picking up the pace, he made it to the pile of rocks that had collapsed from the ceiling. The rocks were large, some even the size of boulders. Standing at the pile, he could feel a breeze coming faintly from somewhere between the rocks. He shined the light and felt with his hand for the spot the air was coming in. He stopped for a moment, watching the beam of light. There were faint puffs of what looked like smoke, but it was pure white. *What is that?* he wondered.

Bending down, he smelled it. It wasn't smoke but rather something refreshing. With his good hand, he picked up one of the medium-sized rocks, where the faint white mist was seeping through. Several rocks suddenly slid down, making the opening bigger. More of the white stuff slithered in as he started picking more rocks off the pile. He worked until there was a good-sized hole on top of the pile near the ceiling.

The white mist became back-lit with sunlight, and Asher could tell it stopped raining. The mountain outside was engulfed in thick cloud cover. He stepped back and watched the fog drift in and travel down the mine. All he could think about in that moment as he laughed to himself were the words of his new friends here in Alaska, talking about living in the Cloud of Glory.

He carefully wormed his way through the hole, and once he was outside, he stood painfully and gingerly in amazement. The fog was so thick that he couldn't see more than a couple of feet in front of him.

"My glory will direct your steps from now on, son. Trust in the Truth and Light of this world, even if it is painful or you don't understand. You will always be safe, no matter what happens."

Asher soaked in the words that were softly spoken to him. He relished being in the open, no longer imprisoned in the dark, claustrophobic tomb of the mine.

Gently taking a few deep breaths of the fresh air, he had not realized how different the air in the tunnel of darkness had been until now. Asher investigated the direction he thought he needed to go up the mountain to find Mia. He still couldn't see more than a couple of steps in front of him, but he started walking across the flattened area nonetheless. He walked until the undisturbed mountain slope came into view.

Following the upward climb, he tried to guess the distance on the outside compared to the distance they had traveled inside the mine. He was determining just how far up he had to walk to reach Mia. Asher plodded along weakly with the spear as a walking stick. He kept his head down, watching each step he took. That was all he could see. This only reminded him of the conversation he had with Rudy about keeping your eyes on the trail in front of you so you don't get distracted or lost.

Not too far up the slope, Asher stopped. He was jolted in shock, bringing the spear into a protective position. Adrenaline was surging through his body.

Holding his breath and not making any sounds or movements, he waited for something to happen. He was staring at a giant grizzly bear lying on the ground only three feet in front of him. Its long arms, the size of Asher's thighs, were stretched out. Its four-inch claws were protruding and pointing at him. With brownish tan fur that puffed out all over, the bear's head was the size of two basketballs.

The bear, however, wasn't moving or making a sound. Asher thought it was sleeping, but he remained at the ready to fight. After a closer look, Asher saw that blood had been draining from the bear's nose and mouth. Becoming bolder, he decided to poke the bear to get a reaction. Slowly, he reached out and jabbed it in the nose, then jumped back, just in case. He braced himself for the worst, but nothing happened.

Asher relaxed a bit, stepped closer to the bear again, and saw blood spots in several areas. He thought to himself, *Well, at least the guy killed it*. Then an incredible thought rang in his head, *If the guy hadn't showed up with a gun when he did, Mia and I would have both been killed by this monster!*

Another thought ran through his mind. A couple of days ago, Mia had said, "God works everything for the good of those who love Him, according to His purpose."

What looked like a tragedy was worked out by the Cloud of Glory, he thought.

Asher turned his eyes up the hill, saying under his breath, "Please still be alive, Mia." This hope pushed him to resume hiking.

It seemed like he had been climbing forever, and he started to question if he simply missed her and the hole in the ground. Suddenly, his eyes ran across a backpack right in front of him. He hesitated to look elsewhere, scared at what he might see next. Gaining courage, he slowly looked up and took a step forward. He saw dark blood splatters on the bare ground, everywhere. With each step, the scene expanded, and a man's lifeless body came into view. Stepping around the body, the gore and what was left of him made Asher vomit. The man's stomach area was ripped open, and his insides oozed out through his torn clothes. The top of his head was crushed in, looking like a pear. Distinct holes had been left behind from the bear's huge teeth. Staring a little closer, he realized that parts of the body were completely twisted in opposite directions. The feet were facing one direction, and the upper torso was facing the other.

He didn't want to see anymore; the horror made him dizzy. Then, he heard a soft moan coming through the fog.

Catching his breath, he whirled around. "Mia, I'm here," he whispered back.

Following the sound, he moved quickly and almost stumbled over her. She lay balled up in a protective fetal position with her back to him. Gently kneeling next to her, Asher delicately reached out to her shoulder. "Mia, I'm here."

Mia flinched, folding her body tighter and bringing her knees closer to her chest. Her arms were up, covering her face as her fingers wove together around the back of her neck.

He spoke again softly, "Mia, it's Asher." With no response, he walked around in front of her. He ducked his head toward her to get a line of sight to her eyes. He wasn't able to clearly see her face, so he reached out gently and touched her arm. He talked to her, but she didn't respond. It occurred to him that she might be in shock. Her body was shivering, and her clothes were soaked from the rain earlier.

This time, he held her arm harder and pulled on it, but she refused to relax. So he began talking louder, thinking he wasn't getting her attention. "Mia, you're all right. Let me help you." She moaned again as though she heard something, so he repeated himself.

When he pulled on her arm again, she slowly released her grasp.

"Mia, you're safe now."

As though she were waking up from a dead sleep, Mia tried to open her eyes and mumbled something.

Asher was unable to understand her. He pulled her arm down, revealing her face, and his eyes went wide in disbelief at the damage the bear had done. Asher tried to relive the horrifying scene that had taken place here when he was helplessly down in the mine. His thoughts then turned to how this could affect the rest of her life. He forced himself to clear his mind, knowing her health and welfare were more important right now.

"Mia, can you hear me?" He gently touched the bottom of her chin, trying to lift it up so they could see eye to eye. However, there was so much blood that even if she did open her eyes, she probably couldn't see.

You've got to control the bleeding, Asher told himself, forgetting his own pain, as he stood up and frantically searched for the backpacks. Finding them, he opened his next to her and pulled out a bottle of water and his last long-sleeved, flannel shirt. Pouring water on the shirt, he started to wipe the blood away slowly. He exposed four long, deep slashes down one side of her face. They started at her forehead, missing her eye, and angled down to her right ear. Asher hesitated for a second when he saw that only half of her ear was attached to the scalp.

The blood seeping from the wounds had apparently slowed down. Asher wasn't sure if it was from lack of blood or from the pressure Mia had inadvertently put on herself in the protective fetal position. She had squeezed her head and face very tightly.

The cleaner her head became, the more Mia began to gradually come out of her state of shock. Asher tenderly tried to move her from her protective position. He was trying to inspect her for other wounds when he noticed a large part of her shirt was blood-soaked in the front and back. This blood had nothing to do with the damage to her face.

He needed to find the source and cautiously pulled back the collar of Rudy's shirt that she had been wearing. He examined her back and shoulder area, looking for damage, and then did the same on her front side. Puncture wounds dotted her shoulder. He deduced the bear had bitten down on her shoulder. He relaxed a bit, realizing that no arteries had been punctured. His mind's eye saw the scene, watching the grizzly standing tall as it roared over its prey. It then swiftly attacked, clamping down with its powerful teeth onto her shoulder. She probably screamed out more in fear than in pain.

The scene, in his mind, showed her being tossed away by the beast that then attacked Willie, but not before slapping Mia across her face with its long, jagged, sharp claws. Asher blinked away the shocking depiction, trying not to get sick again.

Mia mumbled, "Asher."

The sweet sound of her voice made his heart leap as he knelt closer to her face. "I'm here, Mia."

Without moving and with her eyes still closed, she asked, "Is it gone?"

"Yes, it's dead."

"Where's the man who grabbed me?"

He paused, knowing it was good news, but he didn't want her to be emotionally tormented by all the gore, so he simply said, "He's gone."

She seemed to relax her body and opened herself up. She rolled to her back, saying, "I hurt really bad."

"I know."

She raised her arm to touch her face, but he seized her by the wrist before she could feel it.

"Don't touch your face."

"Why? What's wrong?"

Asher didn't want to tell her about the serious condition of her face. He tried to think of a way to let her down easily, but nothing came to mind, so he said directly, "The bear clawed you across your face. It's been bleeding a lot, and I need to clean it out, then stop the bleeding."

Mia released a deep and agonizing cry. Living in Alaska all her life, she had seen many pictures of people who had been mauled by bears. What they looked like afterward was never pretty. Giant tears welled up as her mouth opened again with sounds of torture piercing her soul.

Asher remembered the agony he had envisioned earlier, but this was much worse. Seeing it affected him so much; he wanted to take that agony away from her, but there was no way he could. He sat patiently beside her, wrapping his arms around her and letting the emotional pain pour out. Fog enveloped them on the mountainside, concealing them from the world in this moment of heartbreak and tragedy.

Once Mia calmed down, Asher was ready to attend to her injuries. He pulled out his pain meds, deciding the hard stuff would be best for her situation. It would not only relieve the physical pain but also calm her and put her to sleep. He raised her head, saying, "Put this in your mouth and drink some water."

She did it without questioning him, but Asher couldn't help himself as he cringed. He watched her move her mouth as her ripped skin separated in several places. He could see the long strips of exposed tissue when she opened her mouth.

He paused his medical care for a moment, keeping pressure on the areas still bleeding to give the pill time to take effect. Once he saw her relax, he went back to work.

He cleaned out all of the puncture wounds, applied antiseptic cream, and stitched up each hole on her shoulder. He looked through all the backpacks, even Willie's torn-up one, to determine how much gauze and tape were available (plenty) before adhering them over the stitches. He hadn't been sure how much they still had since a lot had been used up on Rudy and on his own shoulder wound.

After finishing with the puncture wounds, Asher delicately cleaned the long gouges in Mia's face. He then applied a healthy layer of antiseptic and carefully positioned the flaps of skin into their original positions. Next, he took a fat roll of gauze and cut up several wide strips the length of her cuts, and he layered them together. He formed a thick, wide pad and covered the entire injury across her face and forehead. He wrapped gauze around her head several times to hold the padded layer firmly against the skin, bandaging in the same direction as the claw marks. He secured it all with layers of tape.

When he was finished with the wounds, he adjusted her body into a comfortable sleeping position and covered her with Rudy's coat to warm her up while she slept.

While everything was out, he removed his shirt and worked on his own shoulder. The only first aid he provided for his ribs was a pain-killing cream on his side. Then he gently wrapped a long, elastic wrap, which would normally be used for an ankle or knee sprain, around his chest several times to give him a little relief.

After Asher put his shirt back on, he also pulled on a jacket. He sat down, facing downhill, with his knees propped up and his arms resting on them. He lay his head down; he was tired. He hadn't been paying attention to his surroundings ever since he first began to doctor Mia. The clouds had risen higher in the sky.

He raised his head and looked out into the valley from where he sat atop the mountain. The scene was lush with varying shades of vegetation below and the river meandering through it. As he scanned from left to right, his eyes stopped abruptly. Over his right shoulder, on the slope of the mountain, he stared at several white spots.

It took a minute for him to get his mind to register what he was looking at less than a hundred yards away. Then it hit him when one of the white spots moved: a small herd of Dall sheep, just like the ones Rudy had pointed out on their flight in, had been watching him.

The moment was surreal, a limitless feast for the eyes. The prominent colors of the plant life mixed perfectly with the design of the landscape. The smooth color of the sky and the silky white clouds that hovered above balanced it all out. The blue sky began to pierce mystically through the billows of heavenly fog as it stirred, making way for the bright and warm rays of the sun.

The family of Dall sheep stood firm as an older ram's full, majestic, curled horns crowned him king of the mountain.

Asher felt, in that moment, that he had been blind his entire life. For the first time, he felt like he was seeing everything for what it truly was and not as figments of his imagination.

Eventually, the Dall sheep moved on to graze in peace. Feeling rested and warmer, Asher looked at the scene around the mine chimney and sighed, asking himself, *What do I do now?*

"She needs refuge, son. The care that is needed is the strength and wisdom that you do not have. All I ask of you is to love her through it. Cry with her, laugh with her, and I will work it all for the good. Be patient and watch closely for the safe steps of passage I will lay down before you. For My fingerprints will be all over everything, and when you start living in the Cloud of Glory, then and only then will My fingerprints be revealed to you."

Silence overtook the mountain as Asher sat, trying to put the pieces together of everything that had happened since he came to Alaska. It was overwhelming. He turned to Mia as she rested peacefully. He thought about her and when or even if this relationship was going to be a permanent one. Would she have anything to do with him since he had gotten her hurt and almost killed?

The silence was broken by the sound of an eagle's wings overhead as one flew extremely close. It glided above, coming up from behind and out into the valley. Perfectly and on cue in front of Asher, the eagle screeched its alarm for all in the valley to hear, forewarning that it was coming.

He watched the magnificent bird with its wide wings stretched out. The eagle seemed to barely be moving as the invisible thermals lifted it up. It soared effortlessly into its hunting grounds.

A memory came to his mind, and it was about a bird, an eagle, in fact. Thinking back, he remembered hearing something a Sunday school teacher had read in the Old Testament. It had been about how trusting God gives us strength to soar like eagles or something like that. He shook his head, trying to remember, and grinned at the irony.

He stood up and stretched out as much as his damaged body would allow. He thought about their next move to safely get to Bettles. Anticipating a long night ahead, the first thing he did was go through all the backpacks. He selected only the essentials they would need to survive and condensed them all down to one pack.

After finishing, he bent down, and with his good arm, though he struggled, he lifted Mia. He carried her as she slept, with the backpack in his bad hand, and painfully made his way down the mountain. They returned to the flattened area next to the entrance of the mine where he was to make camp for the night.

CHAPTER 16

Asher crouched down in agony as he placed Mia on the ground. He remained in that position for a moment, exhausted. After he caught his breath and mustered all the energy he could, he opened the backpack. On top of everything inside was Willie's handgun. Asher removed it. He had reloaded the gun when he had taken the box of bullets from the guy's backpack. The next thing he took out was a bivouac tent, which had also come from Willie's pack (but had originally been in Nora's pack before it was stolen).

Asher set up the low-lying, waterproof, compact tent that was a foot or so wider and longer than a large sleeping bag. It was three feet high at the entrance but sloped down to a foot off the ground at the other end. Putting his extra-large sleeping bag in the small fabric house, he could not wait to get Mia settled in and fall asleep himself.

It was not easy getting her into the tent, but when he did, she looked comfortable as he laid her on her good side. Checking her bandages, Asher thought they were holding up well. A little blood had seeped through here and there, but he thought she would be okay.

Back outside, he removed his newly replenished first aid kit, courtesy of Willie's pack once again. He also removed a snack, the next-to-last bottle of water, his flashlight with new batteries, his stocking cap, and Rudy's coat. He tossed the items into the miniature tent off to one side. He then squeezed himself in. He pulled the backpack in and laid it down sideways at the entrance. Finally, he zipped the bivouac door closed.

Resting on his elbow, he got out a medium-strength pain pill for himself and downed it, along with a few bites of beef jerky. He put his stocking cap on and gratefully opened the sleeping bag. He carefully raised Mia's head and pulled a portion of the backpack under her for her to use as a pillow. Then he scooted most of himself into the bag with Mia. Just like Asher and Mia's last night in the cave, Rudy's coat acted as a blanket over Asher's exposed shoulder. They were again both in one sleeping bag. Finally able to rest, he exhaled in relief and looked up at the thin material of the tiny tent as the evening light shined through. Too tired to care and ready to get this day behind him, he shut his eyes, falling asleep immediately.

Sometime in the night, Mia jerked herself awake, screaming. She opened her good eye and only saw darkness. Something was wrapped around her, and she was unable to move. Having no clue where she was, her mind raced with the horror of her earlier encounter. She blindly fought back, frenzied.

Asher sprung up, grazing his head on the low tent roof. He was bewildered at what was going on and took a moment to collect his thoughts. He reached for Mia, trying to stop and calm her as he spouted, "Mia! Mia! It's okay. Stop moving! Quiet down!" He had to repeat himself and get more physical, clutching her hands to hold them tight.

"Where am I? What's going on?"

"Mia, it's Asher. You're okay."

"Where am I?"

"We're in a sleeping bag in a miniature tent, down at the flat spot in front of the mine."

"Where's the bear?" she shouted.

"Slow down, Mia. Everything is all right now. The grizzly's dead."

She hesitated, taking it all in as things became clearer. "My face and shoulder hurt. Was I mauled?"

Asher scooted closer to her, wincing in pain as he gently took her in his arms and said softly, "Yes."

Pausing, she laid her head down on his shoulder and started to cry. Through the tears, she asked, "Why can't I open my eye?"

"I have a pad of gauze that covers the whole side of your face, including your eye."

"Did I lose my eye?" She was trying to sound brave but waiting for the worst.

With an uplifting tone, Asher replied, "No. The bear completely missed your beautiful eye."

You could hear a sigh of relief from her, but it did not take away the emotional and physical pain. "It hurts. My face and the area around my ear are throbbing."

He didn't want to mention that her ear was only half attached.

"My back and chest feel like something is stabbing me," she continued.

He did reply to that, "That's because the bear bit down on you, along your shoulder. You have four deep holes, two in the front and two in the back. I don't know if you have any broken bones."

She inhaled quickly as it all came back to her. "That's right. I was yelling at the guy when something behind me bit into me. It shook me violently and tossed me away." She paused, trying to lift her head and look at him in the dark. "What happened to you after the guy threw the rock down the hole?"

"Before we get into that..." Asher let go of her, turning to his stash of items. He felt around for the flashlight. "You need to take another pain pill."

Getting a pill and beef jerky out, he had her swallow the medicine and eat some protein, followed by a few big gulps of water. It was painful just completing this simple task, but she managed.

Turning off the light, they both nestled back down to get somewhat comfortable again. The sleeping bag cover and coat had been off for only a few minutes, but they had begun to shiver. This night was definitely colder than the past few nights.

Asher calmly explained how he had gotten to her but did not mention his broken ribs or his encounter with God. He would leave those conversations for a later time. For now, he didn't want her worrying about him. Then they both fell fast asleep.

The sun had long since peaked over the east when Asher woke up. The wet ceiling of the tent was lying on his face. It was a strange sensation, and he could not figure out what was wrong. He slowly reached out from under the warmth of the coat and sleeping bag. He unzipped the tent a few inches and peeked outside. The world outside was a bright white. Snow had piled up a couple of inches deep, and fat snowflakes continued to drift down.

He zipped the tent back up, then swatted at the top several times. The snow slid off, causing the roof to pop back up to its original state. As he lay there awake feeling rested, his thoughts about their next moves to get to Bettles took shape. An idea from yesterday came back to him.

Slowly, he worked his way out of the sleeping bag while trying to keep Mia warm. He poked through the backpack, looking for a warm shirt and his lightweight rain jacket. Painfully, over his thick flannel shirt, Asher put on the extra shirt and rain jacket hoping this would keep him warm.

Digging back into the pack, he pulled out the final prize that he had discovered yesterday. In Willie's backpack was a satellite phone. Working his way out of the tent and zipping it back up, Asher stood stretching until the sharp, stabbing pains from his ribs almost knocked him to the ground. Holding his chest, he took shallow breaths and strode away from the tent. He turned the phone on but wasn't sure how it all worked, so he pressed a button, thinking it had another purpose. Instead, it redialed the last number that had been called. Hearing the dialing tones, Asher put the phone to his ear as someone answered, "Good morning, Willie. I didn't expect your call for another day or so."

Asher panicked slightly and almost hung up. Then, curiosity got the better of him; he wanted to figure out who was on the other end of the phone. "This isn't Willie."

There were a few seconds of silence during which Asher thought maybe the guy had hung up.

"Put Willie on the phone," the person on the other end demanded in a different tone.

"I can't."

"Why not?"

"He's..." Pausing to think about the fact that he had already said too much, he finished, "dead."

"Who's this?"

Asher was somewhere secluded and thought he had the upper hand. He, therefore, assertively answered, "My name is Asher Collins."

"Well, well, Mr. Collins. It's nice to meet you."

"Who's this?" Asher asked, changing his tone.

"That depends. We can either be friends or enemies—your choice."

"I don't understand."

"Simple, I have the parents of Miss Alaska. And how do I put this?" Acting as though he was thinking of something, the voice paused for effect before finishing, "They will suffer painfully and eventually die if we don't become friends. So you'll do what I tell you."

"You can't fool me. You have no clue where Mia's parents are."

"Really? So you want to become my enemy? Would hearing from someone you might know convince you?"

Asher could hear the phone being put down and a few harsh words being spoken in the background. Another man's voice yelled out, "Leave her alone!"

A slap rang out, and Asher heard, "Shut up, old man."

The man told the woman who had cried out in pain, "Say who you are!"

Soft whimpering came to Asher's ears, and his heart sank. "My name is Nora." Then, she had a sudden change of attitude and yelled out, "Kids, stay away! Don't do anything—!" She was cut short.

"Listen and listen carefully, Mr. Collins." The man's tone seemed friendly but was laced with evil. "Let's be friends. You do exactly as I say, and no one else needs to die up here in this icebox. Do you understand?"

Asher hesitated, trying to think of something he could say or do. He felt small and helpless as he stood there in the middle of nowhere. "Yes," he finally answered.

"Good!" the man said cheerfully. "So here's what's going to happen. By this time tomorrow, you will need to be in Bettles. When you reach the Koyukuk River, you will call me for the last time. Just before you get into Bettles, you will beach the canoe. Then, you will make your way to the airport, staying hidden in the brush, and wait for my plane. I'll be coming in from the east end of the runway. Once I'm there, you'll give me the gold you took from Willie, and I'll give you Mia's mother. Do you understand, my friend?"

"I don't know how far we are from Bettles. I don't know if we can make it by then."

"You'll make it."

"I don't even know what time it is."

"Let me see. So..." He paused to find the time before explaining, "by 10:00 a.m. tomorrow, I'll be expecting a call from you. If I don't hear from you by that time, Miss Alaska's daddy will be shot in the leg. Then, for every thirty minutes I don't hear from you, I'm going to shoot another limb until there are no more limbs to shoot. Do you understand?"

"Come on! I don't know if we can make it. I don't know how far away we are!" Asher was starting to panic.

"That's not my problem. Oh, before I forget, if you try to call for help on the phone you're holding, I'll know. My contacts in the civilized world will be monitoring the phone. They'll notify me of any other calls made from it. If you make even just one more call, I won't waste bullets. I'll start cutting off Nora's fingers, then toes, and, well, you get the idea. I'll exchange body parts for the gold. So, if your pretty little girlfriend doesn't want her mommy to be handed back in pieces, you'll do exactly what I told you. Do I make myself perfectly clear?"

"Okay, okay. We'll get to Bettles with the gold on time and not use the phone. Please don't hurt either of them." Asher brought his hand up to his forehead to wipe away the beads of sweat that had appeared.

"Good, Mr. Collins. I'm glad we came to an agreement. By the way, time started when this conversation did, so you better get into high gear." The man hung up.

Asher looked at the phone, watching it disconnect. Pushing the off button, he raised his head, bewildered, and thought, *No matter what happens, it just keeps getting worse!*

Suddenly, he wanted to kick himself. He had left the heavy leather bag of fool's gold up on the mountain, thinking he wouldn't need it anymore. It also occurred to him that he might have made a mistake by pouring out the real gold. He looked up to where he needed to return and the climb ahead. He released a sigh of regret. Turning back to the tent, he quietly unzipped it and hid the satellite phone deep in the pack.

Asher knew he couldn't tell Mia any of this. She was already suffering; she didn't need to deal with the emotional and mental complications as well. Taking a deep breath, he zipped the tent door back up and started to head back up the mountain to the hole in the ground.

"You're going to start this day without Me?"

He stopped and turned back, thinking that Mia had said something. *No*, he thought, *that wasn't her.*

"We are moving forward together, remember?" the voice reminded Asher refreshingly.

Flashes of Rudy praying before each day popped into his head. He looked upward, and his mind started jumping around, trying to find the right words. Then he finally said out loud, "Yesterday, You spoke to me in a dream or vision, and it gave me relief. I'm beginning to understand what this is between us and 'hiding in the Cloud of Glory.' I'm definitely in the dark as to what is going to happen right now. But You know everything, and my part in this…relationship is to trust You.

"I ask that You please get us to Bettles quickly so no one gets hurt." He paused, thinking of the one person in the greatest pain right now. "Mia is hurting. Please take away her pain and heal her face. Give her peace, just as You did for me inside the mine."

He stopped talking as his mind went blank. Then, he raised his hand up toward the falling snowflakes and made the sign for love. He finished with, "Until later on."

Asher opened his eyes and looked out to the valley below. The uplifting, loving voice responded, "Because you trust in Me, My strength will be in you. You will soar high on wings like eagles."

The vision of the eagle that had flown over him yesterday came to mind. It had soared powerfully through the sky, and the imagery made him feel light on his feet. A new boldness filled him and gave him courage and energy.

It had stopped snowing as he turned up the hill. Without hesitating, he started the climb. Arriving at the scene with a clear head, he looked through the packs that had been left behind one more time. This time, he also grabbed Willie's wallet from his pants for identification purposes. With a small armful of items, including the heavy bag of iron pyrite, Asher returned to Mia sooner than he had expected.

Pulling the backpack and stash of items from the small tent, he left the door open to begin waking Mia up quietly. He put another heavy dose of pain cream over his broken ribs and secured the gauze wrap once more. The bullet wound appeared redder than usual, so he applied a fresh layer of antiseptic cream on it. Then he proceeded to make a new gauze pad for Mia's face and took out a medium-strength pain pill for her. He also grabbed a couple of basic pain pills for himself.

Mia began to stir. She was still groggy from the heavy-duty medication she had taken previously, so she did not move much in the sleeping bag. Asher started to make a breakfast of freeze-dried eggs in a small aluminum pot. He added water from a bottle brought down from one of the other packs and set the pot on the burner to get it boiling. Asher knew he needed to get as much food into their bodies as possible. So he also pulled out two energy bars to keep up their strength for the walk back to the river.

While prepping breakfast, a thought hit him: *the canoe*! They didn't have a canoe anymore. He started to worry, but then it came to him: *the dead guy had one*. Relief dissolved the panic. Now the hard part would be finding it, but that could waste valuable time. Thinking about it drove him to work faster.

Before the dehydrated eggs were ready, Mia made her way out of the tent, wearing Rudy's coat. Asher came alongside her to help her out. She squinted at the bright, white landscape and held her hand up to her eye, saying, "It snowed last night."

"Yes, it did. How are you feeling?"

"Terrible. I feel like throwing up, and my entire body hurts. Then this thing..." She nervously lifted her hand to the bandage around her face and held back the emotions as another, more pressing, need took precedence. "I have to go to the bathroom."

Without hesitation, Asher withdrew a waterproof bag filled with toilet paper from the pack. He then pointed in the direction of a cluttered pile of timber where she could have her privacy.

"Thanks," she said, adding new footprints to the fresh blanket of snow as she walked away.

He quickly ate his portion of the eggs, leaving the fork in the bag, and then downed a protein bar. When Mia got back, he politely handed her a sanitary wipe. After she had finished cleaning her hands, he tried to hand her the bag of eggs. Holding her hands up, she replied, "No, I'm not hungry."

"You don't have a choice, Mia," Asher said calmly. "You must eat to have enough energy so we can finish this trip and get you to a hospital as soon as possible."

She knew he was right and ate it forcibly, doing her best not to vomit. He held out the other energy bar, thinking it would be asking too much, but she ate it. He put everything away, including the wet, folded bivouac tent and the rolled-up, semi-warm sleeping bag. He placed them in their carrying sacks and strapped them to the outside of the backpack.

Mia finished eating and drank half a bottle of water. Asher stuffed fresh snow into the nearly empty bottle, just like the one he had emptied for boiling. Putting them away, he asked her to sit on the dry backpack while he bandaged her face once more. At first, she didn't want him to touch her, thinking not only it would be too painful but also too embarrassing. Then, there was a good possibility he wouldn't want anything to do with her or her mangled face, just like all the other guys who had walked away once they knew she had cancer and had attempted suicide.

"Mia, we have to keep the wound clean so you don't get an infection. It needs to heal well. Fresh antiseptic cream and gauze will certainly help." He chose his next words carefully, knowing they could soothe her or tear her apart.

"Close your eyes," he said soothingly. She closed them as he knelt in the snow next to her. "Mia, your beauty goes far beyond looks. Our joking and bickering energize me, and the boldness of your faith gives me peace. I feel that…no, I know that being with you has helped me start to come to life. I'm a new man, and my heart has finally begun to beat with hope."

As he talked, she listened with her eyes closed. Tears formed as he slowly unraveled the gauze wrapped around her head and carefully pulled the padding off her face. It had dried together in spots, pulling on the skin. She cringed and moaned in pain. However, she kept her eyes closed the whole time. She was too scared to open them and see the reaction on Asher's face.

He could not have planned it any better. She was facing the wide-open valley blanketed with fresh snow. The sun peaked through the clouds and shot powerful and brilliant beams of crystal light that warmed the Brooks Range. "Open your eyes, Mia."

She opened them delicately and took in the mesmerizing glow. Asher could feel her relief as she viewed the valley with the eye that had been covered. For her to open both eyes to such a spectacular scene was breathtaking. This gave him an idea, and he pulled out his knife.

"Hold still while I measure this out." He held the new bandage to her face, placing his finger in the spot for her eye.

While he worked, she asked, "What does it look like? Tell me the truth." Her next words came out in a jumbled whimper, "Am I going to be ugly?"

He turned her chin so that she would look at him. "No, you're never going to be ugly. You have four claw marks the width of pencils, crossing perfectly like this." He motioned his fingers across his face, imitating the angle the bear had scratched her. She watched his eyes closely, looking for his true feelings about seeing her face, but there was nothing to be seen except a calm spirit.

He continued, attempting to be positive, "You're fortunate. The bear could've clawed right through your head. Instead, it looks like he only scratched you." He tilted her head, adding, "I think the wounds are going to heal really well. If there is any scarring, it's going to look beautiful. People get tattoos of things they like or that represent them in different ways. What better way to say, 'Hi, I'm Miss Alaska, and my tattoos are the ultimate work of art.'" He played it up and gave her a smile as though he was proud of the marks.

An emotional switch seemed to flip at these last words. She stood up and looked down on him. "You think this is funny?"

"No, you misunder—"

"This is my life right now, Asher! I'm supposed to be perfect. Now look at me!"

He understood he had gone too far, too soon. "Mia." He gently raised his hand to her good cheek and closed the gap between them. With sweet encouragement, he said, "I'm sorry. I was not making fun of you. I'm telling you that it doesn't bother me or change how I feel about you." He leaned in, softly kissing her. Then, he stepped back and motioned for her to sit. "Please sit, and let me finish bandaging you up."

She sat without saying a word as he quickly went to work. When he was done, she was able to see with both eyes because he had purposely maneuvered the bandage around it. It gave her physical and emotional relief from being confined and half-blind.

"How does that feel?" he asked.

"The pain medicine hasn't kicked in yet, but it's somewhat comfortable. Thanks for helping me see with both eyes."

"You're welcome. Now we need to go. We've got to get to the canoe as fast as we can."

"What's the rush?"

Asher caught himself in a pickle and came up with, "We both need to see doctors ASAP before we get infections. Then, we need to give Rudy a really hard time and break his other leg for the terrible trip he put me on."

Despite their pain, they both chuckled. Then, Mia stated, "We don't have a canoe."

"The dead guys have one waiting for us."

That reminded Mia as she thought for a moment about the guy who had pulled a gun on her. "Did the bear kill him?" she asked.

Asher hesitated, remembering the gory scene, and replied with a grimaced look, "Oh yeah, did it ever! His body parts were all over the place."

Mia paused for a second, looking away. Asher could almost hear her thinking. There were no emotions or remorse for the dead man. Looking back at Asher, she said sternly, "Let's get going. If we can find their canoe, it'll be better than walking up and down mountains for a few days."

Setting the pack on the top of a large rock where he had been cooking, Asher retrieved the handgun. He handed it to Mia, asking her to carry it for them. She didn't hesitate and checked it over to make sure it was loaded. She put the gun in the back of her pants like an expert, which took him by surprise at just how smoothly and calmly she behaved with a gun. He lifted the backpack to his good shoulder and buckled the hip strap, biting his lip the entire time to hold in the pain from both injuries.

Heading downhill, they slipped around in the wet snow on top of the rocks. Once they made it off the mountain, they made a beeline for where they thought the canoe would be along the river. Even though they both were hurting, they made incredible time.

After only taking one rest break, they made it back to the river and found the canoe easily. To their surprise, there was extra food, clothing, and additional supplies, along with two rifles. Mia recognized one of the rifles as her mom's—the same rifle Mia had shot many times, killing moose and caribou.

Asher pulled out a waterproof bag that was filled with toilet paper, along with disposable wipes, and told Mia he would be back in a few minutes. Mia nodded, watching him disappear into the tall willows and trees. Turning back to the river, she saw a perfect reflection of the clouds from above in a small, calm pool that barely swirled around along the shoreline.

She stared down at the beautiful scene but couldn't stop worrying about her face. The pricks of pain continually reminded her that she would probably be deformed for the rest of her life. Looking at the blurry reflection in the water only heightened her anxiety, and she actually became fearful. The idea of seeing what she looked like in the reflection was calling out to her. Mia's chin trembled, and her lips tightened as she nervously lifted her shaking hand. She unraveled the bandage; she needed to see her damaged face.

With all the wrapping in her hands, along with the wide, thick sheets of gauze that she had peeled off her face, she took a step to the edge of the mirrored pool. She looked off into the distance, across the river, and inhaled deeply. She was building courage, but she hesitated, trying to calm her nerves. Mia closed her eyes and wasn't sure if she was praying or just thinking, but she said to herself, *Please, don't let me be ugly. I don't want people to stare at me because I'm deformed and have hideous scars. I want to be the beautiful Miss Alaska.*

With eyes still closed, she went to her knees, surrendering to the new Mia, but panic was still coursing through her body.

She tilted her head down when a sudden shout came from behind her, "Mia, no!"

Every muscle in Mia's body tensed at the loud voice that broke the silence of her moment of truth.

"Don't look into the water!" Asher demanded as he ran to her side just in time and pulled her body tightly to himself so that she couldn't move.

"Let go. Let go of me!" Mia shrieked as she squirmed in his arms. "I need to see the truth!"

He held her firmly in his arms as the pain in his own body yelled for him to let go. Calmly he said, "Stop. Stop fighting, and come away from the water with me."

Her emotions suddenly flipped, and tears started streaming down her face. Her body was throbbing from all the crying. Again, agonizing scenes played through her mind of strangers giving her awkward expressions. Her face would be so grotesque that people would avert their eyes. She would be hideous.

Asher gritted his teeth, fighting his own pain, and lifted Mia to her feet. She had bowed her head so he wouldn't have to look at her, but he reached his warm, weather-worn hand up, gently touching her chin. "Look at me, Mia."

She didn't move, so he gently forced her head up. She kept her gaze downward as he said softly, "Look into my eyes, Mia."

There was a pause before she reluctantly looked up at him. She saw a completely different expression than what she pictured in her head. Asher had a loving smile, eyes squinting in a kind sort of way, staring directly at her. Through his eyes, he was telling her, *You are the most beautiful woman in the world.*

Then, he voiced those exact words aloud, and she stopped a moment to let what he said soak in. He proceeded to take the gauze and wrap from her hand and gently put it back on her face as he said, "What you would see now, Mia, is not what it will be when your injury has healed. I can't allow you"—he paused, unexpectantly letting her know he cared for her more than just as a friend—"to see yourself right now. It will do more harm than good."

With the bandaging complete, he tenderly cupped her face in his hands and looked deep into her tear-filled eyes. "When an artist is painting a masterpiece, he doesn't let anyone view it until he is finished. Do you know why?" Asher quickly answered his own question, "Because everyone would get a false impression of what the painting was going to be. They don't have the same vision as the artist, and that unfinished image would stay with them forever."

He wrapped his long, strong arms around her again. He wanted to give her comfort and help her feel safe. He whispered in her ear, "Miss Alaska, please promise me that you will keep the bandage on until we are safely back to civilization."

He leaned back, scanning her face, which was strewn with tears. They locked eyes, and he asked, "Promise me…?"

She struggled inside herself to rebel, but instead, she calmed down. Asher's calm, loving voice was whispering to her, asking her to trust him and to wait. It took a moment, but she nodded and gave him a faint smile. Then she watched him lean forward and slowly kiss her forehead.

Together they took a deep breath. It was as though they were waking up from a nightmare. They looked around at their surroundings as Asher said, "We better get going."

In the aluminum boat, they sat down in the same positions. Mia was happy to have a real paddle instead of the makeshift tree branch she had used in the other canoe. This helped her to refocus her attention on the task at hand. She gave a forceful stroke, propelling them forward in the water.

After several miles, they were in a good rhythm, even with the pain each was enduring. They paddled quietly until Asher said, "Mia, I truly thought I lost you again. That's two days in a row that I thought you were dead, and each time my heart stopped."

She looked back, smiling modestly on the good side of her face.

He kiddingly raised his voice, "If you do that to me again, we're finished! Do you understand? Three strikes, and you better be out permanently, or we're done!" He pulled the paddle in and gazed deeply into her eyes with a kind smile. He couldn't remove the physical pain, but he wanted to alleviate any mental and emotional pain she was feeling. He also thought a joke might lighten the mood.

"You don't scare me, 23C," she replied with a flirtatious look and turned around as they continued to drift downriver.

Several hours went by before Mia asked for a break. Asher was reluctant but knew they needed to check their bandages, take more pain pills, and eat some lunch. He had also had some quiet time while they paddled to think things through, and he knew there was no way around it—he was going to have to tell her about their time crunch. He figured that telling her sooner would probably be better than later so they would have time to prepare themselves.

He beached the canoe after finding a safe spot and looked through the items that were left in the pack. They agreed on something to eat and sat down. The sun had fully come out, and the clouds escaped somewhere unknown. The snow was gone, and the temperature was very comfortable, so they had both taken off their outer jackets.

Apprehensively but calmly, Asher broached the subject, "Two different things happened to me when I was in the mine without you."

He said it so casually that she responded without looking at him, "What were they?"

"I either fell asleep or was knocked out. Not sure which one, but nevertheless, I had a dream or vision, if you want to call it that, about God and me discussing my relationship with Him."

She stopped midchew and asked with her mouth full, "You did not!"

"Yes, I did."

"What happened?" She adjusted herself to show that she was completely focused.

"Well, he said that I had to stop walking and looking backward in life and letting those things control me. They were substituting as my god."

A slight smile started forming as she saw the direction he was going.

"And I had to choose to follow the Truth and Light of this world or take the dark path without Him." He hesitated and wrinkled his face, looking away from her as his insides stirred with emotions. "I'm beginning to understand what a relationship with Him is. The one big piece is having the Holy Spirit in my life." He looked at her directly with a smile and added, "Living in the Cloud of Glory."

She almost choked on her food with unbelievable excitement and teared up.

"What did I say?" he asked, concerned. His face went blank, having jumped to the wrong conclusion. "Is the pain coming back?"

She calmed down and said, "No, it's not that. I've been praying for a man to come into my life who would say and believe…what you just said!" She looked at him with watery eyes and asked cautiously, "Are you in my life, Asher?"

Asher raised his eyebrows. "Are you letting me in?"

Mia's eyes brightened as her muscles strained to control the giddiness that wanted to burst out and overtake her. She looked away, trying to compose herself. She then turned back confidently, answering, "I think so."

They both went quiet for a while as they basked in the clarity of where their relationship was now headed. Then Mia asked, "You said there were two things that happened in the mine without me?"

"Um, yeah, what I didn't tell you earlier was what happened when the guy threw the rock down into the hole." He hesitated.

"Yes?" She tilted her head, knowing he had been holding something very important back from her.

Deliberately, Asher said, "I fell onto the rock with this side of my body, and I may have a couple of broken ribs."

She stood up, looking down at him, and raised her voice, "You what?"

CHAPTER 17

"Why didn't you tell me, Asher? You carried the backpack with broken ribs when I could have carried it." She placed her remaining food on the pack next to her and faced him squarely.

"You've got deep puncture wounds on both sides of your shoulder. You couldn't have carried it," he pointed out, staring directly back at her.

She folded her arms, scowling as she knew he was right. "Still, you should've told me."

He grinned at her. "I knew you would react this way. I didn't tell you because too much has happened to you already, and you didn't need to be worrying about me."

He stood, reaching for one of her hands as she unfolded her arms. "This isn't what we need to be discussing right now," he said. "There's something much more important that you need to know."

By his serious tone, she knew it was important and understood he was not joking around.

"The guy who attacked you had a satellite phone in his backpack."

"That's good, right?"

"Not after the accidental first call I made." He kept his emotions controlled as he relayed the full conversation, including the part about her parents possibly being killed. He did, however, leave out the threatening, gory parts of the conversation.

She absorbed the story and then thought through everything that was happening. He could tell she was fighting the urge to become frantic about her parents being hostages, but he was impressed she was so under control. She calmly asked, "So who is this guy, and how did he find my parents?"

Asher shrugged his shoulders. "I've thought about it over and over. The only explanation that I can come up with involves the plane that was looking for us when we were making our way to the mine. There was only one person we could see, unlike the two we could see when it first flew over us, going upriver.

"They must've fixed the flat tire on the plane that almost hit your plane. Maybe one of those guys stayed behind to pick up the two who were chasing us…the same two in the canoe that originally were supposed to meet them in Bettles for the gold. As for your parents, they must've disregarded the locker they were heading to when I left them."

Mildly satisfied with the explanation, she surveyed their current location, searching for landmarks. She bent down and started to return the items they got out of the canoe, saying, "We need to get going. There's a lot of river to go down before tomorrow morning."

He paused, shocked by her calm reaction, but was greatly encouraged and relieved she didn't break down.

Silently and as quickly as possible, they collected their supplies and packed their bags. They both got into the canoe, and Mia started to press off from shore when Asher interjected, "Are we forgetting something?"

She looked toward land and didn't see anything. "I don't think so…"

As she turned around to see what he was talking about, he gave her a half-smile. "This is definitely a journey we don't want to continue without talking to Him. Am I right?"

It took her a second before a smile spread across her face (until she winced in pain when she wrinkled the wounds under her bandage).

"You have more experience with this than I do. Would you pray? I'd like to hear you."

They closed their eyes, and she prayed for her parents, for their trip downriver, for everything to work out, and for no one to get hurt. Just before she finished, she paused. In the far distance, she thought she heard something out of place. She waited a few seconds but didn't hear the sound again, so she finished talking to God as they both said, "Until later on."

"Did you hear something, Asher?" she asked worriedly.

"Yeah, I thought I did, but it was so faint I thought maybe I was just hearing things. Then you stopped talking to listen too."

"What do you think it sounded like?"

He looked back in the direction he believed the sound had come from and said, "I don't know. But if I were to guess, it kind of sounded like a wolf howling or something."

"That's what I was thinking. I hope a pack isn't following us. We're leaving a bloody trail. They can smell it from over a mile. Let's get going."

"I agree, but from what Rudy showed me after a few days here, we'll be safe as long as we're in the water." He was remembering the cow teaching her calf to get into the water to keep the killers away from them.

They pushed off, getting into the main current. Now on a mission together, the canoe seemed to move faster as they put more effort into it. Occasionally, they gave their arms a rest and continued to keep up on pain meds when it became too much for them to handle. Asher often found himself lightheaded and took each rest period to close his eyes, take slow breaths, and pray for strength. His ribs plagued him as he sought to paddle hard and effectively. At times, it was difficult for him to even breathe. When he would exert himself, he was unable to inhale deeply.

As late evening came, the wind picked up dramatically, clouds came in swiftly, and the temperature dropped. They figured snow would be coming again.

Mia was feeling comfortable with the miles they had put in today, so she told Asher that the Koyukuk River was down about a couple of miles and they should easily make the deadline. They made camp a little way from the river under a small clump of short trees. The wind had gained speed, making it difficult to cook a hot meal, but they managed. After eating quickly, they got out of the wind and slid into the bivouac tent.

Asher's shoulder had been getting hotter as the day went on and was throbbing with pain. He took a hard look at his bullet hole while Mia was turned the other way. The skin around the hole had become a darker red, and he saw milky-colored seepage.

Putting a healthy amount of antiseptic cream over it and covering it back up with gauze, he tried not to think about what was happening. He knew it had become infected, and soon a fever would start.

They snuggled up together as before while the wind flapped the fabric material like a flag. Sharp, snapping sounds gave it a haunting feel. Mia and Asher lay there together silently, knowing it was going to be a long night.

Asher looked up while it was somewhat still light outside and broke the silence, "About tomorrow and the exchange of the gold: the plane will be at the end of the runway. I've been going over and over the many scenarios that could happen, and I think it would be best if we consider the worst case."

"And what's that?" she asked, without emotion, trying to give her body a rest after the hard day of rowing through pain.

"Do you remember what the guy at the mine said to us?"

"Not really, it happened so fast. He grabbed my hair and jerked my head around while he pointed the gun at me."

"He said he couldn't trust us. We knew too much. Then, he told me I was in my grave and threw the rock down. He didn't think twice when he tried to kill both of us."

She didn't say a word but waited for him to explain what he had planned.

"We have to believe the man tomorrow is going to kill all of us once we've seen him and know what's going on. That would include your mom, your dad, you, and me. He'll leave us all dead at the end of the runway while he easily gets away."

"But…he's getting away with a bag of fool's gold," she said with a frown.

Asher smirked at the thought. "Can you picture the look on his face when he goes to sell it and finds out what it really is?"

Mia nodded in agreement, then asked, "So what do you have in mind?"

"Well, there's no way I'm going to let you near that plane."

"You're not leaving me out; those are my parents."

"I know, but…the guy spoke with me on the phone and told me what I was supposed to do, and none of it included you."

"Still, I need to be there for them."

"You will, just in a different way. What I need you to do…is be my sniper."

"Your what?"

"You said one of those rifles is your mother's and you've shot it many times."

"Yeah."

"So…when we get there, we'll wait for his plane to arrive. I'll be in the bushes where he told me to be. Then, you'll get into position somewhere near the river's edge. Stay hidden, parallel to the end of the runway, where you'll have a clear shot."

The wind continued to blow outside, and she said, smirking, "You've been watching too many movies. I'm not shooting anyone!"

As they looked into each other's eyes, he let her know that he was serious. He said firmly, "You may not have a choice, Mia, or we'll all be dead. I'm not willing to take that chance."

Rolling her head back, she went silent. After a few minutes, she spoke up, "Thou shall not kill is one of the Ten Commandments."

Asher heard the thoughts and worries of her heart and gently replied, "You've had a relationship with God much longer than I have, but the one thing I do know is the Ten Commandments. When I was little, my parents made me go to church, and my Sunday school teacher would give out prizes for remembering scriptures. I loved getting prizes. What the sixth Commandment says is, 'Thou shall not murder.'"

He let that sink in for her, then said, "If God had said not to kill, then your boy David killing Goliath with the power of God that you lectured to me about would have been a sin. All the other people David killed later on with his armies when God was with him would also have been a sin. One sin after another after another.

"Here's the difference: when King David got one of his higher-ranking soldiers' wife pregnant…what was her name?"

"Bathsheba."

"Yes. The great and mighty King David ordered Bathsheba's husband to the front lines of a battle. He did this knowing that Bathsheba's innocent husband would be killed. David wouldn't have to have an embarrassing confrontation with him and could just marry the woman that he had committed adultery with." He paused for effect, finishing with, "Now that's murder."

Mia was not clueless to the difference. She heard Asher's explanation and knew that God had still loved David and blessed him because he repented. He was truly after God's heart, and that helped settle her stirring stomach a little. But still, the thought of shooting someone was the last thing she ever thought of doing.

"I don't know if I can actually go through with it, Asher. How is that going to look on my resume alongside the title of Miss Alaska?"

"Are you serious?"

She smiled, letting him know she was kidding. "I understand the thought of it isn't good," Asher conceded, "but look at what I had to do to save you and myself in the mine a couple of nights ago. The guy was going to kill us. I had to stop him. It will be the same tomorrow, but you'll be saving your parents and me."

She gave out a regretful sigh and became fidgety just thinking about it.

The fierce weather outside shifted their attention as they unconsciously leaned closer to each other. After listening to the howling wind and the thrashing of the trees surrounding the small tent for a while, it lost its strangling hold on them. It was eventually just a rocking sensation that swayed them to sleep.

They hardly moved during the night as their bodies desperately needed a good night's sleep. Stirring in the morning, Mia opened her eyes and blinked several times. She was trying to clear her fuzzy view, and in doing this, she realized her bandage had slid to the side. Gently trying to move it back into place, she accidentally pulled on some damaged skin and gritted her teeth, sucking in air. Asher heard her, which woke him up, and he asked, "You okay?"

"My bandages moved on me, and I was trying to reposition them." After wiping his eyes, Asher reached over and carefully corrected it.

"Thanks."

"It looks like you were a little rough with it while you slept. There are a few fresh blood spots."

"I don't remember a thing after we fell asleep."

"Me either," he said, gingerly touching his shoulder. It was hurting much more than yesterday. Suddenly, his mind became alert, and he burst out, "What time is it?"

She immediately understood his urgency but didn't know how long the sun had been up. "We've got to go!"

"What time do you think it is?" he asked, wrestling his way out of the cramped tent. They needed to wrap everything up and get back onto the river.

"I don't know. I need to get outside and see the position of the sun."

He stopped and looked at her. "See the position of the sun?"

Mia smiled. "Remember I'm half Indian. We know these things."

"Give me a break," he replied sarcastically.

She smiled jokingly as she followed him and crawled out of the tent. "I don't know what time it is, but I'd have a better guess if I could see where the sun is located."

"I know that." He smiled back.

They grabbed some dried fruit and picked out two energy bars for breakfast before they closed up the backpack. Then an idea came to Asher. "How far did you say we are from the Koyukuk River?"

"About a couple miles."

"I think we should call the guy now instead of waiting to get there, just in case we're running behind."

"Good idea. We should definitely be able to beat him to Bettles from here."

Asher opened the backpack and dug down deep, pulling the phone out. His heart started to race, and butterflies erupted in his stomach. "I don't think I've ever been this nervous."

"You can do it. I trust you," Mia said, putting her hand on his chest.

They locked eyes as both of them took a deep breath.

"Here we go." Asher pushed the on button and waited. The signal bars raised, and he pushed dial, just like before. The phone rang a couple of times, and the same male voice answered, "Good morning, my friend. You made good time; you're ahead of schedule. I trust you're where you need to be?"

"Yes, we are," Asher answered firmly.

"Good, good. So let's go over the plan again. You'll be hiding at the east end of the runway along with Miss Alaska." Asher looked at Mia and then away with a frown. "When I land, this is going to happen very quickly. I don't want to give the Bettles airport people time for anything.

"When I turn the plane around into take-off position, I'll shut one of the engines off near the door. You approach the plane there, and I'll open the door so you can hand me the gold. Then, and only then, I'll give you Mia's mom."

"How about her dad?"

The guy laughed and answered, "I'm leaving him behind here at the house."

Asher pulled his shoulders back, not caring about the pain. He got the same look on his face when he was about to tackle someone and said sternly, "No, you're not. Now you're going to listen to me if you want the gold."

Mia's eyes widened, and she tilted her head toward Asher, not understanding what he was doing.

"You're bringing them both with you, alive. I know you plan on killing him before you leave his house. And I know you're going to kill us all anyways. Your buddy William had planned on doing the same thing before his painful death." Asher had found the guy's name when he took the wallet off his body to give to the authorities.

The other end of the phone was quiet as Asher's tone became increasingly aggressive.

"When her mom and dad walk safely off the plane and are with us, I'll gladly hand you the heavy bag of gold. Then, it will be your move."

"My move, you say? Well, that tells me you have a plan. Are you sure you know who you're dealing with and what you're doing, my friend?"

"Not really, but the one thing I am sure of is that there are state troopers all over this. They were notified over three days ago. And no matter what"—Asher dropped his voice—"you will lose!"

There was a brief silence on the other end of the phone. Asher relished it, knowing he had him up against a wall if he wanted the gold. Then the guy said, "So you think I'm going to lose?" He chuckled. "The troopers have already been taken care of. Why haven't they already come to the rescue if they've known about it for days?" He paused to let Asher think about it and finished, "Just so you know, I don't like being threatened, and this is the length I will go to get my way." Sudden screams broke out in the background, and someone shouted, "No!" Then, the blast from a gunshot rang out. Asher could not believe his ears, and he quickly put his hand over the phone. He tried to muffle the sound so Mia couldn't hear it. He looked at her. Mia's face went blank as she stumbled back and collapsed to the ground. She had heard it all and was in shock.

"Are you still there, my friend?" the voice from the phone asked with a laugh.

"I'm not your friend," Asher answered forcefully. He could hear Nora in the background, crying out her dead husband's name over and over.

"Whatever, but you better get moving because I'm leaving in a few minutes. Oh, again, no other phone calls, remember? Because it wouldn't be pretty for your girlfriend to see her mother in pieces."

The man hung up, and Asher stood there, feeling like he was going to throw up. He couldn't wrap his mind around all the appalling events that continued to happen. He looked at Mia, who was sitting on the ground, staring into space in shock. He then turned away as he gathered their belongings to put in the canoe. He felt the weight of the world on his shoulders.

I just got her dad killed. Why? Why did I say anything? How will she ever forgive me? he thought. Then, out of nowhere, his own father's face came to his mind, and Asher heard, "You failed again. You're always failing, and now her father is dead because of you."

He dropped what he had in his hands, ran behind a tree, and vomited. Pain screamed in every part of his body. He dropped to the ground, and his emotions overcame him. With every heave of his chest, the hard fall made his ribs feel like knives were stabbing his sides, and his shoulder throbbed in excruciating pain.

He stayed bent over for another few minutes until his breathing finally slowed, but his mind swirled in confusion. As he straightened up, he grabbed his broken ribs with one hand and wiped his mouth with his filthy shirt sleeve.

He hadn't realized that Mia had walked up behind him. When he turned around, her expressionless face startled him. He didn't know what was going to happen next.

She closed the gap between them as she raised her arms. He flinched, thinking she was going to hit him. Instead, her arms continued upward, gently wrapping around his neck. She squeezed him close to her, and he relaxed. She whispered into his ear, "It's not your fault. You were right. It was going to happen anyways. You were trying to save him."

Asher returned the hug as they stood there silently for a long while, sharing each other's pain. Courage and strength swelled inside them as peace strangely seeped through them.

Slowly they separated, each wanting to say something at the exact same time. Asher said, "You go first."

She gave him an emotional, kind smile. "Asher. 23C. You have been a wonderful gentleman to me. You have helped me, protected me, and saved me, and I want you to know that I don't blame you for any of this."

Asher's heart melted as tears flowed down his face. His body collapsed back into Mia's for support. A rush of emotions was swept away that had been suffocating the truth of life up until now. Until that moment, he had never fully realized how badly he had been drowning in a world of lies. They had been rushing him down a drain into a sewer of hopelessness.

The past couple of years had been filled with painful situations, and now, he felt responsible for what had happened to Mia's father. With choppy words, Asher said, "I'm so sorry, Mia."

In spite of her own aching shoulder and shattered heart, she bravely gave him the support they both needed and replied, "I know. I know. But we need to put this aside for the moment and get going. It's not over yet."

He stepped away from her with more confidence. "No, it's not over." He wiped his face and walked back to the items he had dropped. He picked them up, thinking back to the phone call. "There needs to be a change of plans. The guy said we both need to be at the plane, so our sniper plan is out."

Asher inhaled as deeply as his chest would allow and looked across the river. "I guess it's time to put the David and Goliath battle plan to the test."

As Mia strapped their items securely to the canoe, she responded, "We're going to be taking on a professional killer, and there might be more of them. How are we going to do anything? Look at us. We're pathetic. Our faces are black and blue from being punched. One side of my face is ripped up. You have a split lip and a lump on your forehead. We each have holes in our shoulders, and you've got broken ribs. What are we going to do? Plus, I think you're getting an infection. Your skin is hot, and your face is getting paler by the minute." She reached up to his forehead with the back of her hand. "And you have a fever. Let me have a look at your bullet hole."

He backed away, shaking his head. "You completely missed the point of David and Goliath. Are you forgetting who's in charge of this whole hopeless situation we're in? It's not you or me."

She paused, mentally rewinding and listening to what he said. "You're right…it was faith in God and His power when it came to Goliath. It wasn't David's accuracy and strength behind the rock that killed the giant. He stepped forward into danger, knowing God was with him and that God would take care of it all."

Asher nodded. "So far, every game plan I've had has failed. So this is the only play left in the book. It's like we're six points behind with only a few seconds left on the clock. Just enough time for one more play, and we're sixty yards from the end zone. What else are we going to do? We obviously need to do a Hail Mary pass into the end zone."

Changing the subject, Asher leaned over and placed his hand on his knee. "And you're right, by the way. I think my shoulder is infected, and I'm feeling worse than before; I'm very weak and getting slightly dizzy."

Without hesitation, Mia's nurturing instincts kicked in, and Asher surrendered to her leadership. "Let's get into the canoe," she said. "You get in front, and I'll handle the steering. Just paddle if you can."

As they sat down and each picked up their paddles, they both stopped, sat up straight, and turned their heads upriver. They could hear something over the soft splashes of water against the side of the canoe. They didn't hear it again but looked at each other as Asher asked, "You heard that too?"

"Yeah, it was like yesterday but closer."

"It's like a bark on the wind."

"It's got to be wolves talking to each other."

"The longer this journey continues, the more likely that we'll end up as their next meal, especially if things keep going the way they're going." He looked at her with a joking smile and then turned around, facing downriver. He did his best to help push them off the shallow shoreline with his oar. Without prepping Mia, he raised his hand, making the love sign. He then said out loud, "God, we're needing You now more than ever. Until later on."

CHAPTER 18

Before long, they were leaving the mountains and valleys of the North Fork of the river. The canoe flowed into the main channel of the Koyukuk. It opened into the vast flowing plains south of the Brooks Range. The weather was cooperating, compared to the storm that had blown through last night, and their eyes admired the blue sky. It was brushed with white clouds that hovered high above. The powerful current of the main river whisked them along quickly as they traveled several miles to the edge of Bettles.

Following the instructions from the phone conversation, they carefully beached the canoe out of sight before they reached the township at the east end of the runway. Asher opened the pack and retrieved two things: the leather bag of iron pyrite and the handgun he had taken off Willie.

As before, he handed the gun to Mia, saying, "I have no idea how, where, or when it will be useful, but if we need it or get the chance to use it, we'll have it." He paused, and sick chills ran through his body. He bent over, getting lightheaded as his legs felt wobbly.

Mia went to grab him. "You're getting worse, Asher."

He held out his hand to stop her. "I'm okay. I just need to catch my breath."

"Catch your breath? Look at you, Asher. You can hardly stand, and you're as white as a ghost." She touched his forehead, which was beaded with sweat. "You're burning up. Is there anything you can take in your first aid bag?"

"Later. We have a job to do." He suddenly went to his knees, and Mia thought he was collapsing. Before she could reach out to help him, she stopped in surprise.

In his weakness, he raised his hand to the sky, giving the same love hand signal Rudy always did. Then he spoke weakly, "God...I'm trying to understand this Cloud of Glory thing. Maybe I'll totally get it...once I experience it some more. I don't know what's going to happen next, but so far...it doesn't look good. So, if You're going to show up, please do it now. I want... no, I need...to see You in action right now!

"And if You're the God you say You are...I ask You to protect Nora, Mia, and me. Don't let these people get away with the evil they've done. I will hide in this cloud of Yours...keeping my head down...looking only at the trail You have laid out for us. It's all I have the energy for." He paused, trying to think of more to say, but nothing came to mind, so he finished, "Until...later on."

He stood feebly, trying to stay balanced, and lifted the heavy leather bag. He turned as Mia stood with a glow on her face and tears streaming down. "You're crying again. Did I say something wrong?"

"No, it was perfect." Mia's heart beat proudly for him. He was changing and growing right before her eyes.

He looked out toward the tall brush, where the end of the runway was. "Let's get—" Suddenly, he turned back, looking across the wide river in the direction they had come. Once again, he heard the distant sound that had left them in suspense the last couple of days.

"I heard it again too. It's much closer!" Mia said. Their eyes scanned the area, looking for any movement, but they didn't see a thing, and they didn't hear it again. "I wish it or they would just show themselves. The Indians believe wolves are spirits. They're considered mystical and sacred."

"It's definitely going to take something…mystical or spiritual…to come out of this alive."

At that exact moment, everything seemed to halt: all sight, all sound, and all feeling as they clearly heard a calm voice, full of authority, say, "I've got this. You go do what you need to do."

Both Mia and Asher looked at each other questioningly and asked, "What did you say?"

Together, they realized it had not been either one of them. Asher smirked and cast his gaze up to the blue sky, saying, "I sure hope You do…because we're a pathetic, beat-up…couple right now." Mia gave him a half-hidden smile in agreement.

Then, these words filled their hearts. "Walk forward in faith, believing in Me, and My Spirit will show you My glory that is with you always."

After letting those words settle for a moment, they made their way to the edge of the east side of the runway, staying hidden. As they waited longer than they expected, Asher began to shiver. His clothing was drenched in sweat, and the pain in his shoulder was increasing greatly. It took a concerted effort to keep his eyes open as pain surged through his body.

Finally, in the distance, the hum of an airplane could be heard coming in from behind. Mia looked back. "If that's our guy, he took the long way around. He's too far east; he should've come over the mountains in that direction." She pointed out toward the north/northeast.

They watched the twin-engine plane circle wide and land, coming straight at them from the west. As it slowed with engines roaring, the plane taxied in front of them, then turned around and stopped. The engine closest to the door shut off, the door opened, and steps flipped out to the ground.

No one came out of the plane, so they decided it was their move. "You have the gun ready?" Asher whispered.

Mia nodded her head with a look of dread. Asher stood, reaching out to help her stand up. He understood her reluctance and gave her a little mental boost like his football coaches would do when it looked like they were going to lose. "You told me you confronted death two times before we met and now two times on this journey." He gently stroked the unharmed side of her face, giving her an encouraging smile. Trying hard to stay alert, he then said, "God said He's got this, remember…like He's had you many times before. We just have to do…what we need to do… like David did…going out to confront Goliath…and believe… God will take care of the rest."

Holding his hand against her face, she inhaled as though the air was filled with courage and confidence. Just then, a distinct howl followed by several loud barks came from behind them, somewhere near the river. They both froze as Mia whispered, "We're surrounded by killers, and they're coming for us, Asher."

He stayed focused, saying, "We'll take them on one at a time." He turned and started walking to the plane as she followed his lead.

They walked up to the side of the plane that was facing the open runway and saw movement through the small plane windows. At the bottom of the stairs, they waited until Nora hesitantly stepped to the frame of the door. She locked eyes with Mia as they both experienced overwhelming emotions of relief, excitement, and complete fear. Nora was given a hard push to make her step onto the top rung of the stairs. A head poked out the door behind her.

A shockwave hit them both, forcing Mia and Asher to step back. They were looking up at the man who had pushed Nora.

Mia was the first to speak. "Trooper Clay? What…what's going on?"

He answered arrogantly, "Surprised? Me too. This didn't go down the way it was supposed to. No one was supposed to know that I was involved, but"—he shrugged his shoulders and cocked his head, thoroughly unconcerned—"it is what it is. I'm truly sorry to hear about your father, Mia. That wasn't in the plans."

Adrenaline was overriding the pain of Asher's injuries as he piped in, "How could you? You're an officer of the law! You're friends with Rudy!"

"Not after he finds out about this, let me tell you. Tug is going to be madder than a caged wolverine."

"This doesn't make sense," Mia said, still beside herself.

"It's simple. I was made an offer that I couldn't refuse. You see, Willie and his business were being investigated by the state for questionable, illegal practices. I got wind of an idea that he had from an undercover officer after Willie had coincidently run into a gold mine." Clay started laughing as they heard a stranger's voice behind him in the plane join in the festive moment. "Just last year on that moose hunt with Nora, he saw Martin's collection of gold." Nora lowered her head, taking complete blame as she heard him tell the story, remembering that she had been the one to show off Martin's setup. "I had to get in on the action. My valuable knowledge of everything up here would make Willie's plan run more smoothly and be a lot more profitable by eventually adding all the other miners' gold in the area that I know."

"But why would you do this to us? You've been a family friend since before I was born," Mia said with her heart crushed.

Clay's expression changed as anger started to brew. "Do you know how much time I've put into my job, Mia? I'm always risking my life. I receive nothing compared to what I'm always having to do.

"I lost my marriage because of it, and my kids live in the lower forty-eight to get away from this icebox. Then, when it's all over, my retirement is going to be pitiful. But now…" He looked back into the plane, smiling again. "Now, I don't have to work another day of my life with my share of the gold. Which greatly increased because of you two. Thank you very much! We have three less people to split the gold with."

"You're not going to get away with this," Asher said, staring Clay down.

"Yes, we are. And we're going far away so I never have to put on long johns or a parka again."

A loud voice came from the plane; Asher recognized it from the phone calls. "You've told them too much; let's get on with this. We've got to get the heck out of here!"

"Agreed," Clay responded as he looked harshly at Asher, but then, unexpectedly, he gave him an exaggerated wink. Asher pulled his head back, not sure what that was all about. Mia stood behind Asher and slowly reached for the gun in the back of her pants.

Clay tilted his head sideways, looked at Asher, and said, "Do you remember the story I told you when you first came to Bettles?"

"Yeah."

Clay, not moving, rolled his eyes sideways and toward the back of his head. He did this a couple of times, then added, "And do you remember what I was doing when I peered through the bush?"

Asher nodded his head as he drew his eyebrows together, trying to figure out where Clay was going with this.

"And the funny thing I was looking at and how my friend got his nickname?"

Asher didn't respond as Clay winked at him again. Asher was beginning to understand that Clay was sending him a discreet message so that the guy behind Clay wouldn't know what he was talking about. Suddenly, Asher realized what Trooper Clay wanted him to do.

Asher slowly moved a hand back to push Mia out of the way. Then Clay said, "I want you to carefully hand that bag of gold to Nora."

Asher looked at Nora. She smiled placidly, letting Asher know that she was aware of Clay's strange behavior; she knew what was going to happen. Asher took a deep breath and stepped forward to the bottom rung of the stairs. Slowly lifting the bag of iron pyrite with both hands, he looked up at Trooper Clay and winked back. Asher suddenly tossed the bag of fool's gold high in the air, grabbing Nora's hands as they reached out to him. He pulled her to him as fast as he could, then spun around and tackled Mia, sending them all to the ground. Asher shielded Nora and Mia from whatever Clay had in mind.

Yelling broke out in the plane as two bodies thrashed and fought around. A gunshot rang out.

"I knew you couldn't be trusted, but Willie wouldn't listen to me!" Asher, Nora, and Mia lay curled up on the ground. They turned around to watch the gruesome scene.

They stared as the stranger picked up the leather bag off the floor. He walked proudly down the stairs, stepping onto the dirt runway. He waved his gun back and forth and said slyly, "I guess all the gold is mine now. Pity, I was looking forward to the big party we were going to have in Mexico.

"Thank you for bringing this to me. And now, I must be on my way." He lowered the gun and pointed it straight at Asher as he courageously sat up straight to shield Mia and Nora. The women squeezed their eyes shut as Asher yelled to Mia to shoot the guy.

Suddenly, the swift movement of something large caught Asher's attention coming from where he and Mia had been previously waiting. The man pointing the gun saw the expression change on Asher's face, then heard something rushing in from the side. He started to turn, but before he knew it, an animal leaped into the air and crushed him to the ground.

In the frenzy of the attack, the man realized a huge, ferocious wolf had overpowered him. His neck now in the jaws of the wild beast, the gunman frantically squirmed and tried to scream, but he couldn't. The thrashing dwindled, and his body went limp. He was dead. The growling and tossing of the body were the only sounds heard, drowning out the sound of the engine on the other side of the plane.

Asher, Nora, and Mia quickly stood up, staring at the gory sight. Stepping back, Mia instinctively drew her gun and pointed it at the carnage before them, but it was unnecessary; the animal hovered over the still body, heaving for air. The wolf stepped off its prey and slowly turned to look at them but lost its balance and collapsed.

Even though the wolf wasn't harmed by the man, it was obvious it had been badly injured. It was the size of a full-grown male, but they could see it was skinnier than it should have been. Its coat was soaking wet from swimming across the wide river.

Pieces of fur were missing here and there, showing bare skin and a sizable wound on its neck. Two paws bled from what seemed to be broken claws. Severely worn-down pads looked to be from running a long distance.

The wolf lifted its head and peered at them, giving out a soft whine as if to say, "Come over here."

"It can't be!" Mia screamed out in horror.

"Oh my Lord Jesus." Nora recognized him as well.

They took a step toward the killer, but Asher put his arms out to stop them. "No, it's too dangerous. It's injured."

"Asher, it's Samson!"

He looked closer at the injured animal and vaguely recognized the big Alaskan malamute. He lowered his arms as they all cautiously approached Samson, kneeling around him.

Samson's tongue hung loosely, and blood dripped from his teeth. He panted in such a manner that no matter how much he breathed, he couldn't get enough air. Asher felt a sudden, strange, but deep connection to Samson as Samson's eyes began to flutter. The big dog reached out with his front leg, with all the energy he had left, and set it onto Mia's lap.

They watched speechlessly; no words could express the overwhelming understanding of what had just occurred: the pure loyalty, love, labor, and sacrifice this animal had selflessly given them.

Samson's chest sank, and his eyes closed for the last time. Asher and Mia both realized that Samson was the one that had been calling out to them for the past couple of days. He was letting them know that he hadn't forgotten about them and was coming to their rescue.

Having survived the rifle injury, Samson had instinctively and passionately been driven to find the ones he loved and protect them. He foraged rivers and fought off predators, stepping into every footprint that his family member had made. Up and down the mountains and across the valley floors, he had wandered.

He never stopped to hunt for food but only to rest. He continually searched for the elusive scent of Mia as she traveled for days on the river. His instincts and persistence would not let up until he found his family.

Mia and Nora cried softly over their friend and protector, stroking his side. Asher stood in awe as he viewed a perfect portrayal of a devoted and loving relationship. Samson had sacrificed his life for them.

The voice of creation gently spoke, "I've got you, Asher. I always have and always will. Believe in Me, follow Me, and live in My Spirit, the Cloud of Glory."

Asher walked a few paces away as a flood of emotion swelled up in him again. He saw flashes of years gone by, flowing into this unexpected journey, which had led to this very moment.

"Asher, you wanted to run and hide from your life, but instead you have witnessed what kind of God I am. You now see Me clearly through these experiences. My Son, Jesus, your Savior, is alive and always tending to you as Our glory shrouds your life with loyalty, love, labor, and sacrifice. We will never give up on you."

***

Asher, Mia, and Rudy sat quietly around a table on the deck of Rudy's home. They were looking out at the lake along his property, sipping hot cups of coffee. It was going to be one of the last warm days of the year. His home was situated far south of Bettles, halfway between Fairbanks and Anchorage. It was a rustic log cabin, well-built to withstand the harsh Alaskan weather. On his property, there were two additional buildings: One was a simple dry sauna with its own deck, which jetted out toward the lake, and the other was a larger-sized garage built behind the house. In the garage, Rudy kept his old four-wheel drive pickup, two ATVs, and his small plane. Next to the house and garage, he had a dirt and grass runway, just like Nora.

They were recovering from their respective surgeries. Rudy had to have the break in his leg reset. Recovery would take some time with his leg now in a full cast. His head wound, however, was healing quickly. Asher needed reconstructive surgery on his shoulder, and the persistent infection was taking a while to treat. His painful ribs were going to require months to recover on their own.

Mia, on the other hand, was facing several more surgeries to reconstruct her face to a more normal appearance. The doctors were very confident that she would heal well—to the point that, unless she said something about it, no one would know how bad her injuries had been. The Miss Alaska committee was providing their full support and assisting with all the medical expenses. In addition, they were giving her space and privacy, out of the public eye, to recover.

Nora was keeping her mind off the death of her husband by staying busy as their nurse. Her husband's body had been cremated, and the family planned on having his funeral as soon as everyone was well enough. It would be a celebration of life back up in Bettles.

It was taking a while for the whole story to come out about what really happened. The investigation was moving slowly. But Mr. Alaska (or "Tug") had high ranking contacts at the state level. Asher asked Rudy how Clay had been involved, and Rudy answered, "Clay took everything on himself so no other trooper would get hurt. He knew he was dealing with people who didn't care if others lived or died. He went deep undercover, by himself, to be a part of everything. He didn't want any of his friends in the Brooks Range to get hurt. That's how great of a man my friend was." Rudy paused, trying not to get emotional in front of everyone, then continued, "Unfortunately, your father was killed, and I blame myself for that, Mia."

"Uncle Rudy, it wasn't your fault." She reached out to place her hand on his.

"Yes, it was. If I hadn't gotten hurt, Asher and I would've passed right by your place, not interfering, and those guys would've been long gone. No one would've gotten hurt or killed."

"Uncle Rudy, you taught me to live in the Cloud of Glory, and that's what I'm going to do. No matter what, you're not to blame! You know God will work all things for the good, and that even means the bad, the ugly, and the painful things…" She pointed up to her bandaged face. "Because we live in an imperfect world, filled with broken people."

Rudy smiled. "You're right, dear one. We lost your father, and that needs to be left in God's hands. Just like when Asher lost his father…we must turn around and walk forward in faith, living in great expectation of what Jesus is going to do. Right, Asher?"

They had all heard Asher's story, the struggles with his dad, and the disappointments. He had been hanging onto the past by walking backward, always stumbling and never getting anywhere. "My life," Asher replied, "hasn't completely smoothed out yet, but"—he looked at Mia with a smile—"I understand now what has been suffocating me: Living in the past has haunted me every day. I'm moving forward and looking ahead as I release the past, even though I don't know what's going to happen next."

"Isn't it amazing how God puts our life's pieces together like a puzzle? Look at you two!" Rudy commented, watching Mia and Asher sitting next to each other, holding hands.

Nora chimed in, having overheard their conversation as she came outside to top off everyone's cups of coffee. "Please don't blame yourself, Rudy. Remember these words, 'And we know that for those who love God, all things work together for the good.'"

Rudy followed her gaze to the new, young relationship, understanding what she was saying. After reflecting back to the past and looking into the future, he said, "Asher, I think I'm going to be retiring after all this, and I need someone to take things over. I never remarried or met anyone that I wanted to hand off my businesses to until now. What do you say?"

Staring deep into Mia's eyes, Asher replied with a smile, "I'm never letting go of this beautiful woman." He gave her hand a gentle squeeze. "I guess that means I'm staying here in Alaska, and I'll need a job. But more than that, I'll be moving forward, living in great expectation, by hiding in the Cloud of Glory—especially if every situation ends up like this." He leaned over and gently gave Mia a kiss.

Extending his hand out to Asher, Rudy excitedly said, "Great, then it's settled!"

Asher shook Rudy's hand while winking at Mia and asked, "Do you think I can trust Mr. Alaska?"

Mia smiled the best she could with her face still bandaged and answered, "There's nothing to worry about. Together, we've got this 23C."

ABOUT THE AUTHOR

D. L. Crager is no stranger to the adventurous and deadly great outdoors. Having grown up in the Rocky Mountains, he has climbed some of the highest peaks, rafted in some of the deepest canyons, and spent a large amount of time in the wilderness.

But his greatest successes in life are with Jesus Christ and his family.

"Without a healthy and loving relationship with God and family, other successes will always be fleeting dreams!"

When you read books written by D. L. Crager, you will never be disappointed. His fictional stories will take your imagination to new heights, as biblical truths are woven through the pages, profoundly challenging and changing lives.